"You know I would do anything you want," Ann said.

"Anything?"

"Why, of course," Ann replied. "What do you want?"

She looked at John with wide eyes, and then suddenly was very still. It seemed to her that for the very first time he held her gaze and she saw past the gravity and quiet seriousness which was so much a part of him and into the man himself. What she saw there she did not understand. It seemed as though some flame burned fiercely within him, so fiercely that she gave a gasp of fear . . . . this man was a stranger . . . . a man whose eyes suggested many things from which she shrank . . . . the man to whom she was married!

Also in Pyramid Books
by
BARBARA CARTLAND

Ask me no more: thy fate and mine are seal'd:
I strove against the stream and all in vain:
Let the great river take me in the main:
No more, dear love, for at a touch I yield;
  Ask me no more

Tennyson

AGAINST
THE STREAM

•

Barbara Cartland

PYRAMID BOOKS • **NEW YORK**

AGAINST THE STREAM

A PYRAMID BOOK

First published by Hutchinson & Company (*Publishers*) Ltd. 1946

Arrow edition 1970

Pyramid edition published July, 1974

ISBN 0–515–03389–8

Printed in the United States of America

Pyramid Books are published by Pyramid Communications, Inc. Its trademarks, consisting of the word "Pyramid" and the portrayal of a pyramid, are registered in the United States Patent Office.

Pyramid Communications, Inc.,
919 Third Avenue, New York, N.Y. 10022

CONDITIONS OF SALE

Against the Stream

One

"I bet you I'm right."

"I bet you a shilling you're not."

"You haven't got a shilling."

"Well . . . thre . . . I mean tuppence, then."

"All right, I'll take you—but you've got to pay me."

"You'll pay me, you mean."

"What are you two gabbling about?"

"Oh, Myra, have you seen Daddy's patient? Antionette thinks he is dead."

"Of course he isn't. I expect he's asleep—or would be if you two weren't making so much noise."

"He is very still. . . . I'm sure he is dead."

"Rubbish! Here, let me look."

"Well, what do you think?"

"I think he is good-looking—very good-looking."

The man in the bed smiled to himself. He had been listening to the conversation for the last few minutes while still half asleep. Drowsy and conscious of a vast fatigue, he tried to move and felt a sudden wrenching pain in his side.

Now it all came back. . . . The big lorry coming too quickly and without warning out of a side-turning, a sudden screech of brakes, the sound of his own voice shouting incoherently . . . and then the crash.

He must have been stunned, for it seemed to be a long time later that he became aware that the car was over on its side and that he himself was pinned down and unable to move.

It was Jarvis he had been most concerned about—Jarvis who he knew would have received the full force of the impact on his side of the car. He remembered shouting for help and when help appeared he had kept saying, "Get a doctor for Jarvis."

After that things had become a little hazy. He could recall the almost excruciating agony when they lifted him on to a stretcher, and then he must have fainted. . . .

What happened after that? He had a vague recollection of coming round and finding himself on a bed; of a man—presumably a doctor—putting a glass to his lips and saying,

"Drink this and don't ask any more questions."

He had not realised that he had been asking questions, but he supposed they must have been about Jarvis. . . .

He remembered nothing more; nothing until his dreams, indistinct and disconnected, had dissolved into young voices talking, he presumed, about himself. They were still there. . . .

"I don't think he is good-looking, he is much too old."

This was a child's voice.

"He would seem old to you." There was scorn in the more mature tones.

"What are you children doing?"

Somebody else had arrived on the scene. "There must be quite a crowd outside this room," the man in the bed thought to himself.

"Oh, Ann, we're looking at Daddy's patient, and Myra thinks he is good-looking."

"You have no right to be doing anything of the sort. Go away at once and play at the other end of the garden, and Myra ought to have more sense than to encourage you in such naughtiness."

"Don't be so snooty, Ann. You know it's exciting. Why, we don't even know who he is. He might be a prince in disguise!"

"And he might be a commercial traveller. It is no use making this into one of your romantic dreams, Myra."

"Why not? Besides, who knows? I may be right. Just suppose, Ann, that he turned out to be a millionaire and said to Daddy: 'Dr. Shefford, in gratitude for all your kindness to me, here is a thousand pounds. Spend it on those charming children of yours.' "

"I think it most unlikely that he will say anything of the sort. If he is like Daddy's other patients he will thank us but forget to pay the bill. In the meantime, would you mind making your bed? Your room looks as if a bomb had hit it."

"Oh, bother my room! I am sick of housework anyway!"

"I can't think how you can be, considering the little you do."

"Why can't Mrs. Briggs do my room when she does the landing?"

"Oh, Myra, don't start that argument again—not today, there is so much to do!"

"All right, I'll suffer in silence. But don't forget, if he does turn out to be a millionaire, I have staked my claim."

There was a low laugh, followed by the sound of footsteps moving away from the window.

The man in the bed opened his eyes and raised his head a little. He could see across the room an opening between the window curtains through which the sunlight slanted in a narrow golden shaft to reveal a small bedroom with a french window which apparently opened into the garden.

He looked around him.

The bed on which he lay was an old-fashioned brass one and the furniture in the room was a miscellaneous collection.

It was obviously the room of someone with very little money and not much taste; but it was spotlessly clean, with a big bowl of roses on the dressing-table and the faint sweet fragrance of lavender clinging to the sheets and pillow-cases.

The man found himself wondering about Dr. Shef-

9

ford's family. Antoinette and her companion, who sounded like a small boy, were obviously extremely inquisitive; Myra was romantic and Ann strongly practical.

They all had cultured, well-bred voices; but Ann's despite a note of authority had a quiet sweetness which pleased him. He was particular about voices; so many he knew were harsh or shrill. This strange girl's was soft and musical.

There was a knock on the door. Before he could answer, it opened to admit an elderly woman, red-faced and big-bosomed, who moved noisily across the room and drew back the curtains. The sunshine filled the room, golden and blinding.

"Are you awake, sir?"

"Yes . . . yes, I am awake."

"The doctor said as how I was to tell you that he'd been called out, but he hoped to be back soon and you aren't to worry."

"Thank you."

"Miss Ann's bringing up your breakfast in a moment. The doctor said if there's anything you wanted you was to ask her for it."

"Thank you, I will."

"Though if there's anything I can do for you sir, of course I shall be only too pleased. As long as it ain't anything to do with wounds or dressings—I never can abide such things myself. I joined a first-aid class in the war, but I wasn't any use at it. In fact the doctor said to me: 'Mrs. Briggs'—that's my name, sir—'Mrs. Briggs,' he said, 'you stick to the kitchen. I would trust you with anyone's stummick, but not with their limbs.' "

"So you are a cook, Mrs. Briggs?"

"Oh, I wouldn't go so far as to presume to call myself a cook. I can do a bit of everything in the house. Cleaning's my speciality, but I wouldn't be telling you a lie if I told you I can cook as well, if not better than, any other woman in this village."

10

"I believe you."

"Not that you'd be wanting much food at this moment, sir, after all you went through yesterday. I seen the accident myself and I says to the doctor, I says, 'It's a miracle that anyone's come out alive of that smash-up. A miracle, that it is . . .' Ah! here's Miss Ann with your breakfast."

There was a faint rattle outside the door and the man in the bed turned his head to see a girl enter the room carrying a tray.

"Good morning."

Her smile was as sweet as the voice he had heard outside the window. She had dark hair which framed a small oval face, and eyebrows like delicate wings over very wide and surprisingly blue eyes.

"So this is Ann," the man in the bed thought. "And she is pretty—very pretty."

Ann put the tray down beside his bed.

"I don't know if you are hungry, but I have brought you an egg just in case you could manage one."

"Now I think about it, I am hungry."

"That is splendid. My father looked in at you before he went out this morning. He said you were sleeping peacefully and he hoped you would feel better when you woke."

"Your father has been very kind—I gather that I have to thank him for bringing me here. I have very little recollection of what happened . . . after the crash."

"The accident happened just down the road, and luckily Daddy was at home."

She smiled shyly at the man lying in the bed.

"He is nice-looking," she thought, "but rather awe-inspiring."

His clean-cut features were distinguished, and even lying on his back he gave the impression of authority—a man who was used to giving orders and being served.

She waited for his answering smile and when it was not forthcoming was aware suddenly of his eyes, keen

11

and penetrating, as if they considered her critically. She felt the colour rise in her cheeks.

Mrs. Briggs was still standing on the other side of the bed, her hands on her hips. Ann glanced across at her.

"I think I hear the bell, Mrs. Briggs."

"I wouldn't be surprised," Mrs. Briggs answered. "One can never get down to anything in this house but there isn't a bell ringing. I've given the gentleman your father's message."

"Thank you, Mrs. Briggs."

She went from the room and Ann, adjusting the tray to a more convenient angle, said:

"I don't know whether Mrs. Briggs has told you, but nurse will be here at nine o'clock. If there is anything you want in the meantime please ask me."

"There is nothing I want, thank you, except that I would like to know what has happened to my chauffeur."

Ann hesitated. Her eyes softened and the man in the bed knew the answer before she said quietly:

"I expect you would rather hear the truth. He was killed—instantaneously."

"I had a feeling he might have been. Thank you for telling me."

As if she understood that he wanted to be alone, Ann slipped from the room.

Poor Jarvis! But it was something to know that he had died without pain. He supposed, as Mrs. Briggs had said, that it was a miracle that he himself had got off so lightly. He might easily have been driving, in which case their positions would have been reversed—it would have been Jarvis who was lying here while he was found dead.

"Would it have mattered very much?"

He asked himself the question and wondered what in all honesty the answer should be. Would he be missed? If so, who would miss him? It would have

12

been a nuisance in the constituency—a by-election always caused a commotion . . . but otherwise . . . ?

Metaphorically he shrugged his shoulders. One thought oneself so important, and yet a close acquaintance with death brought the realisation of how utterly inconsequent one is. What in reality did anything matter?

Power, authority, possessions, money—what were all those things? Unimportant indeed when compared with the mere action of breathing; let that stop and everything else was so much waste luggage—an empty suit of clothes no longer required.

He thought of Jarvis. Fifteen years of devoted service; a man whom it would be hard to replace. And yet he would be replaced, and then gradually he would be forgotten. It was hard, and yet was it harder to face than the fact that no one, not even oneself, is really necessary in the world?

The man in bed thought of the bitter fight he had just had over sponsoring the Factory Bill. Tempers had run high; the Opposition had been not only obstructive, but virulent. His own party had been apathetic, while he had been both angry and resentful.

Now he wondered if it really mattered. If reforms were necessary, sooner or later they would become law. It was merely childish to think that he or his ideas were essential to progress.

Wearily the man in the bed passed his hand across his eyes. He was aware that this sort of introspection was unlike him. He was a fighter, had always been a fighter; and he was also an autocrat; he hated to be opposed and opposition usually filled him with a steely, unswervable determination to get his own way.

Now he questioned his own infallibility. Why?

"Because of Jarvis," he told himself and added cynically, "This is only reaction!"

All the same he wondered . . . wondered at himself. . . .

His breakfast was getting cold. Carefully he tried to

move himself into a more comfortable position in which it was possible to eat, but not without pain and the consciousness that one side of his body was bruised and aching.

Nevertheless he found that he was hungry.

"I suppose a good night's sleep has enabled me to get over the shock," he thought. "I wonder what it was the doctor gave me that made me sleep. I must ask him for the prescription."

He thought of the nights when he had lain awake hour after hour, his brain clear, calculating and incurably alert. He had tried various sleeping tablets, but without success. Obviously this local practitioner had something new; "or else something which suits me," he added to himself.

The door opened and Dr. Shefford came in. He was a middle-aged man with grey hair, in a worn suit frayed at the cuffs. There was nothing distinguished or unusual about him until he smiled, and then there was both humanity and humour to be seen in his face.

"Good morning. How do you feel this morning?" His voice was quiet and subtly inspired confidence.

"I have had a good night, thank you, and have made a good breakfast, as you can see."

"That is excellent. Now do you mind if I attend to you rather quickly? I have come away from a confinement. I have told a very nervous prospective father that it will be at least another three hours before his progeny is born; but he doesn't believe me and I quite expect to hear the telephone ring at any moment."

The man in the bed laughed.

"I am in no hurry," he said, "and I should hate to inconvenience the more pressing needs of your other patient."

"All the same I want to have a look at you," the doctor said, and pulling back the bedclothes he began his examination.

It was then that the man in the bed could see his

14

own leg, bandaged and in splints. He asked a question, but the doctor dismissed it lightly.

"That is only a bad fracture," he said. "I am not worried about that. It is here . . . and here. . . . Does that hurt? Now take a deep breath. . . ." The examination was thorough and when it was finished Dr. Shefford drew up the bedclothes again with a sigh. "Thank goodness you are all right."

"What were you afraid of?"

"Internal injuries. If you had seen what happened to your chauffeur you would have understood. My daughter told you that he was dead?"

"Yes."

"He has been taken to the mortuary. Do you feel well enough to answer various questions? The police will want to ask you about the accident, I want to ask you about yourself."

"I can give all the information that is required about Jarvis."

"And about yourself?"

"What do you want to know?"

"Well, first, whom you would like notified about the accident; and secondly, if you want to be moved."

"Moved? Why should I be moved?"

"That was one of the reasons why I was anxious to examine you. When you were brought here yesterday afternoon I was in two minds whether I should send you at once to our nearest hospital so that you could be X-rayed and have better treatment than I am capable of giving you, or keep you here.

"But it meant a fifteen-mile journey to the hospital and as I am a great believer in treating shock first and injuries afterwards, I followed my instinct."

"For which I am very grateful—and, may I add, very comfortable."

Dr. Shefford smiled.

"Thank you. I keep this bedroom ready for emergency cases. Strangely enough we have quite a number

15

here, although we live in a small out-of-the-way place."

"I have no idea where I am."

"The name of this village is Little Cople—it is rather off the beaten track. We are about twenty miles from Melchester."

"Oh, yes, I know whereabouts it is now."

"And now for you, family or relations. Would you like me to telephone them or would you prefer to write out some telegrams?"

"There is no hurry. Am I well enough to return home?"

Dr. Shefford hesitated. "I would rather you gave yourself two or three days' rest before you attempt anything—unless it is absolutely imperative for you to get away."

"You won't mind having me here?"

"My dear fellow, of course not. In fact, I should prefer to have you if possible. If there is one thing I dislike, it is leaving a job half done."

"My own sentiments exactly."

"Very well, then, if you will stay we shall be very pleased to have you. And now . . ." A knock on the door interrupted him. "Yes, who is it?"

"Daddy, Mr. Knowles is on the telephone. He says that you must come at once."

"Tell him I am coming."

The doctor turned to the door.

"There you are! These anxious fathers! And there isn't a chance of that baby being born for another two hours at least. However, I will set their minds at rest and go along right away. Luckily it is only half a mile down the road. Nurse should be here by now to give you a wash and brush up. She is an excellent woman; ask her for anything you want. Good-bye."

Dr. Shefford hurried from the room. Only as he took his bag and hat from Ann who was waiting in the hall did he remember that he was still unaware of his patient's name.

"Keep our visitor on a light diet, Ann dear," he said. "And you might ask him his name. I forgot."

"How like you, Daddy!" Ann smiled, and then waved as he drove off in his small, ramshackle car.

She did not, however, go straight away to the new patient's room. She saw the nurse coming down the passage with towels and hot water and wisely decided that his name could wait until he was washed and shaved. Instead she went to the kitchen where she found Myra at the sink peeling the potatoes for luncheon, with a novel propped up on the window-sill.

"Myra, what are you doing?" Ann asked, but with amused affection in her voice. She was used to her sister's little ways.

"Oh, Ann, you must read this book!" Myra answered. "It is absolutely thrilling! Just listen to this: 'Sinuous and subtle as a snake, she wore a dress of silver tissue which revealed rather than concealed her figure, and round her ivory-white neck was the necklace of big pigeon-blood rubies which the Rajah had given her in Bombay.' Doesn't it sound marvellous!"

"It sounds very peculiar to me," Ann replied. "Why was she taking pigeon-blood rubies from the Rajah anyway?"

"I'll give you three guesses."

"I don't need them. I can't think where you get these books or why you bother to read them, they are such trash."

"They're absolutely thrilling," Myra said with satisfaction. "Besides, I need some colour in my life."

Ann laughed. "Oh, Myra, you do say the most ridiculous things."

"Well, it's true. Here I am, living a drab, colourless existence without any hope of any change. Who wants to do a commercial course? Besides, I am so bad at it."

"Oh, Myra, you must pass your exam this time."

"I am quite certain that I shan't. If you only knew

17

how difficult it is to read one's own shorthand, you would sympathise."

"But you promised Daddy you would work hard."

"And I have," Myra answered. "But I am just not cut out for a commercial career and you know it. Much better let me be a shop girl or go on the stage."

Ann sighed. They had been through all this before. And yet she wondered what was going to happen to Myra. The trouble was she was so pretty and so completely brainless when it came to doing anything practical. But it was impossible to be angry with her.

She looked at her now and thought, as she had so many times before, that her younger sister was fitted only for a life of enjoyment. Myra's hair, a deep chestnut brown with red and gold lights in it, curled naturally over her small head.

Her blue eyes, surrounded with long, naturally dark eyelashes, were set in a round baby face with a tip-tilted nose. Despite plain, cheap and well-worn clothes and her hands in the potato water Myra had at this moment the appearance of having stepped straight out of an illustrated magazine.

Her only unhappiness was that at seventeen and nine months she was rather inclined to plumpness, and although she tried to be strict with her diet her vanity was not greater than her greed, so that sooner or later she always fell for the most fattening things.

Chocolates and cream cakes were irresistible to one whose hungry adolescence had suffered the stringent rationing of war.

It was characteristic, too, of Myra that she invariably took the line of least resistance, but no one could be angry with her for long. She was ridiculously pretty, so good-natured, warm-hearted and incurably romantic. She saw herself always as a heroine and every man she met was a potential hero.

If Ann, who spoilt her, sighed over her future, she herself was supremely confident that "Mr. Right"

18

in a Rolls-Royce was waiting for her "just round the corner".

All the same, the problem of Myra's future was a very real one. Dr. Shefford had spent already more than he could afford on her education and it was essential that she should start to earn money so that what little there was to spare could now be concentrated on the twins.

Antony and Antoinette were twelve. At the moment they attended a small school in the village; but Ann was hoping against hope that they would be able to afford to send Antony to a public school within the next two years although Antoinette, she supposed, would have to put up with the same haphazard education that she herself had received.

Antony and Antoinette were ridiculously alike. They were not very big for their age, but were in their own way good-looking, though lacking the quiet loveliness of Ann and the spectacular prettiness of Myra.

They were extremely naughty; and while possessed of a special kind of exuberant mischief, to the outer world they appeared unnaturally solemn for their years and so well behaved on formal occasions that when they were caught out people found it hard to believe that they could possibly be the originators and perpetrators of such naughtiness.

The twins would huddle together in some quiet corner cogitating their next escapade; and then, when it had been conceived and executed they managed to look so extremely disarming and innocent that it was only those who were well acquainted with them who could be absolutely certain that they were the real culprits.

Ann, after years of experience, was able to detect shrewdly that something was up when they appeared looking particularly solemn and were abnormally quiet and polite.

Although the neighbourhood had had every reason for branding them as young blackguards, they were

19

generally spoken of as "those twins" in terms of affection and amusement.

That they had both character and originality was, perhaps, shown by the fact that, though their names were long and easy to abbreviate, everyone always addressed them formally as Antony and Antoinette.

There was indeed some kind of natural dignity about the twins and it was only when they were alone together that they had special nicknames one for the other which were never admitted to the outside world.

It being Saturday, neither Myra nor they were at school, and Ann as she started to prepare the luncheon wondered where the two children had gone or what they were doing. Myra had returned to her book, turning over a page every so often with a finger wet and dirty from potato peelings.

"Which would you like for lunch," Ann asked— "cherries or raspberries? We have got both."

There was no answer for a moment, then with a blissful sigh Myra looked up.

"What did you say?" she asked.

"I am sorry to interrupt you," Ann said with heavy sarcasm. "What is the Rajah doing now?"

"Becoming most sinister."

"I was afraid he would want something in return for those rubies," Ann laughed.

And then she added:

"I hate to sound school-marmish, but I do wish you would study a shorthand book with the same concentration. You know, Myra, we have simply got to have some more money soon in this house. We are behind with the rent and I daren't ever guess what the grocer's bill is going to be this month."

"Never mind, the new lodger will pay that."

"Who? Oh, you mean Daddy's patient. He seems nice."

"Oh, you've seen him!" Myra exclaimed. "Tell me all about him. What did he say and who is he?"

"I don't know, and Daddy forgot to ask him, too. Isn't that like Daddy?"

"Exactly," Myra answered with meaning. "But he must be rich. Did you see his luggage when they brought it out of the car? A pigskin case that must have cost pounds and pounds, and the car, too, was an expensive one."

"It might not have been his."

"Of course it was his," Myra retorted. "It had a crest on the door, too."

"How do you know?"

"I went and looked. It was a swan with a kind of sprig in its mouth. Oh, Ann, suppose he is a duke!"

Ann laughed. "And what good would that do us?"

"It would be thrilling to meet a real live one. But perhaps he is quite ordinary—and I expect he has a wife and six children, they usually have."

"And what do you mean by 'usually'?" Ann asked in amusement.

"In real life," Myra explained. "I once met a charming man in the train—it was when you sent me to stay at Eastbourne after I had the measles. He was so nice to me and gave me some chocolate."

"Oh, Myra! And I have told you never to speak to strange men in trains!"

"It was quite all right. There were lots of frightfully respectable old women with baskets in the same carriage. Anyway, I was quite certain that he was somebody terribly exciting and important; and then he got out at the next station and there was a large fat woman in a badly cut check coat and skirt waiting for him, and three grubby little boys who simply screamed 'Daddy,' so there was no mistaking who he was—a family man!"

"Poor Myra. That should have taught you not to be so romantic."

"Hope springs eternal . . ." Myra replied dramatically.

"Well, I will go and ask our guest," Ann smiled.

"I will say to him, 'If you please, sir, we wish to know your name, your address, if you have a wife and how many children.' Is there anything else?"

"But of course. You have forgotten the most important thing of all."

"What is that?"

" 'Have you any money?' And if he hasn't, he had better pay in advance."

"That sounds Irish to me," Ann replied.

But she was laughing as she went out of the kitchen. . . .

Two

"I have brought you your tea."

Myra set the tray down beside the bed and gave its occupant a friendly smile. He looked up at her with what seemed to be momentarily an expression of astonishment.

She turned round and shut the door. "I'm Myra," she announced, "and I want to talk to you. Do you mind?"

"Not in the least."

"It is about yourself," Myra said challengingly, adding in a lowered voice: "I have found out all about you. Do you want me to keep it a secret?"

The man in the bed stared at her and his mouth twitched slightly at the corners.

"What exactly have you found out?" he asked.

Myra moved to the end of the bed and leaning against the brass rail in an attitude which was unconsciously graceful and artistic she said:

"When Ann came back this morning and said you had told her your name was John Melton, I was a bit suspicious. I felt you were not just an ordinary person."

"But my name is John Melton."

"Yes, so it is; but didn't you forget to tell her that it was prefixed by 'Sir' and that you were the owner of Gulliver?"

"I answered the questions that your sister put to me," John Melton said briefly, then added: "And how did you discover all this interesting information?"

"I found an envelope in the pocket of your coat which is hanging in the hall," Myra said somewhat defiantly.

"So easily as that? I thought at least you had put a detective on my track?"

"Now you are laughing at me. Honestly, I am being friendly. If you don't want anyone to know, I will keep it a secret, I really will."

"I have no reason to hide my identity or to disguise myself," Sir John said. "Your sister asked me my name and I gave it to her."

"And you don't mind anyone knowing who you really are?"

"No, of course not."

"Oh, but how exciting! Think what a thrill this will be to the village and what a feather in Daddy's cap!—although I expect you will be going away almost at once to get some London specialist to treat you."

"Why should you think that?"

"Why shouldn't I think it? I have seen pictures of your house lots of times and now I remember seeing photographs of you too—in the *Tatler* and papers like that. You are something to do with politics, aren't you?"

"I am a Member of Parliament."

"I think it is all terribly exciting. I had an idea from the beginning that you might be somebody important. Ann laughed at me, but I felt clairvoyant about it."

"If I remember rightly you thought I might be a prince in disguise."

23

Myra looked startled. "What do you mean?" Then she flushed. "Oh, you were listening. We thought you were asleep."

"You woke me up."

"It is a good thing you didn't tell Daddy, he would have been furious."

"I can't imagine your father being furious."

Myra smiled. "He is a poppet, isn't he? If only he would be a bit more sensible about money. We are starvingly poor."

"I remember something being said about that, too," Sir John said with a smile. "But I think it was your sister who remarked that most of his patients went off without paying their bills."

Myra sat down in the chair beside the bed. "I say, you must think we are awful . . . as a family, I mean. But you don't know how rotten it is being poor. I don't suppose you could even imagine what it is like."

"Perhaps I have a vague idea."

"How could you have, living in a place like Gulliver?"

"I don't live there all the time: I have other contacts." Sir John's voice sounded almost apologetic.

"Besides, you are a man," Myra went on, "and men don't feel poverty half as much as women. You don't have to worry about clothes, for one thing."

"No, thank goodness. But tell me about yourselves. Why are you so hard up?"

"I haven't the slightest idea, except that there are too many of us," Myra answered. "It certainly isn't Ann's fault; she is a wonderful manager. She has been paying the accounts and doling out whatever money there was ever since Mother died—and that was seven years ago.

"But Daddy is hopeless! He would give away his last penny and the shirt off his back if somebody was ill; and as for making anyone pay after he has cured them, why, from the way he talks you would think he considered it a privilege to be allowed to doctor them."

"So you all suffer in consequence?" Sir John asked.

There was a slightly cynical note in his voice. He was watching Myra, noting the almost breath-taking prettiness of her colouring, her tip-tilted nose and her swift smile. She seemed so frank and honest—child-like indeed—as she talked with an engaging absence of self-consciousness. And yet he wondered. Some nagging, sophisticated little voice at the back of his mind asked,

"Is this genuine? Are you quite sure this isn't a plant? Has the girl been put up to this?" If it was a trick, it was a clever one.

"Suffer? Of course we suffer," Myra answered. "What do you think I am having to do?"

"I have no idea."

"I'm learning to be a shorthand-typist and I can imagine nothing more nauseating!" There was a world of tragedy in Myra's voice.

"What do you want to do instead?" Sir John asked.

"Well, that's a difficult question," Myra dimpled at him. "To tell the honest truth, I don't want to do anything in the way of earning my living. I hate women with a career, don't you? What I really want to do is to go to parties and have fun and meet interesting people."

"What do you call interesting people?"

Myra hesitated a moment.

"Oh, society people mostly. I see their names in the paper; I see photographs of them when they stay—well, at houses like Gulliver."

Sir John's eyes narrowed.

"So what you would really like would be to be invited to Gulliver?"

"Of course I should," Myra exclaimed.

Then her face fell.

"But what is the use of even thinking about it? Even if you asked us—out of gratitude—we shouldn't be able to come."

"Why not?"

"What should we wear? How could we possibly afford the sort of clothes your friends have. Can't you imagine them turning up their noses at my Sunday best? You should see it! It is four years old and Ann had it before me."

John laughed outright. It was no use trying to be suspicious. This engaging child amused him.

"And did Ann get a new frock after she had given you hers?"

"It was a coat and skirt," Myra corrected, "and actually I am being rather mean about it. It was given to Ann by one of our rich cousins."

"So you have some rich relations?"

"Had," Myra remarked briefly, and explained: "Nell is dead. She was rather a nice girl, about Ann's age; but she was killed in the blitz."

"I see. So there will be no more smart clothes?"

"Not a hope," Myra said cheerfully. "So there you are; now you see how the poor live."

"Tell me more about yourselves. You have got a younger sister, haven't you? I think I heard her also at the window this morning."

"You mean the twins—Antoinette and Antony. They are awful little nuisances—and yet one can't help loving them. I shouldn't be here now if it were not for them."

"Why?"

"Because they have got into trouble again and Ann had to go and settle it. That's why she asked me to bring in your tea. I shouldn't have got the opportunity otherwise, although I was dying to see you."

"I am flattered. But I thought you had seen me."

"I couldn't see much through the crack in the curtains. But when I found out who you were, I was determined to get in somehow and have a talk with you all by myself."

"And Ann would have prevented you?"

"I expect so. She usually looks after Daddy's patients when nurse isn't here. But this afternoon she

26

heard that Mrs. Burrows was simply furious with the twins and she had to hurry off to apologise. You see, Mr. Burrows is our butcher and we owe him pounds; so you can see it was important."

"Very important, I should imagine," Sir John said solemnly. "What had the twins done?"

Myra giggled.

"One cannot help laughing," she said; "the Burrows boy, Eric, is a horrible little beast—a spoilt only child, you know the sort. Besides, he always gets the best cuts off everything—at least, so we think—anyway, he is terribly fat and overfed.

"We have caught him out on several occasions being cruel to animals and the twins saw him this morning trying to tie an old kettle on a string to one of the village cats. The twins watched him till he had nearly got it fixed and then they released the cat and took Eric down to the salvage dump.

"There they tied all sorts of old rubbish all over him. When they had made him an absolutely fantastic spectacle with kettles and old tins trailing behind, and a saucepan on his head and goodness knows what else, they made him run through the village.

"Of course he was yelling with anger and fright by this time and his screams and the rattle of the salvage tins brought everyone out to have a look."

"How did they make him run?" Sir John asked.

"Eric Burrows has very fat legs," Myra replied, "and the twins were carrying a bunch of stinging nettles apiece."

Sir John threw back his head and laughed.

"It is all very well for you to laugh," Myra said, "but it is poor Ann who has to deal with Mrs. Burrows."

"I am sorry for Ann; but at the same time I feel that justice has been done and the twins are really to be congratulated."

"On the contrary, they have been sent up to their room in disgrace. But they won't worry about that; they will sit up there planning some other hideous crime if I know anything about them."

"I feel I should make the acquaintance of the twins."

"You had better ask Ann or Daddy," Myra replied. "If I let them in here and they made you worse, I should get into awful trouble."

"I will risk it," Sir John answered. "I have had a thoroughly lazy afternoon sleeping peacefully and to be honest I am feeling surprisingly well."

"You can't tell what your reaction will be for forty-eight hours. But if you feel so much better I suppose you will be leaving here." Myra spoke wistfully.

"I haven't said so," Sir John answered; "and I see no reason why I should hurry away. I am very comfortable."

"Oh, but you can't be! You can't really like being here," Myra exclaimed. "Just look at this room! Why, you must be laughing at it when you compare it with your own house."

"I am certainly not laughing at it," Sir John said sharply; "and it would be very silly to compare places so utterly different."

"Now you sound cross."

"I am not cross," Sir John answered, "I merely think you are being rather snobbish about Gulliver. It is a famous house because it is historical, not because I . . ."

He did not finish his sentence, for the door opened suddenly and Myra started to her feet. Ann came into the room. She was wearing a light coat over her summer dress and carried her hat in her hand.

"Oh, here you are, Myra! I wondered where you had got to."

"I was talking to Sir John," Myra answered with a faint accent on the "Sir."

"Sir John?" Ann repeated the words and looked towards the bed.

"Your sister," John Melton explained in an amused

28

voice, "has accused me of deliberately misleading you this morning, Miss Shefford. I assure you that was not my intention."

"But in reality he is Sir John Melton," Myra said quickly, "and the owner of Gulliver. You know whom I mean, Ann. You remember we saw some pictures of his house once and you admired them so much."

Ann looked from Myra to John Melton in bewilderment and the colour rose in her cheeks.

"I am sorry if I misunderstood you this morning," she said a little stiffly.

"But you didn't," Sir John protested.

"And now, Myra, perhaps you will go and get your own tea," Ann said. "Tell the twins they can come downstairs."

She bent forward to feel the teapot.

"Won't you have your tea while it is hot, Sir John?" She spoke formally, avoiding his eyes.

Myra moved towards the door. As she reached it, she looked at Sir John behind Ann's back and made a little grimace; then she slipped from the room.

Sir John felt that something was expected from him.

"I kept your sister talking here, Miss Shefford; I hope you won't be annoyed with her."

Ann looked at him and he realised what a tremendous difference there was between the sisters. Ann's eyes too were clear and candid, but there was intelligence in her broad brow and the expression on her face now was of someone who was worried and a little anxious.

She looked towards the door and then she said in a low voice:

"Please, Sir John, don't encourage Myra. She is going through an extremely romantic phase and if it is true that you are the owner of Gulliver, she will dream all sorts of impossible and absurd dreams about it and you will seem to her a fairy-tale prince. She is very young and unsophisticated. I don't want her spoilt more than is necessary."

29

"And does a romantic imagination spoil anyone?"

Sir John was arguing for the sake of arguing, watching Ann's face, noting the perplexed pucker on her forehead, the way she considered his question thoughtfully before she answered.

"It seems to me," she said at length, "that Myra will want a good deal more common sense before she goes out into the world . . . but perhaps I am wrong. She is so very pretty and sometimes I get frightened as to what will happen to her."

"You are very young yourself to mother such a big family," Sir John suggested.

"Oh, not really," Ann answered, "I am twenty-one. Besides, they are all very sweet, including Daddy who is the biggest baby of the lot."

"And you have this afternoon already settled the little trouble about the twins?" Sir John asked.

Ann smiled, and the smile drove the anxiety from her eyes.

"Myra told you about it? Yes, Mrs. Burrows has forgiven them, but I am going to make them both write letters of apology—not to Eric Burrows, he is a horrid little boy, but to his mother. She feels humiliated in the eyes of the village and that is what matters far more than Eric's suffering."

"And will the twins write the letters?"

"Of course they will if I ask them to. They are very good really. It is just that they haven't enough to do; they ought to go to a proper school . . . they ought to play games and have . . . but I don't want to worry you, Sir John, with our troubles. I only hope Myra hasn't bored you."

"I assure you that nothing either you or Myra could say to me would bore me," Sir John answered.

"That is very nice of you," Ann said. "And now please have your tea before it gets cold."

She had left the room before he could think of an excuse to keep her. But when she had gone, it was some moments before he poured out his tea or took a piece

such a wallop in the passage when the master wasn't looking that they kept their mouths shut after that."

Ann sighed. She was not going to say so in front of Antony, but she loathed the rough village boys with whom he had to associate. They were jealous of him in many ways and she knew that when they got the opportunity they took it out of him by teasing and ridicule.

Now she said quickly, as if to escape her own thoughts:

"Come along, now, both of you; and I have got something nice for tea."

"What is it?" Antony asked.

"Strawberries and cream," Ann replied.

"And cream!" Antoinette echoed. "Oooh! where did it come from?"

"The farm. I stopped there on my way home to say we wanted some extra milk for our patient, and Mrs. Drew gave me a jugful for 'the little ones'."

"The little ones indeed!" Antony exclaimed scornfully. "But all the same she is a jolly good sport. I'll race you, Antoinette."

They were down the stairs before Ann had reached the end of the landing, and though she felt they were being noisy she hadn't the heart to rebuke them.

There were so few treats in their lives these days, and both Antony and Antoinette had got to the stage where their food was of intense interest to them. All the same, as they sat at tea she wondered if it would be polite to ask Sir John to have some; then she remembered Myra's stories of Gulliver and hardened her heart.

"He has so much," she thought, "and the children have so little."

When no one was looking, surreptitiously she transferred two of the largest strawberries on her own plate to Antony's. Their portions had all been fairly divided up by Myra at the very beginning of tea, but

33

it was a usual thing for tit-bits allotted to Ann to be given to Antony.

There was something about her little brother which touched her heart, and though she had for Myra and Antoinette a deep affection, it was Antony whom she loved the best. He always seemed so small and courageous and, despite his relationship with Antoinette, peculiarly alone.

Ann wondered if of them all he did not miss his mother the most. He was only five when she died and yet she had an idea that he still remembered her vividly.

Sometimes he would talk about her, asking strange questions, and Ann knew without being told that afterwards he pondered these things in his heart.

Antoinette adored her father; she was in many ways a self-sufficient small person, finding all she needed in life from the spoiling of her father and the companionship of her twin. Antony was different.

Ann was sure of that; and when she went to bed at night she would pray earnestly and with a passion that sometimes surprised herself that she might be allowed to make up to Antony for all that he had lost in not having a mother to love and guide him.

They were just finishing their tea when a sudden thought struck Ann.

"Did Sir John ask you to send a telegram for him, Myra?" she inquired.

"No. Why?"

"Daddy said at breakfast that he must find out whom Sir John wished to notify about his accident. Of course he didn't know who he was then. But I am sure he didn't give Daddy any messages and if he did, Daddy is certain to have forgotten them."

"Perhaps he gave them to the policeman who came after luncheon," Antony suggested.

"Oh, perhaps he did," Ann said, "but I had better go and ask him all the same."

"I will go if you like," said Myra with a too elaborate casualness.

"No, don't worry, I can manage."

Ann went along the passage to Sir John's room. She knocked and entered to find him lying with his eyes closed. She waited a moment, until he turned his head slowly to look at her.

"I am so sorry to disturb you," Ann apologised, "but I have just remembered that you might want to send some telegrams about your accident. My father did speak of it this morning, but I am afraid I forgot until now."

"Your father mentioned it to me, too. Actually I thought I would do nothing. . . ."

"But surely," Ann said, "they will be worried about you."

"Who?"

"Well, there must be someone . . . your mother . . . your wife. . . ."

"My mother is not expecting me back for three or four days at least. And I have no wife. Hasn't your sister informed you of that fact?"

For a moment Ann stiffened, feeling that he was being horrid about Myra. She might deprecate Myra's inquisitiveness herself, but she wasn't going to let anyone else criticise her. Then she understood that Sir John was only teasing and she smiled.

"In this household we don't even listen to Myra's fairy stories," she said. "But if you are sure there is no one . . ."

"I will write to my mother; I think it would be less of a shock for her," Sir John said. "And my household in London are well-trained; they expect me when they see me. So there is no imperative need for any telegrams to be dispatched. All I should like later is some writing-paper and a pencil."

"I will get them for you now."

Ann spoke shyly and when she had fetched him the things he required she slipped from the room without further conversation. She was suddenly aware of the tremendous gulf that lay between them.

One could not reconcile this rich, important man and his subservient household awaiting his commands with their own gossiping, chattering little family circle.

This dramatic intrusion into their small humdrum existence was simply chance. They must not allow a transitory visitor to disturb or disrupt the even tenor of their ways.

"The sooner he goes the better," Ann thought to herself. "He is exciting Myra, and no good will come of us peeping into his big, extravagant world with which we shall never have anything in common."

Three

"So this is the kitchen!"

Ann, who was kneeling with her back to the door scrubbing the flagged floor, gave an exclamation and turned round to see Sir John standing in the doorway. He was supporting himself on a stick and she thought that she saw in his face some amusement and surprise at the sight of her.

"Whatever are you doing here?" she asked severely. "I thought you were resting in the garden."

"So I was," Sir John replied, "but I got bored, so I came in search of a book or someone to talk to. For a moment I thought you were Mrs. Briggs. What are you doing?"

"Can't you see what I am doing?"

She held out the scrubbing brush in one hand and the soap in the other.

"But surely you don't have to clean this floor?"

"Of course I do!—that is, when Mrs. Briggs won't come. She usually gives us three mornings a week, but she has got one of her "turns" and that means at least a fortnight before we see her again. They are the result of asthma, high blood pressure and too much beer on Saturday night—at least, that is what Daddy attributes them to."

"But isn't there someone else?"

"To do this?" Ann with a gesture indicated the big expanse of flagged floor, damp, but clean.

"Yes, of course. You are not fitted for this sort of thing."

"That's all you know about it," Ann retorted. "I have done it often enough; and if I didn't—well, even if we could get anyone 'to oblige' while Mrs. Briggs is ill they would want to be paid."

"But it is ridiculous! I can't understand your father allowing it!"

Ann looked up at Sir John's scowling face and chuckled.

"Darling Daddy imagines that floors clean themselves and meals are cooked by magic. It would be no use complaining to him. Now you go back to the garden, Sir John, and forget our domestic politics; and if you are good, I will bring you out a big glass of iced coffee in a few moments; I have made you some and it is just getting cold."

She spoke as she might have spoken to a small child who was making a nuisance of himself.

Instead of obeying her Sir John walked slowly across the kitchen and sat down on a chair in front of the window.

"I want to talk to you," he announced.

Ann opened her mouth as if she would have argued with him, but seeing the determination on his face, she said:

"Oh, very well then; but you will have to wait until I have finished—there is only this corner left to do."

She turned her back on him and bending over

scrubbed hard. Sir John watched her without comment, until finally she threw the scrubbing brush and cloth into the bucket and standing up announced not without pride:

"There, that's done."

Still Sir John said nothing, and Ann, picking up the bucket in one hand, the soap and kneeling mat in the other, carried them into the small scullery. He heard her pour away the water, then she came back into the kitchen.

Taking off the enveloping apron of brown sacking which had covered her linen frock, she hung it on the door, and going to the corner by the dresser slipped off the old and battered shoes she wore and put on another pair that were waiting there.

Then she drew off the coloured handkerchief which had neatly covered her hair and, shaking her head to loosen the compressed waves, said with a smile:

"Now I am ready. Is it as serious as all that?"

Sir John noted as she walked towards him how fresh and sweet she looked. The dress she wore was old and faded from many washings, but it was freshly laundered and at the neck she had slipped into a plain gold brooch a half-opened rosebud which in its pink perfection accentuated the whiteness of her skin.

She stood in front of him, one hand on the kitchen table, the other smoothing the dark hair back from her forehead. He did not speak for a moment and she said gently:

"Don't look so worried. Are you in pain?"

"No, I'm all right."

"You oughtn't to be walking on that leg," Ann said swiftly. "You know that Daddy said you were to rest. I shall tell him that you are disobeying orders."

"I am not afraid of your father," Sir John said humorously. "And you give me far more orders than he does."

Ann laughed.

"That's one for me, isn't it? I suppose at any moment you will say I'm a domineering personality, just because someone has to take command here."

"It is because you do take command that I want to talk to you," Sir John answered. "I have been here ten days and so far I have paid nothing. Unlike your father I know that food costs money and service means wages.

"I have been thinking things over and I feel it might be awkward for you if I asked you to quote a price for having me as a lodger. I therefore suggest—and I hope that you think it fair—that I should pay you the same amount that I paid to a nursing home where I stayed when having my appendix removed three years ago. Do you agree?"

"It sounds reasonable," Ann answered. "And what did you pay?"

"Twenty-five guineas a week."

Ann gave a little gasp.

"And you are suggesting that you should pay us that? Oh, but it is ridiculous! Of course we couldn't take anything like so much!"

"Why not?"

"Well, for one thing, the sum is fantastic; and secondly it doesn't cost us anything like that to keep you here. You talk about wages, but nurse works in the dispensary every morning anyway, so your being here doesn't cost Daddy any extra so far as she is concerned, and my attentions—such as they are—aren't purchasable!

"So there is only your laundry and your keep—and as for that, we have given you very simple food—practically the same as we have had ourselves. Besides, look at the fruit that you have had sent here from your home.

"Peaches, nectarines, strawberries and all those lovely things which you have insisted on the children sharing! As a matter of fact I have already thought about what you ought to pay and I think that thirty shillings a week would be plenty."

39

Sir John made a gesture of impatience.

"Miss Shefford, I have been very comfortable here. I have stayed because I wanted to stay. I have had exactly the same medical attention as I would have received in the most expensive nursing home, with many extra comforts and kindnesses which would have been quite unprocurable in such surroundings, and I see no reason why we should not be properly businesslike over a settlement."

Ann looked obstinate. "It is too much."

"And yet you need the money."

"Yes, I know that; but that is our problem, not yours. We can't rob you because we are stupid enough to get into debt."

"I wouldn't call your father a stupid man; I would call him a philanthropist and a great Christian."

The unexpected softness in Sir John's voice brought the tears to Ann's eyes.

"Thank you for saying that," she replied. "It is true, of course. Daddy is a wonderful person. He just doesn't understand that even necessities cost money and that, however happy one is, one cannot live entirely on love and friendship."

"At the same time," Sir John replied, "your father has the good sense to realise that money isn't really important. That is why I suggest to you, without making any more fuss, that you accept what I wish to pay."

"But I couldn't!" Ann exclaimed. "It may sound silly to you, but I couldn't take all that money, not even for the sake of the children. You see, I don't want you here . . ."

She stopped suddenly and the blood rose quickly to her cheeks as if the words had slipped out unexpectedly. Then with an obvious effort she went on: "Now I have said that I may as well continue. Sir John, I wish you would go away."

"Why?" The question was hard and sharp.

"Because you are upsetting us all. Daddy likes having you, I know that. He enjoys talking to you in the evenings. It is a long time since he has had a man with whom he could have discussions and political arguments. But when you have gone, he is going to miss you terribly.

"He was quite contented before you came; he didn't know how lonely he was with only a pack of children in the house—no wife and no one of his own age.

"When you go away, you are going to leave a great gap in his life and the longer you put off going, the greater his loss will be.

"And then there is Myra!" Ann was speaking quickly now, almost breathlessly. "Myra thinks she is in love with you. She moons about the place, trying new ways of doing her hair, badgering me for money so that she can buy new clothes with which, poor little stupid, she hopes to fascinate you.

"She hasn't done a stroke of work since you arrived. It won't matter to you when you have gone back to your own life and your amusing friends, that Myra will fail for the second time in her examination and that all the money Daddy has spent on her career will be wasted! You won't care! You won't even know!

"But I shall be left to cope with it! Antony will suffer in consequence because with Myra unemployed we can't send him to a proper school, and Antoinette will have to go without even more things which would make her happy.

"But what will you know about that? Or care? There is much more I could say, but what is the use? Won't you try to understand, Sir John? And please go back to the world in which you belong!"

Ann finished by speaking passionately and pleadingly, her hands clasped together, her dark eyes wide and shining with unshed tears.

Sir John had listened to her without moving. Now there was a long silence between them, so that the only sound in the kitchen was the ticking of the big clock on the mantelpiece. Ann thought as she looked

41

at him that the expression on his face was stern and hard.

"Yes, he is hard," she thought wildly; "hard and selfish. He doesn't understand and he doesn't want to!"

Abruptly she turned and walked across the kitchen. She stood at the dresser with her back to Sir John, staring at a plate—an old willow-patterned one which had been left in the oven too long and was brown at the edges with a great jagged crack across the middle.

Resolutely she fought back the tears which threatened to overwhelm her. It was her world that was in danger, her own complete little family world enclosed within the four walls of the house; a world in which she asked only the love and happiness of her father, of Myra and the twins.

What did anything else matter—politics and national issues, the pomp and circumstance of other people's lives, the glamour and wonder of such places as Gulliver?

She drew her handkerchief out of her pocket and wiped the tears which slipped down her cheeks; then at last she heard Sir John's voice.

"Will you come back here a moment?"

She turned towards him half defiantly, ready to continue the fight yet conscious at the same time of a weakness within herself, a disinclination for further argument.

To her relief the obstinacy and hardness had gone from his face; instead he was looking at her with a new expression—one that she fancied was faintly apologetic.

He said nothing, only looked at her, and she found herself moving across the kitchen towards him.

"Sit down," he said gently, "and let us talk this out."

Ann took the chair he indicated on the other side of the table.

"First of all," Sir John said quietly, "I am going to say I am sorry. I had no idea you felt like this. Secondly, I want you to know my own view-point. It is a selfish one, if you like, but here in your home I have had a holiday and a rest.

"It is the first time for many years that I have been able to relax and forget the troubles of office; to set aside the constant cares and responsibilities which have always seemed to surround me whether I was at home, in London, or staying with friends.

"You would be surprised, Miss Shefford, if you knew in the past week or so how often I have blessed this accident of mine. You are aware, as I am, that from a health point of view I could have left a long time ago.

"But I didn't want to, and the reason for that was that I had been very tired for a long time, and I had forgotten how to be young; forgotten—though it may seem impossible to you—how to enjoy myself. I have rested and I have had a surprisingly enjoyable time as your guest.

"I have felt in your father's company and—if you will let me say so—in yours, too, that I was accepted simply as myself, as a man—plain John Melton without any trappings. It has been a new experience and one which I have enjoyed more than I can say. Can you understand?"

Ann put up both her hands to her forehead as if in a little gesture of helplessness.

"I wish you hadn't told me that," she replied. "It was easier to go on hating you."

"Must you hate me?"

There was something whimsical about his smile.

Ann thought for a moment.

"I suppose to be honest it is because I am afraid of you," she said. "I have admitted that to myself a long time ago. We are a very small pond here and you are a very big stone to fall into it. I have tried to tell myself the damage was done, that it is no use my worrying and that I must make the best of it. But all the same, I feel that if I can get you to go away quickly, perhaps things will return to normal in time."

"Aren't you making a mountain out of a mole hill?" Sir John asked.

"I don't think even you would be so modest as to call yourself a mole hill," Ann answered. "Things have changed—we have all altered since you have been here."

"Even you?"

"Yes, even me. When I have been listening to you talking, when I have heard of other places and other people so absolutely alien to this quiet, uneventful life of ours, I have begun to think that I, too, am missing something; and it has made me restless. Not for long, but long enough to make me afraid, to make me hate you because you have threatened the one thing I have of real value."

"Isn't it greedy of you to hoard your happiness and keep it exclusively yours while the rest of the world is starving and hungry for what you have in plenty?"

"Is the rest of the world like that? How do I know?" Ann asked. "All I know is that we were happy and complete. We had our little problems, of course, but now you have made them so much bigger, so insurmountable.

"You have injected us with the germ of discontent, we have begun to question ourselves as well as our environment. Oh, Sir John, do go away, and perhaps when you have gone we shall settle down again."

"And if I refuse?"

There was a sudden sharpness in Sir John's tones.

"Why should you refuse?" Ann was not pleading now, she was fighting him. "What are we to you? I am not deceived, Sir John, nor am I a dreamer of fairy stories like Myra. I know that any interest you have in us is merely momentary—the amused patronage and benevolence of a rich, important man towards a wandering freak show which has crossed his path by chance.

"What has Sir John Melton got in common with a

small village doctor, unknown and from a financial point of view not even successful at his own job?

"What has Sir John Melton got in common with two semi-educated country girls who have not read the books he has, or met the people he has met, and who have no knowledge at all of his interests and his ambitions? No, Sir John, others may be fooled by you, but I am not.

"When this rest by which you set so much store, this quiet oasis in the middle of a busy life begins to pall, you will go away. You will be generous enough to pay us well, that I quite understand; and the money will mean as little to you as the ten shillings and sixpence you would pay for a seat in the stalls of the theatre.

"You will have seen the show, and that will be that. It won't worry you that you will have left an empty place in somebody's life, an ache in some stupid, susceptible heart, or an atmosphere of doubt and distrust which will not be dispelled until long after you have forgotten that amusing holiday interlude."

Again Ann spoke passionately, but there were no tears in her eyes this time.

"You are certainly not afraid to say what you think," Sir John suggested.

"Not when it concerns the people I love."

"Very well, then; I will accept your decision, Miss Shefford. I will do what you want."

Ann drew a deep breath.

"Oh, thank you."

"But on one condition," he added quickly, "and in this I mean to have my own way. I shall pay for my treatment and my stay in your house at my own price, and you will accept it because you know it will benefit those very people for whose sake you are driving me from your home."

Ann raised her chin unconsciously and with pride, and then her eyes met Sir John's across the table. For

45

a moment it seemed as if they battled with each other silently.

Something strong and magnetic vibrated in the air between them, they were both tense and Ann's quickened breathing parted her lips, while her eyes were wide and dark.

Quite suddenly she capitulated.

"I accept your terms, Sir John, so long as you will leave us."

"I will go tomorrow," he said. "I will telephone for a car and make arrangements to leave immediately after luncheon. Will that be convenient?"

"Perfectly."

Ann could afford to relax; now that the battle was over, she seemed cool, collected and sure of herself. It was hard to remember how young she was and how but a few moments ago there had been fear in her voice and tears in her eyes.

Sir John got to his feet.

"That is settled then. And thank you for your hospitality."

"You must thank my father for that."

Sir John moved a few steps across the kitchen, then turned to look at her.

"You are a formidable fighter, Miss Shefford. It isn't often that I acknowledge myself the vanquished."

For a moment formality disappeared as Ann smiled at him.

"You make me sound rather terrifying."

"All the same," he replied grimly, "that doesn't worry you because you have won."

"Have I?" Ann was serious again. "I will not be able to tell you that with any certainty for at least three months—perhaps longer."

"And will you tell me?"

"Of course I shall not. Why, by that time you won't even remember our names. 'Shefford? Shefford?' you will say. 'That must be the name of the people in that

46

ghastly little village where I had the accident. I wonder what has happened to them.' "

She mimicked a social accent, but there was a touch of disdain and bitterness underlying the superficial tones.

Sir John smiled grimly.

"Miss Shefford, there is one other condition which I ought to have made before I capitulated to your quite unreasonable request. I am very sorry now I didn't include it."

"What was that?"

"I should have insisted on being allowed to give you a good spanking," Sir John said. "You deserve it."

Ann laughed even though her cheeks flamed suddenly and her eyes were shy.

"It is too late now for amendments," she said. "The treaty has been signed."

The shrill summons of the telephone bell echoed down the passage.

"The telephone!" Ann exclaimed. "I had better answer it; there is no one else in the house."

She slipped through the kitchen door and ran down the passage as if glad of the interruption. Sir John followed slowly. The telephone was in the hall and he could not help hearing Ann's conversation.

"What? . . . Who is it speaking? . . . Yes, this is Ann Shefford. . . . What? . . . What do you mean? . . . Yes . . . Yes. Dr. Shefford . . . but I don't understand . . . who is that speaking? . . . What? . . . Yes, I know, he has had them before. . . . Oh . . . he seems—what have you done? . . . Yes, I will get Dr. Ashton. . . . At once, of course, and I will come myself. . . . Yes, at once. . . ."

Sir John reached the centre of the hall as Ann put down the receiver. She stood there for a moment as if stupefied, her face drained of all colour. He thought for one moment that she was going to faint; then with an obvious effort she pulled herself together.

"What is the matter? What has happened?"

She turned to answer him, and Sir John had the

47

impression that she had no idea who he was, that her eyes did not even see him.

"It is Daddy," she said dully, her voice very low. "He has had one of his heart attacks and they think he is . . . dead."

Four

Dr. Ashton bolted the last mouthful of the steamed pudding which, having been kept hot for him since one o'clock, was now at two-fifteen dry, hard and not particularly appetising.

Then he pushed back his chair from the table and got to his feet, giving a quick glance at the clock; he was forever racing time, and time was invariably the winner. He hurried from the dining-room into the small oak-panelled and rather dark hall.

"I am going now, Evelyn," he called.

"Very well, dear. Try not to be late."

It was the response he expected, the one he had in fact been hearing for over twenty years, and automatically he replied to it with a familiar "I will do my best."

He picked up his hat and the black bag which was lying ready for him on the side table and turned towards the door. As he did so, a car stopped outside and almost unconsciously he swore mildly beneath his breath. If this was a patient, it would make him later than ever. He flung open the door.

A man was getting slowly and with some difficulty out of a big grey Rolls-Royce. He held a stick in his hand and his chauffeur was assisting him. When finally he reached the pavement and raised his head a little, Dr. Ashton recognised his unexpected visitor and hurried down the steps to meet him.

"Good afternoon, Sir John."

Sir John Melton held out his hand.

"Good afternoon, Doctor. Can you spare me a moment of your time?"

"Of course I can."

Blithely Dr. Ashton swept on one side the appointments which were already overlapping and told his conscience cheerily that one didn't prevaricate when a man like Sir John Melton was concerned.

"Come inside, Sir John," he said, leading the way through the front door, noting that after all his guest was fairly surefooted and not too clumsy in his movements.

"How are you getting on?" he inquired as they reached the hall.

"My leg is practically well, thank you," Sir John replied. "It is only that it gets a bit stiff when I am driving or sitting in one position for a long time; but when I use it the stiffness soon wears off."

"Well, don't use it too much for another week or so," Dr. Ashton advised, opening the door of his study.

Sir John preceded him into the room. "It is lucky that I caught you. I gather you were just going out."

"The usual afternoon round of visits," Dr. Ashton said with a smile, "but they can keep. None of my patients are so desperately ill that they can't wait half an hour for me. Besides, I am honoured that you should visit me, Sir John."

"I wanted to ask your advice about the Shefford family," Sir John explained.

"The Shefford family. Yes, I wondered whether that, perhaps, was your reason for coming here. It is a sad business altogether."

"You knew Dr. Shefford well?"

"Very well indeed. He was older than I am so that we were not at the university together; but we have been friends ever since we started to practise. We have always lived in this part of the world and he

49

has helped me on many occasions; I think I can say that in return I have been able to help him. It was a great shock to me, as well as to his many other friends, his dying so suddenly."

"He had suffered from his heart for some time, I imagine?"

"For years: he knew all about it, too, and knew the risks he took. We had all warned him—in fact only three months ago I made him go and see Sir Gilbert Hewett—the great heart specialist—and Sir Gilbert told him frankly that unless he eased up and took life more leisurely, he would kill himself. Well, like so many other people, he disobeyed orders and you know the result."

"Yes, I was staying at the house when he died."

"Ann told me. And I thought it was exceedingly tactful of you to turn out at a moment's notice like that."

"I felt they would want to be alone," Sir John said quietly. "Both the elder girls were extremely fond of their father."

"And the youngest," Dr. Ashton added. "Little Antoinette is absolutely broken-hearted. She adored her father, and I think of them all she was his favourite. But they are all delightful children; I am terribly sorry for them now."

"That is exactly what I came to see you about. I have waited until after the funeral before I inquired if there was anything I could do to help."

"Well, Arthur Shefford was buried the day before yesterday, and now comes the reckoning," Dr. Ashton said. "As a matter of fact I sent my secretary over yesterday to see if she could make anything of the chaos in which he left his affairs.

"She is a clever woman, has been with me for years, and she told me last night that she had never seen anything so pitiful as Arthur Shefford's accounts. As for his finances—well, quite frankly, Sir John, there is not much hope as far as I can see of there being anything for the children to live on.

"There isn't even the money to pay the tradespeople. there is a mortgage on the house and his income tax doesn't bear thinking about. And what is the solution?"

Dr. Ashton asked the question dramatically; but if he hoped for an equally dramatic reply, he was disappointed. Sir John took his cigarette case out of his pocket and opened it.

"Do you mind if I smoke?" he asked.

"My dear Sir John, I do apologise! I'm a pipe smoker myself or I would have offered you one before. Now let me see—where did I put the matches. . . ."

"Don't worry," Sir John said; "I have a lighter."

He flicked it open and lit a cigarette.

As he did so, Dr. Ashton studied him. He wondered just exactly how much help Sir John was willing to give the Sheffords. He had known him by reputation for years and no one had ever suggested in his hearing that Sir John was a particularly generous man.

He was known, of course, to have a good brain and for being very much a coming man in politics. His position and money made him a power in other ways; but nothing that Dr. Ashton could remember about him suggested that he was particularly charitable or philanthropic or likely to help to any large extent an obscure doctor's family left—as Dr. Ashton put it to himself—on their beam ends.

"Nevertheless," the doctor thought, "a little is better than nothing and it certainly won't hurt John Melton to hand them out some money. He won't miss a hundred or so and it will mean a great deal to them."

He remembered Ann's face at the funeral. She had been very pale, as was to be expected, and there were dark lines under her eyes as if she had spent a sleepless night in tears. But what had struck Dr. Ashton more than anything was the look of strain and anxiety on her face.

Once during the service she had put out a protecting hand to touch Antony and draw him a little closer to her, and another time he had seen her make the same gesture towards Antoinette.

"She is fond of those children," he told himself, and added, "almost maternal about them; she might be their mother."

He had known then that the anxiety in her face was connected with them.

"She is worrying about their future," he decided, "and not without reason."

He had not been certain at that moment what would be the result of his secretary's investigation, but he had a very good idea. Arthur Shefford had always been hopeless where money was concerned; he just hadn't seemed able to concentrate on finance or anything connected with it.

He had devoted his life to the healing of the sick, rather as another man might devote his life to the worship of God to the exclusion of all else.

But whereas Arthur Shefford had now escaped from the consequences of his years of negligence, his family could not, and Dr. Ashton could not help feeling that it was rather hard that the children should pay the debts incurred by their father through his lack of self-interest.

Well, perhaps after all, help was likely to come from an unexpected quarter. Dr. Ashton admitted to himself that he had misjudged Sir John. He had thought when he had learnt of his departure that they were unlikely to hear anything further from him except a cheque sent in settlement of his account.

On the contrary, here was the great man in person and apparently interested enough to make inquiries as to what he could do. Dr. Ashton had no intention of mincing his words.

"The position, quite frankly, is this, Sir John—and I think Ann will forgive me if I betray any family confidences in making things quite clear to you. My old friend has left his family heavily handicapped.

"There is no money even to pay for his funeral. I

shall, of course, because I am the oldest friend he had, make every effort to get at least a few of his patients to pay up; but even if twenty-five per cent of them are honest enough to meet their bills, it will not be nearly enough to cover what is outstanding.

"It is quite impossible, therefore, for the family to go on living as they are for more than a week or so.

"My wife and I have already discussed the matter and we thought we might offer hospitality to Ann for a few weeks, to give her a chance to look round; but we can't take more than one, we just haven't got room.

"There is, I believe, one relation of the Sheffords who might be helpful. She is a first cousin of Arthur's— an elderly woman who turned up at the funeral and who I gather from some slight conversation I had with her intends offering a home to the twins.

"She seemed to have little affection for Ann or Myra and I came to the conclusion she was one of those elderly spinsters who does not approve of the modern girl."

"But surely," Sir John interrupted, "it will distress them all very much to be separated?"

"I am quite certain it will," Dr. Ashton replied. "At the same time, Sir John, we have got to be practical. Ann and Myra are both at the age when they can earn money; but without experience—and certainly where Ann is concerned without training—they are not likely to be able to earn enough to keep the home together.

"Actually I have not had a chance of discussing with Ann what career she might undertake. She is a capable girl as far as the household is concerned—I might try to get her into one of the hospitals.

"There might be an opening there for a housekeeper, although she's very young; but if she's willing it might be managed; and, of course, if the twins were out of the way and provided for it would simplify things a good deal."

Sir John got to his feet.

"You have told me exactly what I wanted to know, Dr. Ashton. I am very much obliged to you. I am going over to Little Cople now to see Miss Shefford, but I didn't want to put her to the embarrassment of telling me just how bad things are for them."

"I hope you will be able to help them, Sir John?"

There was a note of interrogation in Dr. Ashton's voice. He was both anxious and curious to know what Sir John intended to do. But Sir John, holding out his hand in farewell, had obviously no intention of telling him.

"Good-bye, Dr. Ashton," he said, "and thank you."

The journey from Dr. Ashton's residence to Little Cople took Sir John about twenty minutes, during which he was obviously deep in thought. It was only as they neared the village that he remembered his new chauffeur did not know the way and roused himself to give directions.

The house was not hard to find. The car drew up outside the green front door, which was badly in need of a fresh coat of paint, and the chauffeur jumped out quickly to hasten round to the other side and assist Sir John.

But before he opened the car door he rang the bell, giving a good hard tug to the old-fashioned chain bell-pull which hung, rusty and in one place mended with wire, beside the door.

Yet even after Sir John had been helped from the car and was standing waiting on the front door step, there was no response.

"Shall I ring again, Sir John?"

The chauffeur put out his hand, but Sir John shook his head.

"It doesn't matter. I will go in. Perhaps everyone is out."

He turned the door handle and entered the cool quietness of the hall. Closing the door behind him,

54

he walked slowly and limping a little towards the sitting-room.

The door was open and on the other side of the room the french windows were also open, and Sir John moving across the sitting-room saw, as he rather expected to see, someone sitting at the far side of the lawn under the big cedar tree.

It was Ann's favourite seat and whenever her work in the house was done she would escape there with a book or some sewing, being in this obvious retreat isolated and yet within reach should she be wanted.

Sir John passed through the french window and started to cross the lawn. Ann had her back to him and as he drew nearer he saw that surprisingly her hands lay idle in her lap.

She was staring ahead of her, looking towards the orchard with its ancient, unpruned fruit trees and its golden carpet of buttercups. Sir John drew nearer.

The lawn, which was badly in need of cutting, muffled his footsteps. It was only as he reached her side that Ann sensed rather than heard him and turned her head. She gave a quick exclamation and as if at the shock of his sudden appearance one of her hands sprang to her breast.

"Oh, Sir John, you startled me!"

"I'm sorry," Sir John answered gravely. "I did ring the bell, but nobody seemed to be at home so I let myself in. I thought perhaps you might be here."

"I forgot about the bell," Ann said. "And if I had remembered it I expect I should have thought that it didn't matter now that no one in need of a doctor would ring it."

She tried to speak naturally, but despite herself the tears sprang to her eyes and she bent her head to hide them.

"May I sit down?" Sir John suggested.

"But of course. I am sorry, my manners are all at sea this afternoon."

She indicated the empty space on the rough wooden

seat she was occupying and Sir John moved past her to sit down, his bad leg stretched out stiffly in front of him.

"How is your leg?" Ann asked.

"Better," he answered briefly, as if the subject had little interest for him.

Ann took a deep breath.

"It is kind of you to come to see us, Sir John. And I want to thank you for leaving as you did. I knew, of course, why you had gone. I don't remember very much about that day—not after I had seen Daddy and brought him home—but Myra told me later that you had left and she realised as I did, that you had slipped away because you knew we should want to be alone . . . with . . . with our unhappiness.

"I am glad you understood, Sir John; and I want to thank you, too, for the wreath; it was a very lovely one . . . it was kind of you."

"Your father was very kind to me, I shall always remember him with affection."

"I am glad about that," Ann said. "He liked you, too, and he thought you were very clever. In fact, the morning before he died he said to me that he thought you would go far and be one of the great men who would help this country through her many problems and difficulties."

"Thank you for telling me that," Sir John said. "And now, shall I tell you why I have come here?"

"Yes, of course," Ann replied.

"I have come," Sir John began slowly, "because I know that in this moment of difficulty as well as unhappiness your father would like me to help you.

"I am not exaggerating when I say that during those evenings when we talked together, when I was here as a guest in your house, I found in your father not only a man with whom I had a great deal in common, but one whom I shall always be proud to have numbered among my friends.

"And therefore it is as your father's friend that

I have come here this afternoon. Things are, I know, very difficult for you all; but I believe that if you will let me prove that friendship, those difficulties will not be insurmountable."

Ann smiled at him—a small, tremulous smile, but it managed to lighten the strain and suffering on her face.

"Thank you, Sir John. But quite frankly there is very little you can do. Dr. Ashton's secretary has been looking into our affairs and we have learnt that the first thing to be done is for us to leave this house. It may sound silly to you, but I never expected that.

"Somehow I had imagined that if I worked and Myra had a job we should be able to carry on. But we can't and therefore our family will be scattered. Antony and Antoinette are going to a cousin of my father's—Aunt Ella we call her—and Myra is going to live with a school friend of hers until she has finished her commercial course; after that she and I are going to try to be together. We shall find a room in Melchester perhaps. . . ."

"And you?—what do you intend to do?"

"I have got to find work of some sort."

Ann had spoken calmly and there was no hint of tears either in her eyes or her voice. And yet Sir John was aware of the anguish which underlay every utterance she made—the breaking up of the family, the losing of the twins, the relinquishing of every last link with their father, with each other and with their home was an agony almost beyond expression.

"And do you think that you will find it easy to get employment?"

Ann made a little gesture with her hands.

"There must be something I can do," she replied, "even if it is only housework. I am a very good cook and people are very short of cooks."

"But you can't go into domestic service!"

"Why not? You will admit that I can scrub a floor well, and when you were here you always praised the food we gave you, even though you did not always know that I had cooked it."

Sir John was still for a moment, and then he said: "I have another proposition to make. I wonder if you would listen to it?"

"Of course I will," Ann replied. Then impulsively she added: "Sir John, I've felt terribly guilty about you. Please, I would like to apologise."

"For what?"

"For being so horrid to you that day . . . the day . . . that Daddy died. Yes, I was horrid. I know that now and you have been so kind and considerate . . . in fact you've heaped coals of fire on my head. I was hostile and rather beastly and I've thought about it often and felt ashamed.

"Daddy liked you and you liked being with him. That ought to have been enough to make me keep my mouth shut and realise that I had no right to interfere; but I thought that what I was doing was for the best.

"And then, when you went away so tactfully and sent those wonderful flowers, I felt awful; I saw that I had been both disagreeable and unchristian in my attitude towards you . . . so now I am asking you to forgive me."

"There is nothing to forgive," Sir John said. "I told you at the time I was fortunate enough to take a very enjoyable holiday in your house. I blessed my accident then and I have blessed it since. Don't let us say any more about it. But if being sorry will help you to listen to me receptively now, I shall be glad."

"I am listening," Ann said quietly.

"I, too, have been thinking of many things since I left your house," Sir John began, "and I have thought a good deal about you. I saw when I was here how you looked after Myra and the twins, giving them the love they might otherwise have missed because they had no mother."

"That is true," Ann whispered under her breath

and exclaimed: "Oh, Sir John, I'm afraid for them now! Afraid! You haven't met Aunt Ella."

Sir John looked at the sweet distressed face beside him and realised that Ann's troubles had been pent up inside her far too long.

"Tell me about her," he suggested, knowing that his simple question would break the dams of Ann's self-control.

"It's not really any use my talking," Ann replied wildly; "yet the thought of the twins being with her haunts me—haunts me all the time! Aunt Ella is a stern, rather severe person. She is well off and I think she means to be kind to the twins; but she won't sent Antony to the sort of school I should choose for him, and I can't help thinking she will restrain and crush them both so that after the freedom they have had all their lives they are going to find it hard—desperately hard—to adjust themselves to her ideas and her standards.

"She thinks I have spoilt them both. Perhaps I have. And she thinks that Daddy was a weak muddler, unsuccessful from a business point of view, simply because he hadn't got the brains to be anything else. She doesn't understand, as you understand, that he was something much bigger and finer than that.

"But if she didn't understand him, I can't believe that she will ever understand the twins or see that there is so much that is sweet and good in both of them.

"They are naughty at times, of course they are, but they have been cramped even here because we have had so little money.

"What will happen to them later on when they are repressed and forced into a mould for which I am certain—quite certain—they are unfitted?"

Now Ann was speaking passionately; her voice vibrated with pain.

"I am afraid, Sir John, yes, afraid," she repeated, and she covered her face with her hands.

Sir John waited a moment, letting the violence of

the tempest which shook Ann's thin shoulders abate a little.

"Listen, Ann." He used her Christian name for the first time and neither of them seemed aware of it. "Listen to me. I have got a solution for all your troubles, but I am having difficulty in making you listen to it."

"A solution? What solution can there be?"

Ann took her hands from her eyes. She did not attempt to disguise the tears which lay wet and shining on her cheeks.

Then as she tried to brush them away, fumbling for her own small handkerchief which had somehow got mislaid, Sir John took his large white linen one from his coat pocket and laid it on her knee.

"Thank you."

She wiped away her tears, making a determined effort to still the catch in her breath.

"I am being very stupid," she said at length. "I am not usually like this, but you have caught me at a disadvantage this afternoon."

"There is no need to apologise," Sir John said. "You have had a tremendous shock, and I think, if you will remember, your father—who was a great exponent of shock—would have told you that this is a very natural reaction."

Ann tried to smile.

"I can almost hear darling Daddy telling me to relax and take it easy." She gave her eyes another determined wipe with Sir John's handkerchief and then handed it back to him.

"Thank you. I can't think why women do not have more sensible handkerchiefs."

Sir John put it into his pocket.

"And now," he said, "can I say my piece without interruption?"

"I will be quiet," Ann promised him.

Sir John hesitated for a moment before, looking at Ann, he said:

60

"I suppose if a fairy appeared at this moment and granted you a wish, it would be quite simple. You would want to keep Myra, Antony and Antoinette with you."

"Yes, of course, that would be my wish."

"Well, my suggestion makes that possible."

"Possible for all of us to be together?" Ann asked; and then she looked at him and added quickly, "If you are going to offer us a lot of money, we can't take it."

"That wasn't my intention," Sir John replied. "But as a matter of interest, why not?"

"Because . . . oh, because we have got to have some sort of pride," Ann answered. "I had a feeling when you started that that might be what you were going to say.

"It is sweet of you, of course, and terribly, terribly kind; but you must see, Sir John, that if we are to have any self-respect left—at any rate as far as Myra and I are concerned—we couldn't take money from a complete stranger; or if that is too sweeping, from someone who was a stranger until a few weeks ago—not without giving anything in return. . . ."

Here Ann's eyes suddenly lit up.

"But if you know of a good job—a job in which I could make a lot of money, that would be a different thing altogether. And perhaps as soon as she has passed her examination, you could find Myra a secretarial post with somebody nice. I would accept that, Sir John, and be grateful, yes, terribly grateful for your help.

"I was horrid to you the other day; I must have sounded proud and priggish. Well, I am not so proud now and, I hope, not quite so priggish, and if you can help us in the way I have mentioned I should say thank you very much."

"It wasn't exactly the suggestion I was going to make," Sir John said.

"Oh," Ann's face fell.

"Neither was I going to offer you large sums of money. I already had the idea, strangely enough, that you wouldn't accept money from me."

"Then what is your suggestion?" Ann asked.

"I am coming to it," Sir John went on. "I may seem a little long-winded, but I want to put my point of view very clearly to you. Your position is simple. You want to keep your family together, but you will not accept help except on what you consider honourable terms. In other words, you won't accept charity; you wish to work for what you earn. Is that correct?"

"Quite correct."

"Well, the proposition I have to make is this," Sir John said. "I am a man leading a very busy life. I have at the age of thirty-two achieved for myself a certain position in the political world and also, from a quite considerable fortune left to me by my father.

"I have certain responsibilities and commitments in the world of finance. I have a house in London, and I am also the owner of Gulliver. Despite all this or perhaps because of it I am lonely; unlike Antony and Antoinette I have no one to look after me or to worry about me.

"I don't think I realised how lonely I was until I came to your house. I had never seen family life at close quarters or known one which was so united.

"You seemed complete in yourselves, fortified by your relationship and affection for each other against the rest of the world and all its troubles and difficulties.

"I realised then, perhaps for the first time, what I was missing. That is why I have come here today to offer you a position whereby I shall benefit as much as you, if not indeed more."

Ann looked at him with puzzled eyes.

"I am sorry to seem stupid," she said, "but I don't quite understand what you want me to do. Is it the post of housekeeper at Gulliver or your house in London that you are suggesting?"

"If you like to put it that way, yes; housekeeping will certainly come into it; but the more proper description of your work would be that of chatelaine at Gulliver, and the mistress of my house in London."

Ann drew in her breath in an audible gasp.

"I am asking you to marry me," Sir John said quietly.

For a moment there was silence. Ann thought wildly that this was some kind of joke; then as her eyes searched Sir John's face she knew it was no joke but the sober truth.

"You want me to marry you?" she repeated the words slowly—incredulously. "But why?"

It was as if the question disconcerted Sir John. He did not answer and for the first time turned his eyes from hers and looked across the garden.

"Does it seem so extraordinary a request?" he asked at length.

"You can't mean it," Ann said quickly. "Why, we hardly know each other and I didn't . . ."

She stopped.

"Go on, I can guess what you were going to say," Sir John prompted.

"Very well. . . . I didn't like you, that was what I was going to say," Ann finished. "I made it quite clear, didn't I, the last day you were here? Now . . . You've been kind . . . and I . . . but . . . but why should you want to marry me?"

"I have my own reasons, some of which I have already explained to you."

"That you are lonely? But your mother is alive."

"You haven't met my mother," Sir John said.

"Oh." Ann was silent for a moment, before she added: "I can, I suppose, understand your being lonely in a big house with all that money. I am sorry for you. At the same time . . ." She looked down at her hands, then said hopefully: "I suppose Myra wouldn't do instead of me. She thinks that she is madly in love with you."

"I am afraid Myra is too young." Sir John spoke quite seriously.

"Yes, I suppose she is," Ann replied. "And she knows absolutely nothing about housekeeping—though of course I could do that for her."

"I am afraid I must make it quite clear that neither Myra nor Antoinette are included in this . . . er . . . proposition," Sir John said. There was a faint smile at the corners of his mouth.

"I think the whole thing is a little crazy," Ann exclaimed.

"On the contrary, I think it is very sane and sensible," Sir John argued. "And from your point of view at this particular moment what could be more satisfactory? You will be together; your home for as long as they remain unmarried will always be open to your family. That I promise you. Myra can have all the things she is longing for—including a social life which she imagines is so delectable. Antony can go to Eton when he is fourteen."

"To Eton?"

"Or any other public school that you prefer."

"Oh."

There was something very different in the intonation of Ann's exclamation now.

"And Antoinette can also have the advantage of schooling or private tuition. You will be able to provide all this for your family, and all I ask in return is that you will bear my name and that you will, when you have the time, try to make my life a little more comfortable."

Ann twisted her fingers together.

"It sounds . . . it sounds all too marvelous to be true," she said, "except one thing which you have forgotten."

"What is that?" Sir John asked.

"That I don't love you."

Ann dropped her head and her voice was very low.

"I am quite aware of that," Sir John answered, "and I haven't asked for your love. If you will marry

64

me, Ann, I promise you one thing: I will never force my attentions upon you in any way. Perhaps some day you will grow fond of me, but until that happens we shall be friends—good friends. I hope—but just friends."

"Do you mean that?" Ann turned to look at him.

Sir John's eyes met her steadily. "I am not a man who makes a promise lightly."

Ann turned her head away.

"I know that," she murmured. "It is only that somehow it doesn't seem quite fair on you. I will do my best, of course. I will try to do everything you ask of me. At the same time, isn't it rather one-sided? I shall be getting so much."

"I shall be content if you will marry me, Ann."

She was still looking away from him, her eyes very wide and dark. There was a faint colour in her cheeks and her hands which had lain in her lap, had crept upwards towards her throat, as if she would still a tumult which fluttered there.

Her lips were parted; she looked very young and very defenceless. Sir John watched her. He said nothing and his face was quite expressionless. Then at length Ann spoke.

"Have I got to give you a decision now?"

"Of course not. You can have time to think it over; as much time as you want. But is there any point in waiting?"

"No, I suppose there is none."

She still did not look at him. It was as if a battle went on within her—a battle tense and sharp which left her breathless and weak. Sir John waited. He was very still, hardly seeming to breathe.

Then at last the battle was over. With a gesture of helplessness Ann dropped her hands and turned towards him.

"If you are quite, quite sure that you want me," she said, and there was a piteous note of childishness in her voice, "then I will . . . marry you."

Five

Ann closed the suitcase and stood up to take a last look at her clothes left hanging in the wardrobe.

"Bring only a few things with you," Sir John had said. "You will want new clothes and you and Myra can buy them when you get to London."

New clothes! Ann wondered how long it was since she had thought of having even one new frock, let alone an entire trousseau; and yet somehow the prospect did not fill her with excitement as she might have expected.

Sir John had said—no, she must remember to call him John even in her thoughts. It was difficult; as difficult as trying to convince herself that tomorrow she was being married—married to a man she hardly knew.

She walked across the room and curling herself up on the low window-seat stared out into the garden. She wanted to consider her own future; but somehow her thoughts were too chaotic, she could not concentrate on anything for more than a second.

She was going to be married. That at least was an unalterable fact. What did it mean to her? What did she feel about it? It was hard to say. It seemed all unreal, a dream from which sooner or later she would wake to her father calling her, tenderly inquiring:

"Ann, Ann, where are you?"

Every evening he had called for her and when he had come back to the house at luncheon time too, arriving usually long after everyone else had finished. He would go to the end of the passage leading to the kitchen where he was certain she would be, washing-up and keeping his portion hot.

"Ann, Ann, where are you? I'm home!"

Daddy was home! What had that meant in the past? But now his home and their home had ceased to exist. Yet in gratitude to John she must remember that leaving it would not be the desperate, agonising parting it would have been if they had all been forced to separate.

She could hardly imagine what her feelings would have been at having to say good-bye to the twins and to Myra. In marrying she was indeed stepping off into the unknown, but not alone—at least, only for three or four days while she went to Gulliver to meet John's mother; and then they would all be in London together.

Myra and the twins were going there direct immediately after the wedding. More than once Ann had caught herself wishing that she could go with them, that she could watch and share their excitement at seeing London for the first time.

Everything would be an adventure—John's house, the unaccustomed luxury, the traffic, the shops, even the atmosphere itself, so very different from Little Cople.

But of course she had to do what John wanted and John wanted her to meet his mother.

"You are not having much of a honeymoon, are you?" Myra had said in surprise; and Ann replied:

"I wouldn't dare leave you in London alone for long. Goodness knows what mischief you would all get up to."

"If I were marrying John . . ." Myra began.

But Ann shut her up with a hasty:

"You're not, so don't let us waste our breath talking about it."

It had been hard in the face of Myra's frank curiosity to hide her own feelings of . . . reluctance . . . yes, that was the word; she was reluctant to be married; reluctant to renounce her own name, to give herself into the keeping of a stranger—it was impossible to think of John as anything else.

Ann put her head down on her arms on the window-sill and tried to consider John as an individual, as a man whom she was about to marry. What did she know about him?

That he was tall and good-looking; there was some satisfaction in that; but his good looks seemed to her rather austere, almost indeed stern. Yet he looked distinguished and she supposed that in time she would feel proud to say, "This is my husband." And he not only looked distinguished, he was distinguished.

It was Antoinette who had remarked on the night after she had told them she was to marry John:

"Do you realise, Ann, that you'll be Lady Melton? Golly, won't it be funny to hear you called 'my lady'?"

Lady Melton—John's wife! What exactly did that entail? Ann moved restlessly. He had promised them all so much and she was so afraid that she would not be able to fulfil her part of the bargain.

She had contracted to make him comfortable, to try to make him less lonely. Could she ever succeed? He seemed so much older, almost as if he belonged to another generation. He was grave and quiet and she felt that her conversation must seem terribly stupid and unsophisticated to him.

What did she know of the world—his world, of people clever, talented or important? Of people concerned with affairs of state, people born and bred in luxury and extravagance? She knew only how to love the people around her, to make friends with the simple, kindly village folk.

She knew how to make a very little money go a long way, how to cook an appetising meal out of a few odds and ends and make it enough for five. What good was that sort of knowledge going to do her in a house like Gulliver?

She tried to remember what she had heard of Gulliver, but she had only a confused impression of words, without context and without meaning—of "rococo" "baroque", "stucco", "calcined porticoes"—until all she had read about it seeemed now to have become confused with the descriptions of other houses, mansions and palaces none of which she had ever expected to have the opportunity of visiting. But now, what did the future hold? Where would she find herself? At what places and in what society?

Ann raised her head and looked across the garden. The evening shadows, long and pointed, were stretching across the grass. The scarlet roses glowed passionately against an ancient oak; the lilies, virginal white and golden centred, swayed gently in the rising breeze.

The sun was setting; high in the sky the first evening star had appeared. It was very quiet and very peaceful, and to Ann at that moment it all seemed small and cosy and enclosed.

A little place, but a place in which she had reigned as queen. It was home—and she was leaving it!

She looked across to the seat under the cedar tree where John had asked her to marry him and where she had so often sat in the evening with her father.

They had talked together there, from the times when first as a small child she had willingly sought his advice, up to the very day before he died.

If only she could ask him now! If only in some way he could tell her what was the right thing to do! Silently she called to him:

"Oh, Daddy, I am afraid. Am I doing the right thing?—the right thing for Myra, for Antony and Antoinette and, indeed, the right thing for John?"

Her father had understood John and had liked him. Ann decided that—now—she liked him too. It would be difficult not to like somebody who was so kind and was so willing to agree to everything she suggested.

She remembered Myra's rapture when he had suggested that they should go to London and had promised that he would arrange for someone to take them

69

sight-seeing and to theatres while Ann and he were at Gulliver.

"Do you really mean it? Oh, John, how angelic of you! I couldn't be more excited!"

Myra had almost danced at the thought, while Antoinette had said quickly:

"Can we go to the Zoo? Antony wants to so much, but he doesn't like to ask you himself."

"Of course you shall go to the Zoo," John said, smiling.

He had gone on to suggest other places they might visit—the Tower of London, Westminster Abbey, the Mint . . . and watching their radiant faces Ann had kept telling herself over and over again as if to quieten her conscience that she had done the right thing.

She remembered how after she had accepted John she had left him in the garden for a while and had gone into the house alone.

"I want to think," she said. "Myra and the twins will be back for tea in a few minutes from now. May I be alone till then? Do you want me to tell them?"

"I want you to do exactly what pleases you best," John replied quietly.

Ann stood irresolutely before she said:

"I will tell them before you come in to tea."

She had spoken breathlessly as if the mere thought of making such an announcement left her almost voiceless, and then before he could answer her she had turned and run swiftly as in sudden flight towards the house.

John Melton watched her go, then he sighed as he reached for his cigarette case.

The twins had come into the house quietly, but Ann who was getting the tea ready had heard them and her heart contracted because she knew only too well why they were quiet.

They had said very little since she had told them that because their father had died in debt that they would have to go and live with Aunt Ella. They

70

merely looked at her with the eyes of a faithful animal which accepts blows and kicks from its master because it knows there is no appeal.

But from that moment the twins had been very subdued. Ann noticed that they kept very close together, sometimes walking hand-in-hand as if wordlessly they comforted one another.

Only when she went up to say good night to them had they each clung to her with a passion which said more than words. In the darkness of one bedroom she had felt Antoinette's cheeks wet beneath hers. But she dared not attempt to comfort her, her own self-control was so perilously near breaking-point.

She kissed Antoinette and slipped through the communicating door which led to Antony's room. His curtains were not drawn and he was kneeling at the window looking out on to the garden.

When he saw Ann, he scrambled down, got into bed without a word and then held out both his arms. She had gone down on her knees beside the bed, holding him tightly, very tightly to her. He said nothing for a long time, he only clung to her, until at last he asked in little more than a whisper:

"Ann, do you think that Daddy is with Mummy now?"

Ann had nodded.

"Yes, darling," she managed to say after a moment.

"And do you think she knows about . . . us going to Aunt Ella?"

Ann couldn't answer this question. She felt the tears blind her eyes; gently she had extricated herself from Antony's arms to seek her own room where she could cry alone . . . unheard. . . .

The next day the twins had come down to breakfast late with dark lines under their eyes. Ann had known without being told that they had sat up late against all rules and regulations discussing their future. Listlessly they left for school.

She let them go, although she felt it was immaterial

whether they went or not, simply because from her own view-point she couldn't bear to see them about the house knowing that they, like herself, were saying good-bye to everything that was familiar.

She finished cutting the sandwiches for tea and put them on a tray. Then she heard the front door bang and knew that Myra had returned.

"Where is Ann?"

She heard Myra's voice and guessed that the twins were sitting, as they often did, on the bottom step of the stairs in the hall.

"We haven't seen her yet." It was Antoinette who answered.

"I expect she is in the kitchen. You had better go and help her get the tea. I'm hungry."

Myra spoke sharply and Ann knew it was her way of showing that she was disturbed and upset. She slammed her books down on the polished table, flung her hat into a chair and came towards the kitchen. The twins followed her more slowly, dragging their feet as if they had no interest in food or in anything else.

Ann was waiting for them.

"Hullo," she said; and then to the twins: "I heard you come in some time ago. Don't you want your tea?"

"Not particularly," Antoinette replied. "Are we going to have it in the garden?"

"I say, Ann," Myra said, "there is a big car parked on the other side of the road under the trees. It's a Rolls-Royce. Do you know whom it belongs to?"

"Yes, to Sir John Melton," Ann replied.

"Oh, has he been here?" Myra asked, but not with the same eagerness she would have shown a week earlier.

Her father's death and the imminent break up of the home had taken much of Myra's sparkle and enthusiasm from her. She seemed for the moment to have lost even her interest in people, and her imagination was asleep.

"Yes, he is here," Ann answered quietly. "And will you all listen to me for a moment, I have something to tell you."

She took a deep breath and told them how John had come to see her and that she had promised to marry him—which meant that they could all be together. She heard her own voice die away.

There was silence, broken only by the ticking of the kitchen clock. She was conscious of three pairs of eyes staring at her, of the astonishment of Antony and Antoinette's faces, and then of the sudden whoop of joy from Myra.

"But Ann, it can't be true! How wonderful! How simply wonderful!"

Impulsively she flung her arms round Ann's neck. Then the twins were kissing her too, and they were all crying together.

"You are all coming with me . . . all of you," Ann kept saying over and over again. "We haven't got to leave each other . . . you won't have to go to Aunt Ella . . . Myra won't have to work in an office . . . we can all be together . . . always. . . ."

It was sometime later before she remembered that it was tea-time and that her future husband was waiting for his tea. She and Myra ran up to their bedrooms to bathe their eyes and powder their noses, leaving the twins to carry the tray into the garden.

When Ann came downstairs she found the whole family gathered round John, staring at him with slightly dazed expressions while he expounded plans for their future. . . .

She left him to make all the arrangements concerning their marriage.

"We will be married in three days' time," he told her. "It will mean buying your trousseau after the wedding, but I don't think that will worry you. I expect you would like to be married in a church? That can be arranged as I will get a special licence. As you are in mourning I am sure you won't want anyone there except the family."

They had all agreed with him at the time, though Myra had said afterwards rather plaintively:

"I would have liked to be a real bridesmaid with a proper dress and a bouquet, and all that sort of thing."

"But Myra, you couldn't be—not when Daddy . . ."

"Yes, yes, I know," Myra interrupted. "But, oh, Ann, it does seem such a pity that you can't have a wedding with white satin, orange blossom, a huge cake and your photograph in the *Tatler*."

"But I don't want anything like that," Ann said.

"Well, I should want it," Myra stated firmly; "especially if I was marrying Sir John Melton."

"It is a pity you are not," Ann said without thinking; and then was somehow relieved when Myra said:

"What does it matter who has him, as long as he is in the family?"

Now as Ann thought of the much-cleaned blue dress which she would wear tomorrow, she felt that it was indeed a pity that John could not marry Myra. She would have loved all the pomp and circumstance, being seen and admired, having money to spend and expensive cars to ride in and a position to keep up.

"And I am frightened of it all; quite frankly, I am terrified," Ann told herself.

Once again she wished she could ask her father's advice. She remembered how snobbery always used to amuse him. She could recall an occasion when a rather important person had broken his collarbone out hunting and Dr. Shefford had been fetched to attend him.

When he returned, Myra had asked him with excited curiosity what the patient was like, and wasn't it thrilling to attend someone so well known? Dr. Shefford had laughed.

"When you are as old as I am, Myra," he had

74

replied, "you will find that all men and women, whatever their status in life, bleed red blood when you prick them."

Ann had remembered it because she was the shy one of the family. Myra never minded meeting strangers; in fact she adored a party of any sort, whether it was a committee meeting of church dignitaries or a bazaar in aid of the Waifs and Strays.

But Ann would find herself tense and a little nervous when entering a strange house, and then she would hear her father's humorous tones saying, "They all bleed red blood if you prick them," and unconsciously she would lift her chin higher and smile.

She must try not to be shy for John's sake. She must be a good hostess and learn to entertain distinguished people without showing either her fear of them or her fear of her own stupidity.

All these things were to be a part of her married life. And what of the relationship between John and herself? Ann sighed. Somehow she had never imagined that she would feel like this on the eve of her wedding day; and yet, unlike Myra, she had never even for a moment believed herself in love.

She had loved so many people—her father, Myra, the twins, especially Antony, the girls with whom she had been at school, the old women in the village whom she visited when they were ill.

Even Mrs. Briggs she loved in a sort of way because she was a dear and kindly soul who had been one of their own little household.

But she had never met a man who had made her heart beat quicker, who had made her eyes drop before his or left her breathless because of some magic passing between them.

Now that she came to think of it, she had met very few young men in her life. Either they had been away at the war or else the families round Little Cople had not run to young sons.

Yet she had imagined that sooner or later someone

75

would come along and would want her as she would want him, and that they would settle down together and have children.

Ann had often thought that she would love to have children of her own—a baby soft and cuddly as Antony had been, a baby which would be her very own, to whom she could give so much of what seemed at times a heart overflowing with love.

She had, too, imagined her wedding—pictured herself going up the aisle on her father's arm, wearing white satin and the veil which had been her mother's and which lay in the bottom drawer in her bedroom.

She would be carrying not lilies because they were too conventional, but the white roses that blossomed every summer on the big bush at the bottom of the garden, roses which her father had told her had always been her mother's favourite flowers.

Yes, that was how she had meant to be married; but the reality was very, very different. Daddy wouldn't be there; she would be married in the blue dress which had been her only decent summer frock for three years.

A strange wedding gown except that Daddy had always liked it. He loved colour, and he had told them again and again never, never to wear black for him; he hadn't allowed mourning in any shape or form for their mother—

"We weep not for them, but for ourselves because we are so long without them," he had said.

How often had Ann heard him repeat that when someone they knew died. But still, to be married without Daddy, without his steady hand on hers, his quiet voice advising her, was to know poignantly and painfully the true meaning of being alone.

Tomorrow she was marrying John Melton, and what did she know of Sir John Melton, or, indeed, what did he know of her?

He would be kind to her, she was sure of that. What was even more important, he would be kind to Myra and the twins. But they had struck a bargain in which this was to be no marriage but a union of friendship and friendship only.

"I wonder why he wants to marry me?" Ann asked, she repeated over again as she had done already many times before the words he had actually used in asking her.

He had been sensible enough to understand that she could not take money from him, and in a way it was a compliment that he had known her well enough to realise that whatever the consequences she could not allow herself and Myra to live on charity even if it were the charity of Sir John Melton.

And then he had seemed to understand too what she was feeling after her father's death when he had slipped away from the house, making all his own arrangements so that it was only hours after he had departed that she had realised that they were alone.

Yes, that showed a considerate, understanding nature.

And what else was there to go on? So very, very little. But did it matter so long as John was content, which he obviously was?

Ann sighed, and as she did so she heard someone calling her name.

"Ann! Ann!"

It was Myra.

"I am here," Ann called, getting to her feet, realising that her legs were cramped and that she must have been sitting in the window-seat for a long time.

Myra burst in at the door.

"Oh, so there you are," she said. "I couldn't think where you had got to. John is here and he wants you."

"John!" Ann exclaimed.

"Yes, he has motored over. He said he particularly wanted to see you; and, Ann, he has brought your flowers for tomorrow. They are perfectly lovely, and he has brought me a bouquet too, isn't it wonderful of him?"

77

Ann had turned towards the dressing-table and was smoothing her hair.

"He said he won't see us again until tomorrow at the church because it would be unlucky," Myra said. "That is why he has brought the flowers now. Did you know he was bringing you a bouquet?"

"No, I had no idea," Ann answered. "But he did ask me what colour dress I should wear."

"Well, do hurry and go down to him," Myra said. "He is in the sitting-room and he wants to see you alone."

Slowly Ann went downstairs. In the hall she saw lying on the table a big bouquet of flowers. As she descended she stared at it, remembering how, only a few days before, wreaths had lain there, brought by so many friends for her father's funeral.

And then she saw what the flowers were—small, very white orchids with crimson centres, exquisite, exotic flowers and, of course, ridiculously expensive. For a moment Ann felt rebellious.

"They are not right for me," she thought. "I want to be myself; I want to go on as I always have with the simple things, the ordinary things, the things which are suitable to Ann Shefford."

But she knew she was being absurd.

There was another bouquet on the chair which she had not noticed before. Myra must have put them there when they were half unwrapped. Pink roses, perfectly shaped, the buds just opening to the fullness of their beauty.

"How appropriate for Myra," Ann thought, and she gave a quiet chuckle.

She was smiling as she opened the door of the sitting-room.

John was standing by the empty fire-place with his back towards the door. He turned as she entered and she thought how tall he looked in the small shabby sitting-room. She walked towards him.

"Are you surprised to see me?" he asked.

"I certainly wasn't expecting you," Ann said.

"I meant to telephone you before I left London, but I forgot. I am not going to stay, so don't look worried."

"I am not," Ann replied. "I have finished my packing, but there is very little to pack, and I am pleased to see you."

The words sounded very conventionally polite, even to herself. She thought that John looked at her sharply. Then he put his hand in his pocket and drew out a small pink leather case.

"I wanted to give you this," he said, "before tomorrow."

Ann made no effort to take the case from him and so he opened it.

"Oh, how lovely!"

Ann could not help the exclamation which came to her lips, for lying on cream velvet was the largest blue stone she had ever seen, a stone like the sea on a summer day, set on either side with diamonds which glittered and sparkled like wave-flung foam.

"Your engagement ring," John said briefly.

"Oh, but you shouldn't give me anything like that," Ann said. "It is lovely, really, but . . ."

"There is no but," John said firmly. "It is a sapphire. Sapphire means friendship, you know."

It seemed to her that there was some underlying meaning in his words. She looked up at him inquiringly, but he did not meet her eyes. Instead he said gravely:

"Now let me put it on your finger."

She held out her hand. Her fingers were long and thin and the ring was almost too big for it hung on her finger loosely. Large and shining it seemed to hold in its depths a promise of security and, as John had said, of friendship.

"Thank you."

There was nothing else for her to say. Swiftly the thought came to her that had it been Myra she would have flung her arms round John's neck and kissed him impulsively; she would have been able to express her pleasure so easily and so fluently, while she, Ann, was shy and unsure of herself.

"It is lovely," she said again.

"I am glad you are pleased," John said, and then he put his hand in his pocket again. "I have got you a pair of clips to match, also some ear-rings."

He opened the cases. The jewels, big and brilliant, sparkled and glittered. Ann gave a little cry not of delight but of protest.

"Oh, John, I can't, I can't take all those!"

"As my wife you will be expected to wear jewels."

It was as if he rebuked her. She felt for a moment suddenly cold, as she had when a child after being snubbed for making an awkward mistake.

"Yes, of course, I had forgotten that."

She looked at the sapphires as he held them in his hand, but she made no attempt to take them or to put them on. After a moment John shut the cases with a snap.

"Here they are, then. I thought perhaps you would like to wear them tomorrow."

"Yes, I would, of course, and thank you."

"That is all right then. And you will find your flowers in the hall. I hope you like them too. The orchids seemed to resemble you."

Ann stared at him in surprise. Already he had reached the door.

"Good-bye, Ann. See you at the church."

He had gone before she could think of anything else to say. She was left standing alone in the sitting-room with two jewel cases in her hands.

Somehow she could not explain but she felt perturbed as if in some obscure way she had failed him. But that, of course, was absurd.

Six

"There is Gulliver."

John stopped the car at the top of the rise and Ann, looking straight ahead of her, saw the house of which she had heard so much.

It was a perfect summer afternoon. The warm, brilliant sunshine was offset by a slight breeze so that the shadows beneath the trees wove a moving pattern on the green grass, and every now and then a small white cloud sailed with an air of triumph across the blue sky.

Gulliver, bathed in sunshine, its grey stone warmed to a mellow silver, was reflected in the water which lay at its feet.

Black swans passed gravely under the arches made by its walls, part of this fairy castle which seemed to exist only by virtue of some mirrored magic beyond human comprehension.

"It is not real," Ann thought.

There was no symmetry in the picture Gulliver made, for many builders in many passing centuries had fashioned the stern battlements, the rising turrets and towers, and the mullioned windows shining iridescent in the sunshine.

"You like it?"

She realised that John had turned from the wheel to look at her, and quickly in case he should be disappointed she said:

"It is lovely, of course. But everyone must have said that to you."

It seemed to her that he waited, watching her searchingly as if he expected something more; and then without another word he started up the car, driving, as he had done all the way from London, slowly and painstakingly.

Ann was not certain whether such care was due to his leg or to some other reason—perhaps her own presence in the car. She had protested at first when he told her that he intended to drive.

"I hate sitting in the back of a car," he said, "and the servants are a nuisance anyway; I would rather we went alone."

There was nothing she could say. More than once she fancied that his leg pained him, but if it did he made no complaint.

Earlier in the day they had travelled by train after the wedding from Little Cople to London. It had been a gay, noisy journey and Myra and the twins never stopped talking. It was only later than Ann realised that John had been very quiet, saying little. She herself had felt at her ease because her family were with them; but those moments in the church had been full of shyness.

She had wakened that morning with a sense of fear heavy upon her. When she opened her eyes, it was there waiting, so it had seemed to her, like some animal ready to spring. And then she had remembered —today was her wedding day.

She jumped out of bed and throwing back the curtains and opening the window took in deep breaths of the morning air.

Somehow she felt suffocated, as if a great hand was closing down upon her . . . taking her prisoner.

On the dressing-table lay the three pink leather cases. She looked at them and tried to understand her own feelings. The sapphires were beautiful, indeed they were overwhelming to a girl whose only jewellery had been a plain gold brooch and a bracelet which had belonged to her mother.

As John's wife she must have jewellery. She must do him credit; it would not be suitable for her to be unadorned; and yet somehow she wished that he had waited a little longer.

Always, ever since she had first known him he had been wanting to give her things and always until now she had been able to refuse them; and yet, was that reflection quite fair to John?

It would have been easy to accuse him of meanness had he not given her an engagement ring. But she was afraid of the jewels he had chosen; they seemed like chains—chains which she must accept because of the bargain between them.

It was still very early when having dressed herself she went downstairs to prepare the breakfast as she had done so many thousands of times before. She had everything ready before Myra appeared, yawning, yet looking like a spring morning with her clear, untouched complexion and flung-back hair.

"I can't think why you and John want to get married so early in the day," she grumbled. "An afternoon wedding would have been best and would have given us time to make ourselves beautiful."

"We shall have time to do all that is necessary," Ann said with a smile. "It isn't as if we had a tremendous choice of clothes."

"I am going to buy some new things the moment I get to London. John has said I may—in fact, he has given me some money already."

Myra spoke half defiantly and Ann knew instinctively that this bit of information had been kept from her until now in case she made a fuss. She felt a sudden surge of anger.

Why couldn't John have asked her about Myra's clothes? It should have been left for her to make the decisions, to decide how much should be spent and when.

Then she remembered. Myra would be in London three or four days without her. She herself would be at Gulliver with John.

She said nothing, her silence seeming somehow to

reassure Myra who had obviously been expecting some protest.

"I will spend it carefully, don't you worry," she said. "But oh, Ann, isn't he marvellous? I do think you are the luckiest person in all the world."

"He is very kind." Ann was aware of the slightly priggish tone of her own voice and she added: "I hope you thanked him."

"What do you think?" Myra replied. "I just hugged him and I said: 'If I can't have you as a husband, John, a brother is the next best thing.' I think he was quite pleased."

Ann remembered the way she had received his jewels the night before and she felt ashamed. Yes, Myra would have thanked him prettily, but such words had refused to come from her own lips and she had felt stiff and awkward.

After breakfast she went upstairs to change. She put on her blue dress, then studied herself in the glass and wondered how she could look so dull and lifeless.

"You might be going to the dentist," she told her reflection angrily.

The face that stared back at her from the mirror was grave and serious.

"Why he wants to marry me I can't think," she said out loud; and then quickly she fastened the sapphire clips at her neck, and the earrings on the lobes of her ears.

On the bed there was a little hat of blue tulle and ribbon which Myra had made for her the day before. She put it on and now she was ready.

She picked up her bouquet, white and crimson, exotic and beautiful, the orchids seemed to Ann symbolic of the life which she was just entering and with which she had nothing in common, but she did not anticipate that John's gifts could transform her.

Only when Myra entered the room to exclaim in almost awestruck tones,

"Why, Ann, you look beautiful!" did she realise

84

that the shabbiness of her dress was forgotten. The orchids and jewels gave her a look of sophistication which she was far from feeling and seemed to lighten even the expression on her face so that her gravity was no longer obvious.

Staring back at her from the mirror was another girl; dewy-eyed, soft and tremulous, this girl was a bride—a bride about to meet her bridegroom.

"It is all a dream, a dream," Ann whispered to herself.

As they walked across the fields to the little church she felt as if her feet carried her without her volition. John had suggested sending the car for them; but there was a short cut from the back of the garden which avoided the public streets, and Ann, shrinking at the thought of being seen, had decided that she and the children would make their way by this familiar route.

No one was to know of their wedding. It was to be kept a close secret and John had promised that he would impress upon the Vicar the necessity for secrecy.

When, however, they got to the church they found that the news that there was to be a wedding had spread in some mysterious way of its own, and several of the more curious of the village inhabitants had turned out.

All the same, nothing could have been quieter than the little grey stone church—the Vicar, whom Ann had known all her life and who had so recently buried her father, conducting the service with an affectionate note in his voice as one who gives away a very dear child.

And yet it all seemed unreal, all part of the strange dream that she had been experiencing ever since she had promised to marry John Melton.

As she saw him there waiting for her at the church door, Ann felt a sudden panic sweep over her.

"I can't do it, I can't do it."

Over and over the words seemed to repeat themselves within her heart until she felt that she must shout them aloud, must turn round and run . . . away from all these new commitments, away from the new and strange and fearful . . . away from John.

Then suddenly it seemed that another personality took possession of her; a new Ann, an Ann whom Myra had found beautiful; an Ann who held a great bunch of exotic orchids in her hand and was wearing luxurious jewels with an air.

This Ann carried her forward to John's side, and before she was aware of it he had taken her right hand in his and was holding it in a warm clasp.

"You are all right?"

He asked the question as if she had been ill. She had wanted to tell him then, firmly even if brokenly, that she couldn't go through with it, it was too much to ask of her even for the sake of the children.

Who was this man and what did she know of him? What did he mean to her or she to him?

"Let me go! Let me go!" she wanted to say but she could not.

It was the other Ann who answered him through stiff lips which moved reluctantly but nevertheless spoke clearly.

"I am quite all right, thank you."

His eyes seemed to search hers and then he drew her arm through his and led her up the aisle.

The Vicar was waiting for them. Automatically Ann went through the service. She handed her bouquet to Myra and held out her hand for the ring which John slipped on to her third finger.

She was conscious only of feeling cold, of hearing her own voice as it made responses as if it were the voice of a stranger. And then they were signing the register and she was writing her maiden name for the last time. "God bless you, Ann, may you find great happiness."

It was the Vicar speaking, and he pressed both her

hands and patted her on the shoulder in a kindly way.

"We shall be sorry to lose you, dear child. She has been a wonderful help in the village, Sir John. We are going to miss her a great deal."

Ann had no idea what John replied. She had turned towards her own family who were waiting for her.

She kissed Myra first.

"It was a lovely wedding, darling," Myra said.

And then Antony and Antoinette:

"We could hardly hear you," the latter announced. "You absolutely whispered your words. But John was splendid, weren't you, John?"

The twins looked at him with pride. Already, Ann realised, they had started to hero-worship their new brother-in-law. She was not quite certain that she was pleased; there was a slight stirring of jealousy within her heart; she had had no rivals in the past.

"I have ordered a very special luncheon for us in London," John told them, as they were driving toward the station.

"Did you remember a cake?" Myra asked.

"When you know me better, you will know I never forget anything," he teased.

"I can well believe that," Myra replied. "I think you are terribly efficient."

She looked down at her roses with pride.

"You will have to leave your flowers in the car," John told them. "Ann will feel shy if she is proclaimed publicly as being a bride."

In reply Myra pulled one of the roses from her bouquet and stuck it in her dress.

"I only hope your chauffeur won't lose the rest of them. Do you know, John, it is the first time I have ever been bunched."

"Aren't there any young men in Little Cople?"

"Only one. He is a farmer and he has had a crush on Ann for years."

John looked at Ann.

"I haven't been told about this earlier rival."

To her own fury Ann felt her cheeks flushing.

"Myra is being absurd," she said.

"Oh, Ann, I'm not!" Myra retorted irrepressibly. "And very useful he was, too. We used to get all the best gleanings for our chickens during the war and, what is more, we had new potatoes before anyone else."

"I see I shall have to look to my laurels," John said.

"Oh, he couldn't compete with sapphires," Myra answered.

"I think this conversation is rather ridiculous."

Ann was aware of the sharp note in her voice. She did not know why, but she felt uncomfortable and uneasy. She was thankful when the car drew up at the station.

They arrived at John's house just before luncheon. It was a big, impressive porticoed mansion in Berkeley Square, and as they entered the front door Ann saw that there were several servants waiting in the hall. John introduced the butler.

"Travers has been with us for over thirty years. Isn't that right, Travers?"

"Yes, Sir John. And on behalf of the staff I want to extend to you our very hearty congratulations—and to you, my lady—and our good wishes on this auspicious occasion."

"Thank you, Travers. We are very grateful, aren't we, Ann?"

"Yes, thank you." Shyly Ann held out her hand and Travers shook it heartily.

Somehow from that moment she felt more at home. The servants were mostly old and their smiling good wishes seemed to make the house itself less pompous, less frightening.

It was very big and rather dark; the rooms seemed to Ann enormously high, and the large polished dining-room table with its mass of silver ornaments and crested silver and bowls of hot-house fruit awed the twins almost to silence.

As John had promised, he had not forgotten a cake. It was a big iced one with three tiers and hung with silver bells.

"I had to buy it," he apologised to Ann, "as there wasn't time for our cook here to make one. She was disappointed; I had always promised her that she would make my wedding cake when I got married."

"Couldn't we have waited for it?" Ann asked.

"And disappoint the twins?" he inquired.

She smiled then because he seemed genuinely to enjoy the twins' greedy exclamation, as they sampled the icing, that it would take them some time to get through that.

"We had better have luncheon first," John suggested, "otherwise you will have no appetite for lobsters, fried chicken and ice-cream; I have remembered most of the things you told me you liked."

Again Ann smiled at him and then felt nervous, as she realised that he expected her to sit opposite him at the top of the table. She took her place.

Travers poured out champagne and before they started John raised his glass to her in a toast.

"To the bride," he said.

He sipped his champagne, but Myra protested:

"You ought to say more than that. Wish her luck."

"Surely that is for you to do," John replied.

"Very well, then." Myra held up her glass. "To the two nicest people in the world, and may they always be wonderfully happy together."

The twins drank down quickly the small amount of champagne Travers had given them.

"Thank you, Myra," John said.

"If only I were in love with him," Ann thought swiftly, "how happy I should be today."

The thought persisted through the ensuing hours. They inspected the house. They met John's secretary, Dawson Barclay, a capable and charming young man who promised to look after the family while John and Ann were away. And then they started off in the car to Gulliver.

"If only I were in love . . . If only I were in love. . . ."

The engine of the car seemed to repeat the words over and over again; the very wheels seemed to pick up the sound. . . .

"If only I were in love. . . . If only I were in love. . . ."

"I am being absurd," Ann told herself.

But the words persisted until they began to haunt her, and to escape them she plunged into conversation, talking at random and almost hysterically, until John's quiet replies brought to her a sense of security and peace.

"He is quite happy," she told herself defiantly. "He wants companionship and I will give him that. I can't understand how I can make him more comfortable, but perhaps I shall find out in time."

They drove on and on, leaving the traffic-crowded highways behind, and turning down quiet lanes where the hedgerows were bright with dog roses and the meadow-sweet grew high and white.

"We are nearly there," John said at length. "Are you tired?"

"Not a bit. But I am worried about your leg."

"That is all right. There is nothing more boring than one's own infirmities."

"Unless it is other people's."

"Are you ever bored with other people's troubles? That is the last thing I should have expected you to say."

"Oh, I hear a lot of them. I suppose I always have."

"You certainly gave me that impression—a kind of ministering angel."

"What an awful idea."

"Is it? I thought it rather became you."

John took his eyes off the road for a moment and

glanced at her. Quiet unexpectedly Ann felt the blood rising in her cheeks.

She had an impulse to ask him exactly what he did think about her; but somehow she was too shy to put her question into words and, the moment passing, they both lapsed into silence.

It was then that, topping the rise of the road, John stopped the car.

"There is Gulliver," he said. . . .

He drove on and the car passed over the bridge which in ancient times had been a drawbridge, and stopped before a great oak door set in a Gothic arch.

There were huge stone vases filled with flame-coloured geraniums on either side of the door, and the house itself rose high and massive above them while the water, green and translucent, shimmered beneath them, the sunshine making it hard to tell where the moat ended and the green lawns began.

Ann had a moment of panic.

"You won't leave me, will you?" she asked, and was hardly aware that she had spoken till the words were said.

"No, of course not," John answered. "Are you frightened?"

"Terribly."

"You are not the first person who has felt like that on coming to Gulliver," John said. "It can prove very indigestible taken in a single gulp. It is like the history of England—it should be taken in small doses."

She realised gratefully that he was talking to give her time to regain her confidence, but all the same she felt cold and nervous as she stepped out of the car.

"They won't be waiting for us," John said, "as I told them we should arrive 'some time' during the afternoon; but I expect there will be speeches to be made this evening; the staff will want to meet you."

"How terrifying."

"Oh, you won't have to say anything except thank you, and you will do that very prettily, I am sure."

He opened the door and drew her into the great hall. The marble floor, the panelled walls hung with ancient armour, the great oak staircase with its heraldic lions sitting on top of the newels, the stained glass in the windows and the quiet dimness as if of another age left Ann speechless.

"Wait a moment and I will ring for Barker," John said. "You thought Travers had been with us for a long time, but Barker was here with my grandfather. He is nearly eighty and very deaf, but nothing will induce him to give up. We have tried for years to pension him off, but he says that when he goes he will go feet first, so that's that."

From that moment Ann had only an impression of voices, of long galleries and great rooms, polished floors, tapestries and coats-of-arms, of hot-house flowers and glittering chandeliers, Aubusson carpets, windows opening out on to quiet courtyards and ornamental gardens which bore no resemblance to any garden that Ann had ever seen before in her life.

She was aware that John was showing her Gulliver with pride. She knew that he wanted her to admire so much the things that he not only admired, but loved.

Yet she felt that it was impossible for her to take in everything—it was so big, so fantastic; and in trying to concentrate she grew even more bewildered.

John's mother was out. Barker had told them:

"Her ladyship thought you would understand, but it is her ladyship's Red Cross meeting this afternoon and she had promised to speak and didn't like to disappoint them; but she will be back just as soon as she can manage it."

"We quite understand," John said. "In fact, it gives us time to see the house before tea. We will have tea in the morning-room, Barker."

'Her ladyship ordered it in the drawing-room, Sir John."

"Oh, very well then." John turned to Ann. "That is in your honour."

"Tea in the drawing-room?"

"Yes, the formal drawing-room is kept for very special occasions—marriages, deaths or royalty. Wait until you see it; you will understand."

Ann did understand. It was one of the largest rooms she had ever seen.

"A perfect example of baroque," John told her, but to Ann it was merely overwhelming with its gilded furniture, the pictures in their ornate carved frames, and the mirrors which reflected flashingly the crystal chandeliers.

On every table and banked in the corners of the room were flowers—flowers which seemed even more unreal than the house itself; orchids of every shape and colour, carnations and lilies, arranged so that each was shown to advantage—a picture within a picture.

"My mother is a great horticulturist," John explained. "Amongst other things, of course. In fact, there are very few subjects on which she is not an expert."

Ann felt herself shiver.

"Tell me more about your mother."

"She is a very remarkable woman," John answered. "I hope you and she will get on together."

"Have you . . . when did you . . . tell her about us?"

"I wrote to her," John said briefly.

Ann felt somehow that he was keeping something back from her, and then just as they were going to sit down the door was opened. A short woman in Red Cross uniform came hurrying in.

"My dear John," she said, "I am sorry I was not here to greet you. Barker will have given you my message. It was absolutely essential that I should be at the meeting this afternoon—the secretary had made the usual muddle of the invitations."

John walked across the room to meet his mother. He bent down and kissed her cheek, then turning he led her towards Ann.

"This is Ann, Mother," he said.

Ann looked at Lady Melton. She felt a momentary surprise at her appearance; somehow she had expected someone tall, someone like John, but as their eyes met she knew that although she might be short in stature there was nothing small or inconsequent about her mother-in-law.

Lady Melton held out her hand.

"Well, Ann, I suppose I must welcome you to Gulliver," she said.

But there was no welcome in her voice.

Seven

Ann was always to remember that first afternoon and evening at Gulliver. It seemed to her then and subsequently like a long-drawn-out nightmare when the dreamer knows that he is being overtaken by an unknown terror from which there is no escape.

There were certain people who always had the effect of making Ann feel small and insignificant, of making her retire into a protective silence because she was afraid of them. Lady Melton was one of these.

Ann knew from the first moment of her entering the drawing-room that there was antagonism behind her hard inquiring eyes and a subtle disapproval beneath the clear forthright tones of her well-modulated voice.

"Now you must tell me about yourself," she said in a manner that commanded rather than requested the information.

Ann felt shyness paralyse her tongue and she looked quickly at John as if for help.

"I hope you read my letter, Mother," he said. "I gave you what I thought was a pretty complete history of Ann."

Lady Melton looked at her son.

"Yes, I read it," she said. "It was a considerable surprise to me—not to say shock."

"I was afraid it would be," Sir John said. "At the same time I thought you would understand, Mother, that as Ann has been so recently bereaved it was better to have a completely quiet wedding."

"I'm afraid I cannot understand why such extraordinary haste was necessary," Lady Melton said coldly. "Ann could have come to stay here for a few months and then you could have been married properly."

"Oh, it was quite proper," John said with a humorous twist of his lips.

Lady Melton ignored the interruption.

"After all, John," she went on, "you must remember your responsibility—not only to me, that of course is a detail—but to your tenants, your friends and, not least, your constituency. I feel apprehensive, very apprehensive of what they will all think."

"I imagine it will give them something new to talk about," John said coolly.

The door opened and the butler and a footman came into the room, the latter carrying on a big silver tray a crested teapot and silver hot-water kettle. The tea-table was already laid at one side of the fire-place. Ann glanced at it, comparing it with the teas that John had eaten and apparently enjoyed at her own home.

The tablecloth of white linen was heavily embroidered and bordered with a deep flounce of real lace. On what Ann recognised was very beautiful antique china, food was arranged delicately and tastefully, but in such abundance that she wondered how they could ever be expected to consume even a tenth of it.

There were two plates of tiny scones piled pyramid high, one lot made of brown flour, one of white. There was asparagus rolled around with wafer-thin bread and butter, sandwiches made of cucumber, mustard and cress and tomato, cream buns, prettily shaped cakes each ornamented with a different design in coloured icing, and two large cakes, one of sponge so light that it looked as if a puff of air would blow it away, and the other so heavily weighted with fruit as to resemble a plum pudding.

"Let us start our tea," Lady Melton said, and then as she approached the table she stopped. "But of course, John dear, it is your wife who should pour out now."

She made the gesture of a queen renouncing a throne.

Ann exclaimed quickly: "Oh, no, please, Lady Melton. I wouldn't think of such a thing."

"Very well, if you insist," Lady Melton replied.

There was just a hint of satisfaction in her voice. She sat down and picking up the silver teapot proceeded to make the tea from a silver cannister with the air of someone performing a religious rite.

"I hope our tea will be to your liking," she said to Ann. "We have it specially sent to us from China. My father owned many plantations there once, but although we have long since disposed of them the tea comes to us still."

"How interesting," Ann said.

But when a cup was handed to her she looked a little apprehensively at the very weak, faintly scented liquid.

"Lemon or milk?" Lady Melton asked.

"Milk, please," Ann replied.

Seeing Lady Melton put two thin slices of lemon into her own cup she wondered if she had made the wrong answer.

John was helping himself to the scones as if he was hungry, but Ann felt it impossible to eat anything; her appetite seemed to have left her, her mouth felt dry and she searched through her mind wildly for something to say.

"Now," said Lady Melton. "Tell me about yourselves. Where were you married?"

"In the village church of Little Cople," John replied.

"And who was there?"

"A few village people, Ann's sister Myra and her young brother and sister who are twins."

"Yes, yes, I remember you mentioned them in your letter. Oh, dear, it sounds very informal," Lady Melton said. "I think it was a good thing you didn't ask me, John, I should not have approved."

"That is exactly why we didn't have you there, Mother. I know that you like things done both formally and efficiently."

"Hardly a fault, if I may say so," Lady Melton replied. "And now, Ann, tell me about your family. John has said that your father was a doctor; and who was your mother before she married?"

"My mother's name was Winter," Ann replied.

"Winter? Winter? Now let me see—what part of the country did they come from?"

"I think my mother's family lived in Somerset."

"I don't seem to remember any Winters in Somerset. Do you, John?"

"No, I am afraid I don't. But there are a lot of people in Somerset whom I don't remember and have never known," John replied.

Lady Melton glanced at him.

"Really, John, you seem to resent my asking questions. If you spring a daughter-in-law on me at a moment's notice you can hardly expect me not to be curious about her."

The eyes of mother and son met across the tea-table. Quite suddenly Ann felt that this was intolerable. She had forgotten in her own plans for the wedding, in her efforts to dissect her own feelings, that John's family would also have to be considered.

She was about to speak, to say something—what, she didn't know—when suddenly the drawing-room door was flung open and a girl came into the room.

She was tall, thin and exquisitely proportioned, and

97

her fair hair which shone like burnished corn fell to her shoulders on either side of a distinctive and extremely attractive face.

"John!" Her voice was a cry, and she ran across the room to put her hands on John's shoulders as he rose to greet her and to kiss him affectionately on the cheek.

"Welcome home. So many, many congratulations! We have all been so thrilled at the news! Are you happy?"

She stared up into his face, then without waiting for an answer she turned to Ann.

"And this must be Ann!" She held out her hand, the charm bracelets on her thin wrists jangling as she did so.

"My cousin," John explained to Ann. "Vivien Lynton."

"How do you do?" Ann said quietly.

"Do you mean to say John hasn't told you about me?" Vivien asked. "How remiss of him. Or was it intentional?"

She looked at John as she spoke and her red mouth twisted slightly as if something in the situation amused her.

"I have not yet had time to tell Ann about all my relations," John said gravely.

"Which is perhaps a good thing," Vivien replied.

She sat down on a chair on the other side of the tea-table and crossed her legs—long, thin and very shapely legs encased in sheer silk stockings.

She wore a dress of crêpe-de-Chine, very simple in design, but exquisitely cut, and the two clips which finished the neck-line were of gold set with multi-coloured precious stones.

Ann knew that beside this lovely creature she was shabby and insignificant.

"I know what I must look like to her," she thought.

Ann longed with an almost physical longing for

98

Myra and the twins, for her own background, for the people she knew and understood.

"Tea, Vivien?" Lady Melton asked.

"No, thank you, Cousin Margaret. I had some tea at the Loftons. I told Sam you were married, John, but he simply wouldn't believe it. He thought, as we all did, that you were a confirmed bachelor."

"No, I was merely waiting until I met somebody I really wanted to marry," John said.

He spoke in a tone of voice that Ann had never heard before. It seemed to her that he was looking at Vivien in a strange way, as if they fenced together, he and she.

"And how lucky for you that you have done so now," Vivien replied, speaking as if there was honey on her tongue and yet a little sting behind it.

"I consider myself very lucky," John said.

"And what does the new Lady Melton feel about it all?" Vivien asked. "You must forgive us if we feel somewhat astounded. You see, we have been begging John to get married for years and he always told us there was plenty of time; but now time seems to have been the last consideration where your marriage is concerned."

Unconsciously Ann raised her chin a little higher.

"I am sorry to have been instrumental in causing so much commotion," she said. "But you see, John has told me very little about his family or his relations, so selfishly I only considered my own."

She spoke gently. At the same time she felt inside herself that she had hit back. She even imagined that John glanced towards her with something like approval in his eyes.

Lady Melton put out her hand towards her son.

"More tea, John?" she asked, and added: "Well, it is done now, and I suppose it is no use regretting it. All the same, I imagine we shall be asked for an explanation."

"Which I am quite ready to give," John said. "No more tea, thank you, Mother."

"Oh, well, a Member of Parliament ought to be expert in answering awkward questions," Vivien said.

"Fortunately this one is not awkward," John replied.

"No?"

Vivien raised her eyebrows. They were plucked to a very thin line and then drawn in with a dark pencil. Ann could not help watching her. She was fascinating, there was no denying that, and yet at the same time her face was hard.

"She is not very young," Ann thought—"older than I am."

But if she was prepared to be critical, she could not help admiring the ease and the grace with which this strange girl lay sprawled in the arm-chair—the long, tapering elegance of her fingers, the way her hair was arranged to frame her face.

John got to his feet.

"I am going to change my clothes," he announced. "I am too hot dressed like this, and I will show Ann her room. Where will she be sleeping, Mother?"

"In the Queen's room, of course," Lady Melton replied. "It was prepared as soon as I got your letter. Surely you remember that all the Melton brides use that room."

"Oh, yes, I had forgotten," John said. "We must be careful not to offend tradition, mustn't we?"

"You seem to have done that very successfully already," Vivien interposed. "Melton brides are always supposed to wear the Brussels lace veil and great-great-grandmother's tiara, unless, of course, they have a runaway marriage for some strange reason—or other."

"This has been the other reason," John replied.

He slipped his arm through Ann's as she stood irresolute by his side:

"Come along, Ann," he said to her, "we will go

100

and inspect the Queen's room, and you shall wear great-great-grandmother's tiara at your first Court ball. That will show them!"

He led her across the polished parquet floor towards the door. There was silence behind them and Ann was acutely conscious of two pairs of eyes following their movements until the drawing-room door shut behind them.

She said nothing as they crossed the hall and climbed the great staircase side by side. But when John opened a door off the wide landing, she glanced at his face.

It seemed to her that his jaw was squarer than usual and his lips closed in a tight line.

They went into the room. It was very large and very lofty, the walls, panelled in pale blue brocade, matched the hangings of an enormous carved gilt four-poster bed which dominated the centre wall.

There were great ostrich feather fronds at the top of the pillars and over the bed itself was a royal coat-of-arms embroidered in gold.

"Six queens of England are reputed to have slept here at one time or another," John said; but before he could say any more Ann turned to face him.

He saw the expression on her face and was silent.

"We have made a terrible mistake," Ann said quickly. "You ought never to have brought me here like this. You ought never to have married me. You have upset your mother and it is obvious that she dislikes me."

John did not answer for a moment, then he sighed.

"Listen, Ann," he replied at length, "I'm sorry, but I rather expected this. My mother is a very strange woman. I am her only son and I am afraid that she feels hurt at my marrying without her approval or, indeed, her knowledge."

"Well, why did you do it then?" Ann asked. "I didn't think; I didn't understand what you were doing. I don't know why, but vaguely I had the idea in my head that your mother was an invalid. I suppose

I ought to have asked more questions. Instead I was thinking about myself and my family."

John turned and walked across to the fire-place. He leant his arm on the marble mantelpiece and stood staring down into the grate.

"I can't explain, Ann," he said, "or . . . no, that is not true. I don't want to explain; I don't want to say things which might seem disloyal. I don't want to put anything into words. But won't you try to understand? I asked you to give me—companionship."

Ann felt her anger dissolve at his words; she had been feeling it rise within her like a flood; anger at the position to which he had brought her; anger at her own inadequacy, at her own shyness.

And now for the first time John seemed not a dominating, older man with the world at his feet, with everything he wanted at his command, but a younger man who had troubles and difficulties even as other people.

She choked the words that rose to her lips and tried to remember how much he had promised to do for Myra and for the twins. All he had asked in return was companionship.

If there were to be trials, if there were to be troubles, from whatever source they came, couldn't she by understanding his difficulties and sympathising with him in some way help to repay her debt towards him?

She gave a little sigh and impulsively she capitulated completely.

"I am sorry, John. But don't leave me alone if you can help it, will you?"

She tried to smile at him, but her lips were tremulous.

He straightened himself and turned from the contemplation of the gate. He looked at her and their eyes met across the room. Then he smiled too. At that moment they seemed nearer and more friendly one to the other than ever before.

"Will you trust me to look after you?" John asked.

"Y . . . yes," Ann answered, but without great conviction.

It occurred to her that she had never been looked after herself but had always looked after others. Her momentary anger had gone and now she tried to find excuses for the antagonism she had sensed downstairs.

Not so much for John's sake as for her own because she hated to be disliked and was afraid of unpleasantness. She tried to tell herself that it was obvious any mother would be upset. John had undoubtedly behaved badly.

And what of Vivien, the lovely cousin whom she had not expected? No doubt John had many such relations who would feel hurt by his neglect and by his unexpected marriage.

"Who is Miss Lynton?" she asked, breaking the silence between them and trying to make her question sound casual.

"Vivien's mother was my father's first cousin," John replied. "Both her parents are dead and she and her brother have made their home here for the last five years."

"She is very lovely."

"Do you think so?"

"Don't you?" Ann parried.

"I have known Vivien too long to be an unbiased judge," John replied; and then as if he wished to dispose of the subject he asked: "You haven't told me yet what you think of this room."

"I think it is much too big and grand for me," Ann said. "I shall be terrified to sleep in that bed. Is the room haunted"

"Not that I have ever heard," John said. "The haunted part of the house is in the west wing. That is where the monk is supposed to walk who loved a nun and finally drowned himself in the lake when she wouldn't run away with him."

"How romantic!" Ann said. "But don't let us tell

103

the twins or they will want to stay up night after night watching for him."

"I must remember that," John said. "And now I must go and change. I expect they have unpacked for me in the dressing-room."

He walked across the room to open the door by the fire-place. Ann followed him and saw another room, smaller than the one in which they stood but still very large from her standards.

"Will you be sleeping in here?" she asked.

He nodded. "You can call out if you are frightened," he said.

"You are so far away I don't suppose you would hear me," Ann said.

"I will listen very attentively," he promised.

He had spoken easily and yet she felt the blood flood into her cheeks. Her eyes dropped before his.

"I was only joking," she said hastily.

She turned away from him and went towards the dressing-table in the Queen's room.

"Why am I such a fool?" she asked herself. "Why can't I behave normally and naturally as Myra would do? She would take the situation as a matter of course."

Yet even as she thought it, Ann knew that was untrue, for if Myra was in her place there would be no such situation. Myra would be in love with John. She would love him as a husband—as a man into whose keeping she had given herself.

This present situation was, in fact, ridiculous. Would Lady Melton be surprised, Ann wondered, if she knew that her son had made such a bargain? And why, oh why, had he ever wanted to marry her? She stared at her reflection in the mirror. Once she had thought herself pretty, but now this vast house with its ornate magnificent surroundings dwarfed and belittled her.

She thought of Vivien Lynton and knew that the contrast between them was almost laughable.

John shut the communicating door between their rooms. Ann glanced round her and saw that by the bed there was a telephone. She took off the receiver and after a moment or two she was connected with the exchange. She gave the number of John's house in London; she had written it down on a piece of paper so that she could talk with Myra.

She waited, feeling as if she must hear the voice of someone of her own. She was lost, a stranger in a strange land and she wanted contact if only for a few moments with those she loved and who loved her.

The telephone was answered and she asked for Myra, and after what seemed a long wait she heard Myra's voice.

"Oh, Myra! Hullo! It is Ann!"

"Oh, Ann, darlingest, we've had such a wonderful time! What do you think? We have been to see . . ."

For the next two minutes Myra never drew breath. Her tongue seemed to trip over itself in her excitement to describe her pleasure and her ecstasy. Finally she paused through lack of breath and Ann managed to say:

"I am so glad, darling, that you are having such fun."

"And you? What is Gulliver like?"

"Enormous . . . and . . . and very beautiful of course."

"I am simply dying to see it. And oh, Ann, I wish you had been with us this afternoon."

"Did you miss me?"

There was something wistful in Ann's voice.

"Of course we did." Myra's answer was comforting, but Ann felt that it was not strictly true.

She asked after the twins.

"They are eating," Myra said. "I shouldn't be a bit surprised if they are not both sick tonight with so much excitement, apart from the number of cream cakes they have managed to consume for tea."

"I will telephone you tomorrow," Ann said.

"Yes, do," Myra replied. "We are going to get up

early and go out. We don't want to miss a moment of this. Good-bye . . . and enjoy yourself."

"Good-bye," Ann said.

She put down the receiver, but Myra's excited tones seemed still to echo in her ears. She thought of the twins; they had had so few treats that even a tiny party or an invitation to tea had been talked about and commented on and remembered long after it had happened.

Now they were getting everything all at once—and without her. She felt lonely, a little out of it all. It was wrong, of course, and selfish of her, and yet she could not help it. She felt so lost herself, so apart from all that had once mattered.

There was a knock on the door and Ann, realising that she was sitting limply by the telephone, jumped to her feet.

"Come in."

It was only John.

"I have changed," he said. "I want to show you the gardens, or are you too tired?"

"I am not a bit tired," Ann said hastily. "But wait a moment while I take off my hat."

She crossed the room to the dressing-table. Her things had already been unpacked and she picked up the plain Maison Pearson brush which she had used ever since she was a little girl and brushed her hair.

"I shall have to give you some dressing-table things, shan't I?" John said.

Ann looked at her brush, at her comb with two teeth missing and her poor little collection of face creams and manicure accessories.

"Perhaps these are hardly suitable to my position as your wife," she replied.

Then seeing his face in the mirror wondered if she had made the wrong answer. She smoothed her hair back from her forehead.

"'When we get back to London I want you to go

106

to a really good hairdresser," John said. "Vivien can recommend one. I have an idea that I would like your hair parted in the middle. I may be wrong, but anyway I would like you to consider it."

Ann put the comb down on the table and opened a drawer to look for a clean handkerchief. For the moment she could not trust herself to speak. Already he wanted to change her, to make her look like Vivien.

"Why," she asked herself for the thousandth time, "why has he married me?"

Eight

There was a knock at the door. Ann who had been staring out of the window started guiltily; then, pulling her dressing-gown farther round her, she called out: "Come in."

A maid entered, an elderly woman with grey hair drawn back severely under a starched white cap.

"I came to see if I could help you, m'lady."

"No, no, thank you." Ann said hastily; but feeling that she had been a trifle abrupt, she added: "I am used to looking after myself."

"Her Ladyship said I was to attend to you, m'lady, so if there is anything you need, perhaps you will ring the bell by the bed."

"I will, thank you."

The woman after hesitating a moment said: "I only found one evening dress when I unpacked for you, m'lady."

"It is the only one I have," Ann replied, smiling; but as if she sensed something in the older woman's expression, she continued: "You don't think it is suitable for this evening?"

"Oh, I wouldn't say that, m'lady; I am sure it is very charming. It's just that her Ladyship and Miss Vivien are wearing more formal gowns. You see, there are several guests to dinner, and the tenants and staff are coming up to the house afterwards to congratulate Sir John—and to meet you, m'lady."

"Oh, I see."

Ann felt a feeling of dismay flood over her. Guests to dinner, a formal gathering afterwards, Lady Melton and Vivien wearing beautiful gowns suitable for the occasion, while she. . . .

Abruptly with an almost hysterical desire to be alone she said:

"Well, I am afraid there is nothing I can do about it. As you saw when you unpacked, I have only the one dress with me."

"Of course, I understand, m'lady. I hope you don't think it presumptuous of me to speak."

"No, no, of course not. . . . I will ring if I want anything, thank you."

The door closed behind the maid. Slowly Ann walked across the room to where her dress, her one and only evening dress, was laid out over a chair. She knew without looking at it every familiar line.

She knew its faults, its discrepancies, everything about it; and yet she had to look at it, to look and know all too well exactly how unsuitable it was for this of all evenings when she would be. . . yes, why not admit it? . . . "on show" as John's wife.

It had been her only evening frock for over three years, but she had never cared for it even when it was new. She remembered so well receiving the length of dark grey satin.

"You will look like a battleship in it," Myra had laughed when she brought it home.

But it had been a gift of love, given in the fullness of heart and in gratitude.

There had been an old woman in Little Cople who had been her father's patient for nearly twenty-five years. She was very old and completely bed-ridden, and her sister who looked after her was nearly as old as she was.

Poor, in ill health, with no relations save each other, and few friends, they nevertheless remained two of the happiest people that Ann had ever known.

Their faith, their belief in the goodness of God shone through the frailty of their ageing bodies like a light. It was impossible to be with them and not to absorb a little of that inner joy that came from a belief that God was all-merciful and held them safe within His protecting hand.

As they grew older, the village found them queer and began to laugh at them. Certainly they talked a little strangely of visitations which had come to them in the night, of angels' voices which warned them of trouble to come.

When Miss Jenny, who was the younger sister, began to fail, Dr. Shefford hoped that the neighbors would rally round and give them a hand, for both the old women had one desperate fear that they would have to leave their tiny cottage and be taken to the infirmary.

But the neighbors were frightened of them or else were too selfish to put themselves out, and it was Ann who solved the problem.

Luckily the cottage was not far from her home. She used to slip down three or four times a day to help the old women. She would wash them, make their beds, tidy the rooms and prepare their meals either in their own cottage or at home.

Last thing at night she would go back to shut them up and see that their lamp was turned out and the guard safe on the hearth for fear of fire.

The elder sister died first, and a week later Miss Jenny followed her, dying, Dr. Shefford said, of a broken heart because she had nothing left to live for.

But before she died she had told Ann to look in the

bottom drawer of the big old-fashioned tall-boy which always stood in her sister's bedroom.

There, wrapped in innumerable sheets of tissue paper, she found a parcel.

"Bring it to me, bring it to me," Miss Jenny said, sitting up in bed, her hands trembling with excitement.

Slowly and laboriously she unpacked the parcel, to disclose a dress-length of grey satin.

"My sister wished you to have it, dear," she said to Ann. "It was to have been her wedding dress."

There was a break in the old and quavering voice.

"Her wedding dress!" Ann exclaimed. "And she never got married?"

Miss Jenny shook her head.

"He was drowned, dear, drowned coming back from India. His ship went down."

Bare words, simple words, and yet Ann knew that they hid a tragedy. At last she understood why as Miss Jenny's sister got older she had often rambled on about the sea, and once when she was dying, she had called out quite clearly.

"He is calling . . . he is calling me . . . but the waves are drowning his voice . . . I cannot hear . . . I cannot hear. . . ."

Ann looked down at the grey satin which had been treasured and preserved all through the long, long years by a heart which had always been faithful, by a love which had never died.

"She wanted you to have it, dear," Miss Jenny whispered. "Perhaps it will bring you the happiness she never had."

Ann thanked her and bent to kiss the old and wrinkled cheek. But when she had taken the gift home, she looked at it somewhat ruefully.

The satin was the sort which was unobtainable nowadays, but she knew that the colour would not be becoming to her dark hair and would not set off to advantage the whiteness of her skin.

She was not fond of grey, it always seemed to her a dull, indecisive colour; but as she said to Myra:

"We can't afford to look a gift-horse in the face."

"Well, I don't want it, anyway," Myra retorted.

"Which is good thing," Ann replied, "because I intend to make myself an evening dress. There is plenty of it; I shall have a full skirt and little puff sleeves."

"Whatever you do with it," Myra said scornfully, "you will still look like great-grandmother's ghost."

"At least I shall have something to wear," Ann replied, remembering the threadbare black velvet which had served her for many years as a dinner frock and was really past repair.

She cut out the grey dress, made it and wore it, but she never liked herself in it. She had tried adding a touch of colour at the neck and round the waist, but somehow that had merely made the dress seem rather vulgar and uglier than when it was unadorned.

When she had packed to go away on her honeymoon, it had gone into the suitcase because she had nothing else.

"What does it matter?" Ann had asked herself; but now she knew that it did matter—tremendously.

She stood looking at the dress and suddenly she put her hands up to her face.

"Why did I come here?" she asked aloud, and a sudden surge of anger against John rose up within her.

He had given Myra money to buy clothes, but he had not thought his wife would feel shabby and ashamed in the grandeur and luxury of his home.

"It is King Cophetua and the Beggar Maid!" Ann thought, and a bitter smile twisted her lips.

The clock on the mantelpiece chimed a tiny silver chime. Ann looked up and started to dress hastily. She must not be late. She expected that John would be coming in to fetch her at any moment. What was he thinking, she wondered, on the other side of the door?

She had enjoyed going round the garden with him. He had showed her the lake and the water-lily pond, the ornamental fountains, the herb-garden, which had been planted in the reign of Queen Elizabeth, the hot-houses and vegetable gardens.

It had all been very beautiful and very awe-inspiring, very nearly as breath-taking as had been her tour of the house. But somehow, Ann thought, it had been more enjoyable because it had been more impersonal. She had not felt in the garden that she individually had any part to play; she was just a spectator, a visitor who was being shown round.

It was only as they got back to the house that she felt overpowered by John's home, and the realisation that it would be her background as John's wife.

Alone in her bedroom, she felt a sudden, almost intolerable longing for her father. She had tried all day to put the thought of him away from her for fear that she should break down; but now it swept over her, the thought of being without him, of her own loneliness, and of being so utterly lost without his guidance and his love.

"Oh Daddy, Daddy," she cried within her heart, "how can I bear it? How can I live without you?"

She would have wept then, the tempest of tears was very near, her control was stretched to breaking-point; but strangely, even as she realised the agony of her unhappiness, she felt the moment pass.

Vividly, so vividly that for a moment she thought that it was a real rather than a mental picture, she saw her father's face smiling at her, and she heard his voice.

"But you have never given in, Ann, my dear."

That was true, she had never given in; they had laughed together about it, he and she, so often. When

112

things had seemed difficult or even insurmountable, Ann would always protest.

"I will find a way round it somehow!" or had cried, "I will make it come right, I will!"

"You ought to have been a boy," Dr. Shefford had told her more than once; "you would have made a fine pioneer."

Had not all the household at Little Cople lived on her strength, drawn courage from her, and remained undefeated because she had always been able to hold her head high?

"You have never given in, Ann, my dear!" Ann knew then unmistakably and with a childlike faith that she was not alone. Tremulously, because the moment was so poignant, she had forced herself to smile.

"I won't give in, Daddy, I won't."

But human nature is not capable of sustaining the heights for very long. As Ann dressed and finally slipped the grey satin dress over her head, she felt both dismayed and discontented with her lot.

It was bad enough to face a hasty marriage with a man one hardly knew; but to be pitchforked into a different social stratum of life at the same time was, Ann thought, almost a refined type of cruelty.

She looked at herself in the mirror with distaste.

"A dull, dowdy, ghost-like creature, that's what I am," she told herself and then turned round almost defiantly with her chin held a little higher than usual as there came a knock at the door.

"Come in."

She expected John, but it was the elderly house-maid again.

"Sir John has sent word, m'lady, that he has to see Mr. Brownlow, the agent, before dinner, and he hopes that when you are ready you will find your own way downstairs to the drawing-room."

"Thank you."

Ann hoped that she did not look as dismayed as she felt.

This, she thought, was the last straw. With John by her side she would not have minded so much facing the critical eyes of her mother-in-law or what she anticipated would be Vivien Lynton's contempt. But alone . . .

Quickly she picked up a clean handkerchief and turned towards the door.

"It has to be done," she thought, "and the quicker the better."

She forced herself to walk briskly, but once outside her own room she hesitated. She felt it was almost impossible to drag her feet over the soft carpet which covered the wide landing. The great staircase lay in front of her.

"I've got to do it, I've got to," she told herself, and then as she stood there she heard a movement behind her.

"Are you wondering which is the right way?" someone asked.

She turned swiftly. A young man was standing just behind her. He was slim and fair and extraordinarily good-looking. What was more, his smile was friendly and somehow irresistible. Without thinking Ann found herself smiling back spontaneously and naturally.

"I do know the way," she answered without waiting to choose her words. "But . . ."

"You are frightened?"

His frankness was only engaging.

"Yes, frightened," she confessed.

"Then I must look after you," he said. "You are Ann of course, and I am Charles—Charles Lynton."

"How do you do?" Ann held out her hand.

"Has nobody told you about me?" he asked.

Ann shook her head.

"They will," he promised. "In the meantime I will try to make a good impression, which may in some way mitigate all the bad things you are going to hear."

"Why bad?"

"You will learn all about me in due course," he said, "but for the moment let's forget it because I want to tell you how glad I am to meet you and how happy I hope you will be here at Gulliver."

Ann felt a sudden lightening of the frozen misery which seemed to have encompassed her being ever since she had arrived. Here was somebody warm and human, somebody who wanted to be nice to her and who seemed even on such a superficial acquaintance to like her.

"Thank you," she said with an eagerness which gave the simple words a fuller value.

"And now," Charles said, "I suppose we must go downstairs."

Obediently Ann turned, but he saw the expression on her face and stopped.

"What's worrying you?" he asked.

Without considering Ann told him the truth.

"This dress!" she said and added quickly as if ashamed of her own frankness, "I suppose no woman really likes being Cinderella."

"Of course they don't."

There was sympathy as well as understanding in Charles's tone.

"You see, it's the only one I've got."

"But of course," Charles answered. "And dear John with his usual masculine obtuseness never thought of anything so mundane as clothes when he brought you here."

There was something so humorous in the way he spoke that Ann laughed.

"It is ridiculous to mind, isn't it?" she asked. "Please don't tell anybody I'm so stupid."

"But you are not stupid," Charles replied. "This is a very important moment in your life and you want to look your best. Wait!"

He stood back to look at her.

115

His eyes narrowed, and then suddenly he said: "I have it!"

"Have what?" Ann asked.

"An idea," he answered. "An inspiration if you like. Anyway I know what to do. Leave everything to me. Go back to your room; don't let anyone see you. I shan't be more than three or four minutes."

"But I don't understand," Ann exclaimed and added quickly: "If you are thinking of borrowing a dress for me, I would rather you didn't. I prefer to . . . be myself."

"Of course," he replied. "Trust me."

Ann did as she was told, why she was not quite sure. She went back into her room and waited. She felt slightly perturbed but at the same time curious.

She was aware that she had taken an instantaneous liking to Charles, even as she had taken an instantaneous dislike to his sister, and her cry of fear that he might borrow a dress for her had been because she could not bear to think that anything of Vivien's might be offered to her.

Vivien was her enemy, she was sure of that, though why and for what reason she did not know. Charles was different and yet how could he help her?

Quicker than she had thought possible there came a swift knock at her door and without waiting for her reply Charles entered.

For a second she did not realise what he carried, but as he crossed the room she recognised them. Camellias, pure white, perfect in their symmetry. Charles laid them down carefully on the dressing-table; then he put his hand in his dinner-jacket pocket and brought out a roll of fine, delicate wire.

Swiftly he started to make a wreath, Ann watching his fingers thought they were those of an artist, long, thin and tapering. Hardly those one would expect to belong to a handsome young man.

He stripped away the green leaves from each flower

116

and raised them so that they made a half-circle or as he put it a "halo" for Ann's head.

"Put it on," he said. "It will look like a halo, but it is more suitable and far more becoming than any of the expensive tiaras you will as John's wife wear in the years to come."

Feeling a little dazed Ann sat down at the dressing-table and did as she was told. Charles had left the ends of the wire to tie together underneath her hair.

She fixed the wreath on her head, holding it steady with hair-pins inserted cleverly along the wire where they did not show. Then she looked at herself and gave a little exclamation.

But before she could say more Charles stopped her.

"I haven't finished yet."

There were half a dozen camellias left. He arranged them in a neat little bunch and then held them against the V-shaped neck of her dress.

"Pin them there," he commanded, "and be careful not to bruise the petals."

Ann did as she was told, and then looking at her reflection she gave a spontaneous sigh of relief and excitement.

"It's good, isn't it?" Charles asked. "The Quaker Girl up to date!"

It was good; it was almost perfect. There was something demure and yet very attractive now in the severity of the dull grey dress relieved by the dead white of the velvet-petalled flowers.

On Ann's hair they brought into prominence the vivid beauty of her eyes and the transparent delicacy of her skin. No longer did she look a dull, dowdy, ghost-like creature.

Now she was a woman dressed with originality and with that touch of genius which can transform the commonplace as if with a magic wand.

And she was crowned—crowned with flowers, but also with confidence as she realised that in some new unexpected way she looked prettier than she had ever done before.

"Oh, thank you. It's wonderful; I feel so much better."

"And you look quite beautiful."

He spoke the words slowly and deliberately. There was something in his eyes which made Ann turn swiftly towards the door.

"We shall be late."

"Let them wait for the bride—the new Lady Melton," Charles replied.

But he followed her and they walked down the broad staircase together.

There was a buzz of voices in the drawing-room, but with Charles at her side Ann held her head high as they entered the room. For a moment it seemed to her as though there was silence, and then John came forward quickly.

"I was just coming to look for you," he said. "I was afraid you had lost your way."

"That is exactly what I had done," Ann told him with a faint smile; "but Charles came to my rescue."

Was it her fancy or did an almost imperceptible shadow pass over John's expression?

"Oh, Charles," he said, and without further comment drew Ann over to introduce her to several new people in the room.

There were three middle-aged couples, two young men, a dowager who regarded her somewhat fixedly through lorgnettes; and then John drew her to where, a little detached from the group, standing in front of the fire-place was a small, oldish man.

For a moment Ann thought he was bending down, before she saw he was a hunchback.

"My cousin Sinclair," John said. "He lives here and looks after us all. Isn't that right, Sinclair?"

"I hope it is true, John," the hunchback answered in a low deep voice which was somehow peculiarly charming. "Sometimes I am able to offer you my advice, and sometimes you listen to me. I ask nothing more of life, and I only hope that Ann will one day honour me by also turning to me if she needs a friend."

His handclasp was warm and comforting. Ann longed to ask John about his cousin. She looked at the hunchback's face; it was lined as if with suffering, and yet it was an attractive face, a face of character, fine-drawn, sensitive and somehow unworldly.

"It must be a tragedy," Ann thought, "that such a man should be a hunchback."

She made up her mind to ask John about him at the first opportunity, but now she had caught sight of Vivien and for the moment everything else was brushed from her mind.

Vivien was looking amazingly beautiful. She wore a dress of sea-green sequins, which gave her the appearance of a Rhine-maiden. It was difficult to look at her and not feel that her loveliness was supernatural.

She moved sinuously across the room, smiled up at John, her long dark lashes lifting back from eyes almost translucent in colour. Then she turned to Ann.

"And how is the bride feeling?" she asked. "I feel we are all extremely indiscreet in being present on your honeymoon, John."

"Surely the remedy for that is obvious?" John replied.

There was a steely note in his voice, which Ann had never heard before.

Vivien, however, was quite unperturbed by the snub. She put out a hand and touched his arm.

"Don't sound so cross, darling," she said. "This is *supposed* to be the happiest day of your life."

Ann felt that Vivien had scored a point, but there was no time to wonder what John was thinking for Lady Melton was making the move towards the dining-room. Ann found Charles at her elbow.

"Keep your end up," he whispered. "You have

knocked them flat as Cinderella did when she went to the ball."

"Thanks to her fairy godmother," Ann flashed back.

He bowed mockingly as they were separated from each other, and Ann found herself being led to the end of the table in the great banqueting hall.

She felt a moment of panic.

The candelabra high-branched with their tall candles, the great crested silver ornaments, the egg-shell china dishes piled with hot-house fruit, the orchids which decorated the embroidered lace-edged cloth, all combined with the strange faces around her to make her feel as though the only thing she wanted to do was to run away and hide.

She was trembling and her fingers gripped the carved oak arms of her chair. Then a quiet, deep voice at her side said:

"I have had the honour of being told to sit next to you. May I start by saying how glad I am?"

Ann found herself looking into the kind, understanding eyes of John's cousin, Sinclair. Her lips were dry and for a moment she could not answer him.

"This room is always a bit awe-inspiring the first time you see it," he said, and she knew that he understood and was giving her time to recover herself.

"There are so many first times of everything today," she said unsteadily. "It is the first time I have ever been to a big dinner party or seen . . . well, people like these."

"Tell me what sort of people you are used to," he asked, and she knew that there was not only kindness in the question, but a real desire to know.

Almost unconsciously she began to talk of her home and of her father. The dinner, formal though it was, passed more quickly than Ann had imagined possible.

On the other side of her there was a rather dull, prosy, fox-hunting squire who had brought over his wife and daughter from a neighbouring estate. He had little to say to someone who did not appreciate

120

the delights of the chase, and every possible moment Ann turned with relief to Cousin Sinclair.

Somehow, though they were so completely different in appearance, he reminded her vaguely of her father. He had the same quiet sense of humour, the same genuine interest in people, and the same indifference to their position or the trappings with which they surrounded themselves in life.

Ann found herself enjoying her dinner because of the man who was sitting next to her. She forgot for the moment why she was there or who she was, and it was with a sense of surprise that she heard Lady Melton say:

"We must, of course, drink the health of the bride and bridegroom."

The party rose to their feet, and awkwardly Ann would have risen also had not Sinclair put a quick hand on her arm and whispered:

"You remain seated; we are toasting you and John."

Glasses were raised.

"The bride and bridegroom." Ann feeling the colour rise in her face hoped that she was not disgracing John, who seated at the far end of the table seemed to be taking everything calmly, and in his usual grave manner.

The party sat down. "Speech," someone called, but John shook his head.

"I make far too many speeches at other times," he said, "this is my night off."

"But you must drink your bride's health," someone suggested.

"Of course." He took up his glass and raised it to Ann.

With an effort she raised hers in return, but even as she touched the champagne with her lips she felt how false the whole thing was.

"We are like people on the stage," she thought, "like puppets pulled about by strings. This isn't real,

121

this isn't true; we are all pretending, acting instead of living."

She felt a quick surge of revolt within her. Then looking at her down the table she saw Charles, a twinkle in his eye, the smile which somehow she found irresistible curving his lips.

Almost imperceptibly as she looked at him he winked, and suddenly Ann realised that while she was revolting against the pomposity and the stilted formality he was seeing the humour of it. To Charles it was comedy, not tragedy—a moment for laughter.

Feeling young and suddenly carefree, Ann winked back.

Nine

Lady Melton entered the library and shutting the door sharply behind her advanced briskly towards the desk where her son was writing.

"Now, John, I think it's time that you and I had a straight talk."

John rose slowly to his feet.

"Very well, Mother," he replied. "If you think it will do any good."

"My dear boy, I think you owe me an explanation."

John smiled as if he was slightly amused.

"I suppose it would be ridiculous of me to pretend not to understand what you mean by that."

"Very ridiculous," Lady Melton answered. "You know quite well you have behaved badly."

Then her tone changed and for a moment there was an emotion in her voice which made her sound quite human.

"Oh, John, how could you be such a fool?"

"A fool, Mother?"

"Yes, a fool," Lady Melton repeated bitterly. "What made you marry this girl? She is quite pretty, I grant you that, but she is a nobody, she has no poise, no social sense, and as far as I can make out, no conversation. How could you imagine for one moment that she could fill the position as your wife? You have always been difficult, John, but this time I despair of you. Whatever made you do such a thing?"

John took out his cigarette case, opened it and appeared to be absorbed in selecting a cigarette. There was a pause, but after a moment he said:

"I suppose you would not accept the obvious explanation?"

"That you are in love with her?" Lady Melton questioned. "But why? For what reason? Look at the choice you have had all your life of really attractive women; and I had hoped, yes I have always hoped that sooner or later you would marry Vivien."

"You made your interest very obvious, Mother, if I may say so."

"And why not?" Lady Melton asked. "I have grown very fond of Vivien. She is an extremely sensible young woman and she would be a useful wife to an ambitious man."

"Unfortunately I am not ambitious."

"My dear John, don't be so absurd. What is this new phase of yours? I don't understand you, I tell you that quite frankly. And as to this mésalliance, it is a tragedy. I can't think what we are going to do about it."

"Well, that is lucky, Mother, as frankly I don't wish you to do anything. Would you be surprised if I told you I was happy?"

"I suppose you must be getting something out of it," Lady Melton said acidly, "but I can tell you one thing, John, and that is that the girl is not in love with you. She has married you for your money."

John shut his cigarette case so sharply that the report seemed for a moment to echo across the room;

then he threw back his shoulders as a man might who carried an intolerable burden.

"I'm sorry, Mother, but neither now nor at any time will I discuss Ann."

For a moment Lady Melton looked nonplussed, but only for a moment. Then she attacked in another direction.

"Well, perhaps you will condescend to tell me what arrangements you wish to make. This is your house, of course, John."

"Thank you for reminding me," her son said quietly. "For the moment I wish to make no change. You will remain on here, and so can Vivien, Charles and, of course, Sinclair. Later on I may have other arrangements to suggest, but for the moment I don't wish to burden Ann with having to run a large house. Besides, when Parliament is in session we shall have to be in London."

Lady Melton got to her feet.

"Well, if you expect me to thank you, you will be disappointed," she said. "I will stay here and continue to do my duty; but I am disappointed in you, John, bitterly disappointed. I shall do my best to be polite to this girl, but don't ask any more of me or expect it."

"I have learned never to expect from people more than they are capable of giving," John said quietly.

His mother gave him a glance as if she wondered whether he intended to be rude or not, but she said nothing further.

She left the room, walking with a swiftness which was characteristic of her, but which detracted nothing from her dignity and the almost overbearing impression she gave of being formidable.

In the orangery Ann, who was trying to tempt an ancient and extremely supercilious parrot with a lump of sugar, also heard a voice say:

"I want to talk to you."

124

She dropped the sugar into the cage and turned round with a smile of welcome.

"Good morning, Charles; I have been hoping to see you because I wanted to say 'Thank you'."

"What for?"

"For being so kind to me last night. For saving me from making a fool of myself, and for making me look, well, at least presentable."

"That's exactly what I wanted to talk to you about," Charles said. "Let us go out and sit in the rose garden. There's a seat where I know we shall not be disturbed."

He led the way into the sunshine and they walked until he led Ann to a seat framed in fragant blossom, the crimson and yellow roses making a secluded, almost secret bower from which one could see and yet not be seen.

The rose garden was, although Ann did not know it, famous among horticulturists; but she was conscious only of a wealth of colour, of the humming of the bees as they flew from flower to flower collecting honey, and the sound of the birds as they fluttered around the exquisitely carved marble bird-bath in the centre of the garden.

"How lovely!" Ann exclaimed.

"That is exactly what I was going to say," Charles answered.

There was something in the tone of his voice and in the look in his eyes that told Ann with a sense of shock that he was not speaking of the garden.

"What did you want to talk to me about?" she asked hastily.

"You," he replied.

"And what about me?"

"I want you to listen to me, Ann. You know that I am your friend—that is if you will let me be."

"Let you? Of course I will let you. I need a friend badly, Charles; I'm not so stupid as not to realise that. I was frightened when John brought me here yesterday and still more frightened after I had had tea with my mother-in-law, and . . ." she hesitated.

. . . "My sister," Charles finished, and added: "I know, I know only too well; and when I saw you looking lost and miserable at the top of the staircase, I felt like a knight-errant sent to rescue the imprisoned maiden."

Ann laughed.

"Did I really look as bad as that?"

"Pretty gloomy."

"I felt it," Ann confessed; "but after you had been so kind and changed my whole appearance by bringing me the camellias, I felt different. Aren't we women fools when you think about it? Clothes matter so much."

"Oh course they do, and that is precisely why I have got a suggestion to make to you."

"What is it?"

"That you will let me choose your new clothes for you."

"You?"

"Yes, don't look so surprised. I have designed my sister's dresses for years, and actually a clothes sense is the only talent I possess. A most reprehensible one I admit. You will hear all about it in time.

'Charles, the poor boy, is such a waster. Just does nothing with his life! Why his only interest appears to be clothes, women's clothes! It's really dreadful for his family, isn't it?' "

Ann was laughing helplessly before Charles had finished speaking. He had mimicked cleverly and with exactly the right intonation Lady Melton's voice. Ann could almost hear her speaking.

"That's right, laugh at me."

"Oh, Charles, I can't help it, you are so funny."

"At the same time I'm being practical as far as you are concerned. I am going to tell you something. You may have heard it many times before, in which case it won't surprise you—you are a very beautiful young woman."

Ann sighed.

"If it's true, you are the only person who thinks so."

"But . . ."

"And, of course, there is a 'but'," Ann said quickly.

"Yes," he replied, "there is a 'but', and I am going to tell you what it is. You are badly produced. You are like a valuable picture hung in the wrong light and in an excruciatingly unsuitable frame. You are like a jewel that has never been polished.

"Oh! I could go on giving you smiles—thousands of them, but instead I'm going to cease talking and get down to action. I want your permission to go to London today to buy you some clothes, just a few to go on with."

"Today?" Ann exclaimed. "But how?"

"I've got a friend," Charles explained. "He is a dress designer. Yes, a 'he'. You will get used to these new ideas in time, and he is just beginning to make a name for himself. I've helped him with his designs often enough, and I've sent him quite a lot of people.

"I am going to steal some of his models; he won't mind, not when he knows whom they are for. You are about model size, thank goodness, and later you are going to give him a really large order.

"You are going to have wonderful clothes, really beautiful creations, and I am going to produce you as the most beautiful woman that has ever graced the head of the table at Gulliver."

"It all sounds like a fairy story," Ann said. "I just don't believe a word of it. But I must have some new clothes, that is sensible and reasonable enough. . . ."

"And you are going to let me choose them," Charles interposed.

Ann hesitated for a moment, and then she answered:

"If it really interests you."

127

"It does," he said. "Last night we compared you to Cinderella, if I remember rightly; but we have got our fairy tales mixed. You are really the Sleeping Beauty." He paused a moment and added softly: "One day someone will wake you up."

Ann's eyes fell beneath his.

"I am very much awake, thank you," she said lightly.

"On the contrary," Charles answered. "Shall I tell you a little more about yourself?"

Some instinct within her warned her that this was dangerous ground. She got to her feet.

"I think we ought to go back to the house; John may be looking for me."

"Yes, John, of course," Charles sighed, but he also rose. "I think really you ought to come up to London with me."

"To help you choose my clothes?"

"Heavens, no, I wouldn't trust your taste for a moment; the Ann you are used to seeing in the glass is not the one that I have in my mind's eye. But I would like you to go to a hairdresser."

"Goodness!" Ann exclaimed. "What is wrong with my hair? John wants it parted in the middle and now you start complaining."

Charles raised his eyebrows.

"That's unusually perceptive of John," he said "For it is exactly what I was going to ask you to do."

"I've decided to refuse both suggestions," Ann replied. "I think on the whole I would rather be myself."

"Nonsense," Charles replied. "You have got to shed that old self like a snake shedding its skin. You will part your hair in the middle, my dear; and if you don't like what you see, well then, I will give up dress designing and take to coal mining instead."

Ann laughed.

"It's all so ridiculous really."

"And yet at the same time you would like to be a beauty. But you will have to do what I tell you."

Ann thought of Vivien moving across the drawing-room the night before, the shimmering green of the sequins revealing her figure, and turning her into a creature of fantasy and loveliness which stirred the imagination; she thought of her shining hair, her general air of being perfectly turned out, exquisite in every detail.

Suddenly she made up her mind. . . .

"Charles, I will do whatever you suggest," she said, and there was a solemnity in her voice as though she took a vow rather than made a decision.

"I shall never ask of you any more than that," he replied and somehow the tone of his voice said more than his words.

"And you really will get me some clothes today—at once?"

"On one condition."

"What's that?" Ann asked.

"That you won't allow anyone to awaken you before I come back."

For a moment his eyes held hers. Something strange and magnetic seemed to pass between them. Ann drew a quick breath and turned away.

They had reached the terrace when they saw one of the footmen approaching.

"You are wanted on the telephone, m'lady."

"It must be Myra from London," Ann cried happily and ran impulsively into the house.

The morning-room was empty and she picked up the telephone which lay on the desk before the open window.

"Hallo!" It was Myra who answered her.

"Oh, Ann darling, something so exciting has happened. Dawson Barclay's sister, Mrs. Doughty, has asked me to go down and stay for the week-end. She has a house on the river; they are having a dance on Saturday night and I have bought myself the most marvellous new dress. I must go; do you mind?"

"No, of course not, darling. Tell Mr. Barclay I think it is very kind of his sister. But what about the twins?"

"That's what I wanted to tell you," Myra went on. "Dawson and I both think it would be best if they came down to Gulliver today. Will that be all right?"

"Yes, of course," Ann said, conscious of a sudden doubt, but not wishing to damp Myra's enthusiasm. "I will go and tell John now. I am sure he will agree."

"Oh, Ann, isn't everything thrilling? I have bought myself an evening dress, and two perfectly scrumptious cotton dresses, a hat, some sandals, and a lot of other things that I had better not mention on the telephone."

"Have you spent all the money John gave you?" Ann asked.

"Practically every penny of it, but he won't mind, will he? After all he has got lots more and it's yours too—now."

"But we can't. . ."

"Oh, I know what you are going to say," Myra interrupted. "Don't you worry, Ann. I will wangle it out of him. Dawson doesn't think he will mind, anyway."

"I suppose it's all right," Ann said doubtfully.

"And Ann, about the twins. . . . "

"I think there is someone going up from here by car, so he can fetch them."

"Well, as a matter of fact," Myra answered, "they have left already. I have been trying to get through to you for nearly an hour. Dawson and I are leaving in about twenty minutes and I thought it better to get them off at once. Dawson took them to the station and put them in a first-class carriage, so they should be all right. Their train gets to Crockley Cross at twelve o'clock."

"Very well, I will meet them."

"You do understand, don't you, darling? You're not stuffy about it all?"

"No, no, of course not."

"That's splendid. Well, I will ring you up tonight if I can, and oh, Ann, I am having such a wonderful time!"

Ann put down the receiver slowly. It was no use, she could not help the feeling which swept over her of being neglected and forgotten.

Myra had found her feet, was living her own life, making her own arrangements, buying clothes, doing everything on her own; and only a few days ago she had seemed a little girl, nothing more than a child, clinging to her elder sister and asking her advice over everything.

The old life was indeed finished. Somehow the new one seemed infinitely less attractive.

"Lady Melton of Gulliver." Why should that compare so unfavourably with "Ann Shefford of Little Cople," whose word was law in the tiny house they called home, who ruled her little family with a loving heart, and who received in return their unstinted love and adoration?

For a moment Ann had to fight for her self-control.

"I've got to accept this," she told herself, "even as I have had to accept other things."

But it left a bitter taste behind. She tried to console herself. Myra was independent of her, but she still had the twins.

She went in search of John. For a moment she had no idea where to look for him; then she remembered that the day before when he had been showing her the house he had told her that he did most of his work in the library.

She went down the long passage which led to it and opened the door softly and a little timidly. There was always the possibility that John might not welcome the arrival of the twins, and Ann wondered what Lady Melton would think of them.

As she opened the door she heard Vivien's voice: "Oh, John, how could you, how could you do it? After all we have . . ."

The sentence was broken off in the middle, for Vivien looked up and saw Ann standing in the doorway. In the silence that followed Ann knew that Vivien had been speaking of John's marriage and of her.

John was seated at his desk, the chair pushed a little bit back, his legs crossed and his fingers lightly laced together as his elbows rested on the arms of the chair.

He seemed to be considering Vivien as she sat on the arm of the sofa, a vivid, colourful figure in a dress of emerald-green linen.

It was an attitude which revealed both the grace of her exquisite body, and the loveliness of her legs, and Ann was vividly conscious too of the almost compelling attraction of Vivien's face—her scarlet mouth which seemed to invite kisses, her wide expressive eyes, fringed with long, artificially darkened eyelashes.

"Come in, Ann," John said, apparently quite unembarrassed by her interruption.

But Vivien added quickly, with a spiteful note in her voice: "We were just talking about you."

"So I gathered," Ann said quietly.

Inside herself she felt afraid but she knew that she did not show it as she walked across the room and sat down on a chair opposite John's desk. It was hard, however, to face John while she was conscious of Vivien's critical and hostile gaze.

Quickly, because she was embarrassed, Ann broke the silence.

"Myra has just telephoned me," she said, speaking only to John.

"Everything is all right, I hope?" he asked.

132

"Yes, quite all right," Ann replied, "but Mr. Barclay's sister has asked Myra to stay for the week-end."

"Why on earth should Dawson have arranged that?" Vivien interrupted, her cold and slightly supercilious voice breaking in on Ann's somewhat hurried speech.

"Why shouldn't he?" John asked. "I told him to look after Myra and apparently he is doing his best."

"Well, I don't suppose she will enjoy herself," Vivien said. "Susan Doughty is an awful bore, at least I have always found her so—one of those busy, interfering sisters who consider their brothers very much their own property."

"Myra is looking forward to her visit," Ann said, "especially as they are having a dance tomorrow night."

"Dear, dear, Dawson is getting quite gay in his old age," Vivien mocked. "Or perhaps your sister has something to do with his suddenly stepping out."

"I'm afraid I know very little about Mr. Barclay," Ann replied, and then deliberately turning her face to John as if to exclude Vivien she said: "As they were going away, Myra thought that it would be best to send the twins down here. They are arriving at twelve."

With a sense of relief she saw that John was genuinely pleased.

"That's splendid," he said. "We'll go and meet them, shall we?"

"That would be lovely," Ann answered.

Vivien stood up with a deliberation which drew attention to herself.

"You will be quite a family man before you have finished, John," she said coolly and walked towards the door.

"I hope so," John replied quietly.

Something in his quiet seriousness embarrassed Ann more than Vivien's rudeness. The door shut and she was alone with her husband.

"There's something else I want to tell you, John," she said.

"Yes?"

"It's about my clothes . . ." Ann began, strangely nervous, and feeling now that the whole arrangement she had made with Charles was somehow ridiculous.

"You want some money, of course," John interrupted. "I've been thinking about that and was going to discuss the matter with you."

"It isn't only the money," Ann said, quickly, "but Charles has suggested that he should choose some things for me to wear."

"Charles would," John said. It seemed to Ann a trifle grimly.

Quite suddenly her nervousness left her. Charles at least had been kind and understanding. John did not understand the humiliation of being dowdy and threadbare while there were such creatures as Vivien under the same roof.

"I need some clothes very badly; I ought to have been sensible enough to buy at least a few things before I came down here."

John got to his feet and walked across to the window. He stood looking out for a moment as though he was debating something within his mind, and then he turned back towards Ann.

"I ought to apologise to you," he said.

"For what?"

John seemed a little lost for words.

"For making a mess of several things," he said at length. "I realise now that we should have gone somewhere else for our honeymoon. We should have got to know each other and then have come to Gulliver. But . . . well, I didn't anticipate the reception we should both receive."

He was so obviously finding it difficult to express himself that for once Ann lost her own fear of him.

"Don't worry, John," she said. "I understand of course that your mother and Miss Lynton are upset by your marriage. They don't think I am good enough for you, and . . . well . . . I agree with them."

"That's not true and you are not to say it." John spoke so sharply that Ann looked at him in surprise. "When you promised to marry me, you did me the greatest honour that any woman can do a man. If I have bungled things will you please put it down to my stupidity, or should I say inexperience . . . and in no circumstances blame yourself for anything."

Ann did not know quite what to reply, but after a second, shyly because in her heart she was still afraid, she said:

"I don't want to upset everybody or to get you into trouble."

John looked at her, and then he smiled.

"You are a wonderful person, you know."

Ann gave a little laugh.

"That's the second compliment I've had this morning," she said. "I shall get my head turned if everybody goes on like this."

"And who was fortunate enough to pay you the first one?"

"Charles," Ann replied. "He said . . ." She stopped, and unaccountably felt herself flushing. "Oh, he talked a lot of nonsense, but he says that if he is allowed to choose my clothes he will turn me out looking . . . quite a respectable wife for you."

"How kind of Charles," John said a trifle dryly, and then he added as if determined to be generous: "But he certainly is an expert where clothes are concerned. It is the one thing he can do well, if it comes to that."

"He told me everyone disapproved of him, but he has been very kind to me."

"And that is most important, of course," John said gravely without irony. "Well, if you want my permission, of course you have it. Tell him to buy you anything he likes and send the bill to me. And some-

135

time I would like to talk to you about having some money of your own.

"I am transferring some shares to you which will bring you in a certain income. It will be your own money and you will not have to ask me every time you want something."

"That is very kind of you," Ann said, "but don't make it too much, will you?"

"Why?"

"You know the answer."

"That you don't wish to be beholden to me?"

"No, not that; but I don't want to take too much when I am giving so little in return."

"We have had this argument before," John said. "Why not increase your generosity instead of curbing mine?"

"You know I would do anything you want," Ann said.

"Anything?"

"Why, of course," Ann replied. "What do you want?"

She looked at John with wide eyes, and then suddenly was very still.

It seemed to her that for the very first time he held her gaze and and she saw past the gravity and quiet seriousness which was so much a part of him into the man himself, and what she saw there she did not understand.

For it seemed as though some flame burned fiercely within him, so fiercely that she gave a gasp of fear ... this man was a stranger ... a man who held her captive ... a man whose eyes suggested many things from which she shrank. Her heart was beating faster and yet faster. . . .

Involuntarily she made a helpless little gesture with her hands, and then the power that had held her spellbound was gone.

It was only John facing her, calm, grave, imperturbable, a man whom she hardly knew and yet the man to whom she was married.

Ten

Ann ran down the stairs, a shady hat in her hand. When she reached the hall she could see the car and a chauffeur waiting outside the front door and she hesitated a moment, wondering where John would be. At that moment he came along the passage from the library.

"Ann," he said, "will you forgive me if I don't come along with you? The Chairman of the Urban District Council has just called to see me on a very important matter. He has come a long way because he heard that I was at home. He is an old man and I should hate to be rude to him, but at the same time I don't want to disappoint you."

"It's quite all right, John," Ann answered. "Don't worry. I quite understand."

"You will forgive me, won't you?" John asked seriously.

"There's nothing to forgive," she smiled at him.

"I wish you thought there was," he said, and then, seeing her look of surprise, added: "You might even be a little disappointed that I cannot come with you."

"But of course I'm disappointed—and sorry," Ann said politely, and yet her conscience pricked her.

She knew in her heart of hearts she was glad. She much preferred to meet the twins alone. Of course it would have been nice to have John as a companion.

At the same time she was honest enough to admit to herself that in her longing to see the twins again she would much rather have them all to herself with no one else there to listen to their chatter and confidences.

But John must not guess her thoughts and feelings. He had been kind and she must be polite.

"Of course I'm sorry that you can't come," she repeated and tried to make her voice sound sincere. Then looking at her wrist watch she said: "I had better be going. I hear it takes nearly twenty minutes to get to the station."

"Good-bye then," John said.

"Good-bye." And she hurried away down the steps to the waiting car.

As the chauffeur drove off, she turned her head and saw that John was standing in the doorway looking after her. It struck her at that moment that he looked lonely. But she told herself that such an idea was absurd.

If anyone was likely to feel lonely at Gulliver she was, being very much a stranger in a strange land.

The chauffeur was a young man. He was only the second chauffeur he told her as they drove along. He had been wounded in the war and had a very bad time of it out in Burma.

"It's fine to be home, m'lady, and somehow, though it's difficult to put into words, it's everything to see green fields again. The heat out there was awful; it seemed to cling to you, and nothing you could do seemed to make things any better. I used to dream sometimes when I was out in the jungle of lying in the fields at Gulliver and trying to catch tiddlers in the river like I used to as a boy."

"You have always lived in this part of the world then?" Ann asked.

"Yes, Gulliver's home to me, m'lady. My mother has a little cottage on the estate. She worked in the house until they pensioned her off. And my wife was in the still-room until we got married."

Ann sighed.

"They are all part of Gulliver," she thought, "every one of them except me."

The road to the main-line station was down twisty lanes shaded by trees through which the sunshine fell in a speckle pattern of gold and shadow. There was the smell of hay, freshly cut, and sudden vistas through the high hedges of corn ripening in the sun and swaying gently in the breeze.

"It's all very beautiful," Ann said, almost involuntarily, hardly aware that she spoke aloud.

"No place like it in the world, m'lady," the chauffeur replied.

They came to the small market town of Crockley Cross. There was a grey stone cross of very ancient origin; there were little Queen Anne houses with delicate fanlights over their front doors, bay-windowed shops which went back to Georgian days and balconied houses which recalled the elegance of the Regency. The modern, ugly red-brick station seemed horribly out of place.

"If you will wait in the car a moment, m'lady," the chauffeur suggested as they drew up at the entrance, "I will go and see what time the train is due. Sometimes they get held up by the excursions at this time of the year and there's racing at Midenhurst today, which will result in a lot of extra traffic."

Ann remained in the car as he suggested, and in a few moments he was back again.

"As I expected, m'lady, the train's late. There's not a chance of it getting here for another three-quarters of an hour the station-master tells me."

"That will give me time to look round and see the town," Ann said.

"Shall I drive you, m'lady?"

"No, thank you, I would rather walk."

She got out of the car and set off down the tree-bordered road which led from the station. Soon she was in the market place.

There were few people about, some housewives were shopping or gossiping over their prams as they blocked the pavement, their older children chasing

139

each other to pass the time. Cars crept leisurely down the main street as if even they were not in a hurry.

The whole place indeed had a charm of its own; it seemed never to have awakened from the more leisurely and less speed-conscious era in which it was first built.

Ann looked in the shop windows, but they held little of interest, until a sign, freshly printed above a green and silver door caught her eye. "Lilith, Hairdresser", she read.

Ann smiled to herself and wondered how many of the people in this old-fashioned town would remember that Lilith was supposed to be the originator of all enchantments, the first glamorous and seductive woman in the whole world.

"Someone's got a sense of humour at any rate," she thought, and then as she would have passed on she stopped.

She looked at her watch, debated with herself and quickly made up her mind.

"Why not?" she asked herself.

She walked into the shop. Its interior was as attractive as its front door and sign. Leaf-green hangings, chairs painted silver, and flower prints framed in silver on the palest of green walls. A girl in a green overall came forward.

"Can I help you, madam?"

"I wondered if there was anyone here who could wash and set my hair," Ann inquired. "I have not very much time as I am meeting a train at twelve forty-five."

"I think we could manage it," the girl answered. "I am free myself at the moment."

"That is lucky!"

Ann was led to a cubicle also furnished in silver and green.

"How very charming this is," she exclaimed.

"I'm so glad you think so," the girl replied.

"Is the shop yours?" Ann inquired.

The girl nodded. "I have been dreaming about a shop of my own for five years," she confessed; "in fact all the time I was in the Forces, but now it's really happened I can hardly believe it's true."

"What made you settle here?" Ann inquired, feeling somehow that Bond Street or a more sophisticated town would have been more suitable.

"My mother lives here, and she is very old," the girl answered. "She would have hated to be uprooted; besides, I thought it was time this place was wakened up a bit. Do you know, they have never had a women's hairdresser here before?"

"Are you doing well?" Ann asked.

"We have got as much work as we can manage at the moment. I have got two assistants, one of them has come in as my partner, but later we hope to expand. We want to have manicures and perhaps facials, but it doesn't do to be too ambitious all at once."

She washed Ann's hair with firm, experienced fingers, and having rubbed it partially dry, she put fresh, clean towels round her shoulders and took up the comb.

"Will you part it in the middle?" Ann asked. "Someone has suggested that it would suit me better."

Lilith made a straight, clean parting down the centre of Ann's dark head.

"How do you want it set?" she asked.

"I have really no idea," Ann replied. "Something simple and easy to manage."

Lilith stood back a moment and looked at her.

"But of course you ought to have your parting in the middle," she said, "and your hair should be caught up at the sides to fall in heavy waves on either side of your face, and the ends should be turned up in loose curls. May I do it like that?"

"It sounds perfect," Ann approved. "I wouldn't know. I have really never worried about myself."

"I don't suppose you have needed to," Lilith answered. "Most women would give a million pounds to have a skin like yours and your naturally curly hair."

Ann smiled to herself.

"That is the third person," she thought, "who has paid me a compliment today. I can't think what is happening to me. Perhaps it is the effect of getting married."

Lilith started to work on her head, concentrating in silence on getting the waves exactly to her liking, moulding and sculpting the hair with all the intensity of a true artist.

Suddenly there were voices in the cubicle next door.

"Hallo, Molly, I thought I should find you here."

"Hallo, darling, I hoped you would come and see me. Sit down and have a cigarette."

There was the sound of a chair being brought forward, and the first speaker in a somewhat affected but cultured voice asked:

"What's the local news? I only got back from Scotland last night."

"Don't tell me you haven't heard about John Melton?"

Ann felt herself stiffen as the answer came quickly:

"What has John been doing? I haven't heard of him for ages if it comes to that."

"My dear—he's got married."

"Married? Good heavens! Who to, and why has there been nothing about it in the papers?"

"That's what we all want to know! Apparently he has married someone absolutely unknown. At least so Angela told me. She rang me up this morning about it. The Yateleys went over to dinner at Gulliver last night to meet the bride."

"What's she like?"

"Oh, quite nice, they thought; very quiet, and not a bit what you would have expected of John—or his mother."

"And what has the formidable Lady Melton got to say about it? She won't like being the dowager."

"Well, according to Angela, the Yateleys got the impression that she was furious. Apparently the girl's a penniless doctor's daughter, and how she managed to catch John is nobody's business."

"And what has Vivien to say to all this?"

"I bet she's as sour as quince. I think she thought she was bound to get John in the end, after the way she had made it so obvious that he was her property. Do you remember how she behaved at the Drayton's ball last year?"

"Well, John has pulled a fast one on her, but I wouldn't be in his bride's shoes if Vivien gets her nails into her."

"I expect if she has managed to catch John she can manage to look after herself. But I should like to see her. Let's go over and call."

"My dear, I wouldn't dare. I'm allergic to the atmosphere at Gulliver, and the look in Lady Melton's eyes is more than I can face! She always gives the impression that anyone who is not one of her especial friends is something that the cat has brought in."

"That's true enough!"

There was a burst of laughter. Ann felt that her cheeks were burning and with a sense of utter relief she found that Lilith had finished her hair and was bringing up the heavy drier.

The hood was placed over her head, and once it was switched on it was impossible for her to hear any more.

"So that's what the outside world thinks about Gulliver," she thought. It was apparently not entirely the place of romance and beauty that the illustrated newspapers had made it appear. And she herself had not been mistaken in her estimate of Vivien's character.

That was important, she now knew for a certainty what she originally suspected, that Vivien had wanted to marry John.

Why then had John not married her? She would, Ann thought, have made a very suitable mistress indeed for Gulliver and it was quite obvious that Lady Melton approved of her.

With the noise of the drier divorcing her from the outer world, Ann sat thinking. She had made a number of new acquaintances in the last forty-eight hours.

The men she liked. John's secretary, Dawson Barclay, had been the first. She had seen him only for a short while, but she had liked and trusted him.

A man, she thought, of whom her father would have approved and she had no qualms about leaving the twins and Myra in his care. Charles and Sinclair were both friends and she knew that she would need and value their friendship.

But—and here Ann sighed—the women were a very different proposition.

Her mother-in-law was a strange person, hard and frightening. It was almost impossible to think of her as loving or even being fond of anyone, and yet Ann supposed that she had some affection for her son.

If not, why should she mind that John had married someone of whom she did not approve? Was she afraid that a daughter-in-law might interfere? Ann could not imagine Lady Melton being interfered with by anyone.

The house and grounds were John's, but it was his mother who ran everything and ran it with an efficiency and a shrewd, calculating business ability which might have made her a captain of industry, but which was somehow unnatural and unattractive in an elderly woman in Lady Melton's position.

At breakfast that morning she had told John some of the improvements she had made on the estate and the changes she intended to carry out shortly. Listening to her Ann realised there was very little that went on which escaped Lady Melton's eye.

She had a complete grasp of every detail, and when John argued one particular point, she could invariably advance an extremely convincing argument in favour of her own opinion.

"What would happen if I had to do all this?" Ann thought in some dismay.

She was too well acquainted with the medical profession not to recognise efficiency when she saw it, and she acknowledged Lady Melton's supremacy in this particular, while at the same time she could not help wondering if such an assumption of authority was not rather annoying to a man.

"A bustling, busy woman," she thought, with everything that was gentle, feminine and sweet in her nature subdued or eradicated.

Ann admitted now that she disliked her mother-in-law and that the dislike was mutual, but she was afraid to express even to herself her true feelings about Vivien.

She had never met anyone like her before, had not really believed that such a woman existed outside the pages of a novel.

Her ultra-sophistication, a loveliness which could be hard and acid in quality and yet remain attractive, lips which could appear alluring but could also with a smile speak in bitter cruelty were phenomena beyond Ann's comprehension and simple experience.

Involuntarily she sighed. How was she ever going to live with such people, let alone understand them?

Only with Charles had she felt really at ease, at least when he was not saying things which embarrassed her or looking at her in a way which she knew spelt danger.

"I expect he flirts with every woman he meets," Ann told herself and knew that she was reluctant to believe what her common sense told her must be true.

It was nice to be told that one was attractive, to learn that one had charms which had not previously been discovered in the quiet, uneventful life she had lived at Little Cople.

The thought of her home made her remember the twins. Ann looked at her watch, time was getting on.

She was just going to call out when Lilith returned to the cubicle and removed the drier. Carefully she ran a comb through Ann's hair, turned the ends over into heavy neat curls, and then, giving a last skilful squeeze to the waves, said:

"Now look at yourself."

Ann stared in the mirror. It seemed to her that she saw the face of a stranger. Had Charles been right or wrong? For a moment she was not quite certain that she liked the alteration. Then Lilith said:

"But it's perfect. It shows the shape of your face and that lovely forehead. How you could ever have parted your hair on the side I can't think. But I must admit even I didn't expect it to be so successful when you suggested the change.

"It will be even nicer in a few hours. It is a little bit stiff at present and hair is never quite happy the first time it is changed over, but you look lovely, you do really."

"Yes, I think it is an improvement," Ann said slowly. "Thank you for taking so much trouble."

"I hope if you are satisfied you will come again," Lilith remarked.

"I most certainly shall," Ann promised with a smile as she opened her bag and paid the bill which was presented to her.

"Well, telephone for an appointment, or pop in and make one the day before," Lilith suggested. "We get awfully busy; by the way may I have your name so that if you ring up I shall know who you are?"

Ann hesitated for a moment. She played with the idea of saying "Ann Shefford", and then remembered that John would be well known in the town and it was only a question of time before they knew her too by sight.

"My name is Melton," she said. "Lady Melton." She was conscious that Lilith looked up at her

146

suddenly in surprise, and then a slight sound made her turn her head.

Standing in the doorway of the cubicle which had been next to hers she saw a plump young woman, her eyes wide with surprise and her mouth slightly open.

"Good-bye," Ann said quickly to Lilith, "and thank you again."

She almost ran from the shop, hurried down the street, and arrived hot and panting at the station just in time to see a train come in at the down platform.

She reached the entrance as the crowd came surging out. Most of them were obviously holiday-makers, men in open-necked white shirts, women carrying picnic baskets, and children with butterfly nets and bathing dresses under their arms.

"Ann . . . Ann, we're here!"

The twins had seen her before she saw them. Antoinette's arms were round her neck and Antony was holding on to her hand.

"Darlings, I'm so glad to see you."

She felt as if she had been parted from them for years and with a sudden rush of emotion of which she was ashamed she knew that she was very near to tears.

"The train was frightfully late," Antony was telling her, "and we're terrifically hungry, Ann."

"That's all right," she reassured him. "We will soon be home. There's a car outside."

"Oh, good, is it a big one?"

"Go and see for yourself," Ann suggested and then was arrested by a voice saying quietly beside her:

"I hope you will forgive me, but are you the mother of those children?"

She turned to see a stout, middle-aged man in a somewhat loudly striped grey suit.

"No, I'm their sister."

"I apologise, I didn't see your face when I asked the question or I would have known that you were too young to be their mother. Could I have a word with you for a moment?"

"Yes, of course," Ann replied with a sharp glance at the backs of the rapidly disappearing twins.

What on earth had they been up to now? she wondered.

"Perhaps it is best to go outside the station," she suggested.

She led the way. The twins had already reached the car and were clambering into it, asking the chauffeur innumerable questions about the engine and its horse-power. Ann stopped just out of ear-shot.

"Is anything wrong?" she asked quietly.

"No, nothing, nothing at all," the man smiled. "I'm sorry if I made you anxious. I was talking to those two kids on the way down and if you will allow me to say so they are extremely intelligent children."

"Thank you," Ann said, wondering what was the point of this conversation.

"It is very unusual," the stranger went on, "to find twins who are like each other and yet of opposite sex. It makes them rather unique in my opinion and that's why I ventured to speak to you. Perhaps my card will explain things better than I can."

He drew out a wallet, and extracting a card held it towards Ann. She looked at it and read: "Clarence B. Watney, United Zero Film Company."

"You have heard of me perhaps?" Mr. Watney said in a tone of voice which suggested that a reply in the negative was unthinkable.

"I'm afraid I very seldom go to the films," Ann said apologetically.

"Well, I'm a producer. Producer and incidentally a pretty large shareholder in United Zero. I started the company if it comes to that, and you can take it from me that what I say goes. But to cut the cackle and get to the horses, those twins of yours are what I've been looking for . . . something a bit unusual.

"The public is mad on juvenile leads at the moment

and if you will sign on the dotted line I promise you that they will both be stars before the year is out."

"You want them to go on the films?" Ann said incredulously.

"That's it," Mr. Watney said, "and I promise you that it will be worth their while, and your while too for that matter if you are their guardian. Now, can we make a date right away for them to come to the studio and have a test? Not that the test will be anything but successful or my name isn't Clarence Watney."

"But wait a moment," Ann said. "I must think about this. I have never dreamt of such a possibility. Have you said anything to the children?"

"Not a word," Mr. Watney promised her. "I just watched them, noted their reaction to the things we talked about and the places we passed, and I said to myself:

'Here are two well-bred, sensitive kids who could make a fortune if they set their minds to it and had the right man to produce them.'

"And, madam, I am the right man. You go and ask anyone you like about me. They will tell you I am top of my profession. There's not a producer in England today that has anything like my reputation.

"Those kids want handling with vision and imagination, and that's just what I am prepared to do."

"It's very kind of you, Mr. Watney, but . . ."

"There's no 'but', or if there is, there shouldn't be. Their schooling will be seen to and they will certainly be able to pay for the best. Now, when can we get together and start signing contracts?"

Ann turned the card over in her fingers.

"I'm sorry, Mr. Watney, but you must allow me to think about this. I am grateful, very grateful. May I write to you?"

"Telephone me, it's quicker," he suggested. "The children have given me their names, but I don't know yours or your address."

"Shall I write it down for you?" Ann suggested.

"I would be very grateful if you would," he said.

He drew an envelope out of his pocket. Ann inscribed it quickly and handed it back to him.

"Lady Melton, eh?" he exclaimed. "Well, Lady Melton, I shall hope to hear from you. You will find my telephone number on the back of that card. What I want you to do is to let me know when you're ready to talk business; and if you don't ring me, I promise you I shall be ringing you and that within a very few hours."

Ann held out her hand. "I promise I will telephone you, but I can't tell you yet whether the answer will be 'yes' or 'no'."

"Well, let it be 'yes'," said Mr. Watney, "or I shall be an awful nuisance trying to make you change your mind."

He shook Ann by the hand warmly; then she turned and got into the car.

"What was that man saying?" Antony asked. "We behaved well in the train, we did really."

"Yes, he said you did," Ann answered. "He was not complaining, in fact he was saying very nice things about both of you."

"That's a change," Antony grinned.

"I hope you have been good all the time that you have been away from me," Ann suggested.

Antony looked at Antoinette and they began to giggle.

"Now what have you done?" Ann asked. "I know it's something awful, so you might as well tell me right away."

"It was not really bad, Ann," Antoinette said quickly.

"All the same, tell me about it," Ann pleaded.

"Well, the rotten thing is that we could not wait to see the fun," Antony complained.

"What did you do?" Ann insisted.

"I found a chain," Antoinette began. "I found it in an old cupboard in the hall. I can't think that John

150

wanted it, and anyway he will never miss it, there were so many things in the house. Do you know, there were . . ."

"Tell me about the chain," Ann interrupted.

"Well, it was a long, thin one and at the end of it it had a tiny padlock and key," Antoinette said.

"I put it in my pocket," Antony broke in. "We were going to bring it down here to show you, and if you thought we ought to we would have asked John if we could have it. But when we got to Victoria Station Dawson went to buy the tickets, and while we waited we saw all the porters' barrows all heaped together . . ."

"Waiting for the next train in," Antoinette interposed.

"And what did you do?" Ann inquired.

"We locked them all together with the chain and turned the key in the padlock!" Antony finished.

"And, oh, we did want to see them all trying to get their barrows quickly," Antoinette cried. "But of course Dawson came back with the tickets and took us away to our own platform and was awfully pompous about us behaving well and not falling out of the carriage! As though we would! And so we missed all the fun."

Ann looked at them with what she hoped was a severe expression, but suddenly her lips began to twitch.

"You're laughing," Antony shouted.

"You're not angry a bit," said Antoinette, bouncing up and down on the car seat. "Oh, Ann, it's fun to be with you again."

"You've missed me?"

"We've had a scrumptious time in London, but you should see Myra now," Antony replied. "She's such a grand lady in her new clothes, and all she says is 'Don't, don't, don't'."

"We love you best in all the world," Antoinette confided.

"Oh, twins, you are the naughtiest children in the

world, but I adore you," Ann exclaimed. "Please, for my sake, try to behave properly at Gulliver."

"What's it like?" Antony asked.

"It's a wonderful house," Ann answered.

"And the people?"

Ann hesitated for words.

"You will find them all rather grown up," she said at length. "They will expect you to be polite and good-mannered and to be seen and heard as little as possible."

"Phew," Anthony ejaculated. "Aunt Ella all over again!"

Ann looked at him in surprise. Unwittingly he had hit the nail on the head. She had been wondering vaguely at the back of her mind of whom Lady Melton did remind her.

Now she knew. Aunt Ella, of course—brisk, efficient, hard, and with a place neatly labelled for everything in life.

"Darlings, try to be good for my sake," she begged.

"There it is," Antoinette said excitedly.

They rounded the drive and Gulliver lay in front of them, mirrored in its water, a symphony in grey and silver.

"Golly, it's like something on the films," Antony muttered.

Ann looked at the expression of surprise and astonishment so clearly portrayed on his keen, attractive little face.

"The films!" she echoed in her thoughts.

What part was Mr. Watney to play in their lives? What answer was she to give him?

Eleven

"I consider his offer sheer impertinence. You had better let me speak to him when he rings up." John spoke sternly.

Ann stared at him.

"I don't think he meant it impertinently," she said quietly. "He seemed a very genuine person. Now I come to think of it, I have heard of him. I'm not much of a film-goer, I've never had the time, but I seem to have heard his name. Anyway, it would be very easy to discover everything about him and his company."

"Surely it doesn't matter one way or the other?" John asked. "You are not interested in any proposition he might put forward, and there the matter ends."

"I don't think you quite understand, John," Ann said patiently. "I admit that I was rather astounded myself at first, but on thinking it over I have decided that I must go into this very thoroughly. It may be a great opportunity for the twins."

"Opportunity?" It was John's turn now to look astonished. "You don't mean to say, Ann, that you would consider even for one moment that they should act on the films?"

"Why not?"

"Why not?" John echoed her question quite angrily. "The whole thing is preposterous, impossible, and as I have already said, I consider it a gross impertinence on this man Watney's part to approach you with such a ridiculous suggestion."

Ann got up from the soft chair in which she was sitting, and walked across to the mantelpiece. For a moment she stood looking down into the neatly arranged but unlit fire and then she turned round to face her husband with a look of determination on her face.

"I think we are talking at cross purposes," she said, "and there is something that I had better make clear now once and for all."

"Which is? . . ."

"That when I promised to marry you, you very kindly undertook to look after my family, Myra, Antony and Antoinette; but that is not to say that I cannot make alterations in such an arrangement or that should an opportunity present itself we should not, all four of us, eagerly try to make money on our own initiative. We don't want charity, any of us!"

"I am not offering you charity," John interrupted.

"Dependence, then, if you prefer another word. I wanted to remain free, you know that, but because I was unable to be free and support my family . . . I . . . I . . ."

". . . You married me." There was a bitter note in John's voice.

"Exactly," Ann replied, glad that he had said what she hesitated to say so bluntly. "And now quite out of the blue it seems there is a chance—a marvellous, almost miraculous chance—of the twins becoming independent."

"To their detriment!" John said. "If you do this thing, Ann, I promise you you will regret it all your life. I want Antony to go to a decent public school, Antoinette also should be given a proper education.

"If you let them become child prodigies, force them to mix in a world with which they will have nothing in common either now or later, what do you think their future will be?"

"That is not the point," Ann said. "You have been generous, John, very generous; I'm not saying you haven't, but at the same time is it wise for the twins, for any of us, to make ourselves utterly and completely dependent on you?"

It was John's turn now to rise from his chair. He walked slowly backwards and forwards across the room before he replied. Ann watched him.

There was an expression on her face which was new to John, but which her family knew only too well, an expression of obstinacy, of a determination to get her own way.

"When Ann digs her toes in," Myra said once, "it is quite useless to argue with her."

But John had no intention of relinquishing the fight. He merely changed his tactics. He stopped in front of Ann and looked down at her. His face was grave and his brow knitted, but somehow, as she raised her eyes to his, Ann had the impression that he was by no means as impregnable as he appeared.

"Listen, Ann," he said gently, "can't we both be reasonable about this? I want a chance to prove that my suggestions are right. I want a chance to give Antony and Antoinette all the things that they have never had before in their lives. But I can't do that overnight, and one won't see the result for a year or so at least. Give me my chance, and then if I fail . . ."

"If you fail," Ann said, "they will still remain dependent on you I presume . . . like Vivien?"

She had not meant to add the last two words, but they seemed to slip from her lips, and as soon as she had said them she felt ashamed, feeling instinctively that she was somehow taking a cheap advantage.

John answered her evenly.

"Vivien and her brother are my first cousins," he said. "My mother made herself responsible for them when they were orphaned, and if I have contributed to their upkeep it is because they are relations, not because I had any particular choice in the matter."

"While, of course, you chose me," Ann said with a faint smile which somehow contrived to be bitter. "And I accepted you on your own terms, but it does

155

not follow from that that circumstances should not alter cases."

"If either the circumstances or the case were reasonable, you know I would agree," John said sharply.

"Well, I think they are both reasonable," Ann replied. "And if the twins are offered a really excellent contract in which they can make a lot of money, I consider that neither of us has any right to stand in their way."

"I tell you the idea is preposterous and ridiculous," John exclaimed.

He was as near losing his temper as Ann had ever seen him. She, too, was angry, but she was able to remain outwardly calm, to speak in a dispassionate tone which she knew was more effective than if she showed her irritation at John's assumption of authority.

"I disagree, and as the decision rests with me as the twins' sole guardian, I shall see Mr. Watney and listen to his proposition, at least with an open mind."

"And if I forbid you?" There was a touch of the whip in John's voice.

He came nearer to Ann. For the first time she became aware how big he was and that there was something almost overpowering about him when he was angry.

Defiantly, however, she threw back her head and looked up at him.

"I shan't listen to you."

"I shall make you. After all, you are my wife."

There was something in his eyes which goaded Ann to revolt. She meant to hurt him as she replied: "In name only."

As she spoke, even as the words left her lips, she knew she had made a mistake. John's arms shot out and his hands fell heavily on each of her shoulders.

For a moment she was surprised, and then quite inexplicably she found herself quivering beneath his touch.

John was looking intently into her eyes, and though

she would have resisted him, she found she could not look away. She was at his mercy, and for the first time in her whole life Ann was really afraid of another human being.

A panic rose within her. She wanted to wrench herself free; but somehow she could not move and could only stand there trembling, aware of some strange current passing between them, aware of John's eyes looking deep down into hers as though it seemed he searched her very soul.

And then at last, after what seemed to Ann to be an eternity of time, he spoke softly.

"Don't drive me too far, Ann."

She wondered what he meant and yet was incapable of thinking coherently. She was aware only that she wanted to be free, that she was afraid of him. This was all so different from what she had expected. She could not think, could not even speak.

"One day you will understand." The words were murmured rather than spoken aloud, and John's voice was deep and very low.

Ann felt as if her legs were not strong enough to support her any longer. John's hands on her shoulders seemed to press her down; at the same time she felt that if she showed her weakness she would be lost, defeated, overpowered.

She had the idea that he was drawing her to him, forcing her to surrender by sheer will-power. Every nerve within her body was tense in an effort to withstand him. This silent battle was bitter, fierce and desperate.

Ann felt herself quiver, knew that the world seemed to be slipping away . . . she trembled on the edge of an abyss; one more moment and she would be over the edge—she would fall and be overwhelmed. . . .

"Let me go," she whispered, and the words were faint.

In answer John's hand seemed to tighten still harder on her shoulders. For a moment something

157

flickered in his eyes, something from which Ann shrank in a sudden terror, and suddenly she was free.

John had walked away from her across the room to stand with his back to her, staring out of the window.

For a moment utter relief outweighed every other sensation, and then Ann was aware that her heart was thudding against her breast and that her lips felt curiously dry.

What had happened she did not really know. She could not find thoughts, let alone words for what had occurred. And yet she knew that it had been momentous.

Her reaction was immediate. She felt alone and forsaken, and tears filled her eyes although she was too proud to let them fall. She had so many enemies already in this vast, hostile house, and if she were also to lose John. . . .

She would have spoken then, but at that moment the library door opened and the hand she had already raised towards him fell limply to her side.

"I'm sorry, am I interrupting you?" It was Sinclair who entered and who asked the question in his gentle, half apologetic manner.

John turned round.

"Come in, Sinclair, you are the one person we want at this particular moment. Ann and I are having a slight difference of opinion and perhaps you can help us."

Ann thought it characteristic of Sinclair that he made no comment on the information. Another person might have exclaimed: "A quarrel already!" or made some fatuous reference to the short time for which they had been married, but Sinclair merely crossed the room slowly and sat down in a high-backed chair.

He was small and deformed and yet somehow he was not without dignity. He looked at Ann and smiled.

"You have already been told," he said, "in what

way my sphere of usefulness lies. If I can possibly be of any assistance, I am yours to command."

Briefly and, Ann had to admit, quite fairly John told Sinclair of Ann's encounter with Mr. Watney when she met the twins at the station. He added his own repugnance at the whole idea and explained Ann's conviction that the children should be given the opportunity to earn money and become independent.

"Now, Sinclair," John finished, "you have the facts in front of you. What is your verdict?"

Sinclair had listened attentively, his eyes on John's face while he was speaking. Now he looked at Ann.

"Have you anything to add?" he asked.

"Nothing," Ann replied. "Except that I imagine you have guessed even if you have not been told, the circumstances in which I and my family were left after my father's death?"

Sinclair nodded.

"Well, then," she continued, "you can perhaps understand my feelings. John has offered with great generosity to do a great deal for the twins; at the same time we must never forget that whatever advantages they enjoy they were utterly and entirely penniless except for John's bounty!

"Here it seems to me is a 'gift from heaven'— which John for some personal prejudice wishes us to refuse."

Sinclair leant back in his chair.

"Have either of you," he asked, "thought of discussing this with the twins themselves?"

Ann shook her head.

"No, I have said nothing to them," she said. "I thought it would be best to hear just what Mr. Watney had to suggest."

"All the same, before you either raise that gentleman's hopes or disappoint him by a direct refusal," Sinclair said, "I think it would be wise to consult the twins. They are, after all, directly concerned. Let us ask them what their feelings are in the matter."

159

"I think it would be a mistake to involve the children in this discussion," John said slightly pompously.

His opposition made up Ann's mind immediately.

"I disagree," she said with a flash of defiance which somehow was all the more violent because of her weakness of a few moments earlier. "Sinclair is right; the twins should be consulted. If you will send for them, John, we will tell them the facts and listen to their opinions."

She sensed that John still wished to argue with her, but with Sinclair there she felt safe from his overpowering insistence. He walked towards the bell, then changed his mind.

"I will go and look for them myself," he said, and before Ann could say anything further he had left the room.

Relieved of his presence, Ann felt herself relax and as if the strain was more than she had anticipated, she sat down suddenly on the sofa.

"John is being obstinate," she said. "He doesn't understand what it is to be poor."

"It is always very difficult to put oneself in somebody else's place," Sinclair replied. "At the same time I have often found that people are very unnecessarily proud where money is concerned—they believe it to be of paramount importance, when really both the giving or accepting of it have very relative values."

"What do you mean?" Ann asked.

"I mean," Sinclair replied, "that money is for the giver the easiest gift, and therefore lazy people often gain, quite undeservedly, a reputation for benevolence because they give generously of what they have in plenty.

"I am not referring to John, of course; I am speaking generally; but I can promise you, Ann, my dear, that there are far more important things and more valuable things that human beings can give each other than mere pounds, shillings and pence."

"You mean . . .?"

"Kindness, understanding, sympathy, and of course the real charity which comes from the depths of our hearts," Sinclair said slowly.

"Yes, I understand," Ann said; "but at the same time we all have our pride and nobody likes to be completely dependent on someone else."

"We are dependent one on another," Sinclair said, "and the greatest dependence of all is when a man and woman love each other."

Ann had no answer to this, and for the first time she began to question not John's attitude, but her own. Was her pride and that hard resentment which had always been her attitude towards John's open-handedness something of which she could justly be proud?

Or was it instead something narrow and unfriendly which could not accept graciously what was so kindly offered? In her heart, she knew the truth but tried to excuse herself—money was, as Sinclair said, really unimportant; it was love which ultimately counted where men and women were concerned.

And yet did love enter into this particular problem? One could not command love. Besides, John had not asked for her love; he had asked only that she should be a companion to him. Now she felt that such a position was impossible.

Why, she did not know, save that it seemed there were dangers and perils that she had never anticipated. Had she made a mistake?

She raised her eyes suddenly and saw that Sinclair was watching her, and she had the feeling that he knew where her thoughts were leading her.

"I am very fond of John," he said quietly. "He has had a difficult life. It has not all been as smooth and as easy for him as you might imagine. You will find, Ann, my dear, that happiness does not always go hand-in-hand with great possessions, and incidentally there is no particular virtue in poverty."

Ann felt herself flush, and then she answered humbly:

"I'm afraid I know very little about John."

"You will find out about him in time," Sinclair said, "and I am certainly not going to spoil your curiosity or shorten your voyage of discovery by telling you too much; but believe me, he is a very worthwhile person. You told me that your father liked him."

That was true, Ann recalled, and yet she had from the first been on her guard against him.

"Why?" she asked herself.

Just now she had been afraid of John, very afraid. Had not she sensed that he might sooner or later have that effect upon her?

She put her hands up to her cheeks and spoke frankly and honestly from the depths of her heart.

"I am lost," she said, "lost and frightened. All of this is too big, too much for me to understand."

"Oh, no, it isn't!" Sinclair retorted softly. "You've been through a great deal in a very short time. You have lost someone from whom you drew strength, and you have had to make a great many big and important decisions.

"Don't allow yourself to be panicked into thinking that everything you do is wrong just because things are moving rather quickly. Follow your instinct for what is right and for what is true, and don't let your eyes mislead you, your heart is a far better guide."

"That's the sort of thing Daddy used to say to me," Ann whispered.

"It's the sort of thing he will still say to you if you are prepared to listen."

Ann glanced up quickly. There were tears in her eyes.

"You believe that?"

"I'm sure of it," Sinclair answered.

She gave him a tremulous smile.

"Then nothing else matters, does it?"

"Nothing else will matter if you listen and are guided by those who love you. There are many of them,

was suspicious of this sudden gentleness in case it was in some way a trick to give him an unfair advantage.

"It is three o'clock," she said, comparing her wrist watch with the clock and speaking merely for the excuse of having something to say.

"Is there anything you would like to do?" John asked.

"I really think I ought to go and see what the children are up to. It seems funny not to have a thousand jobs waiting for me and with no time to do them."

"I was hoping that you would let me drive you round the park and down to the village. There is a lot for you to see as yet."

"That would be nice," Ann replied. "I will find the children and suggest that they come too. They will certainly get into mischief if they are left here."

If John was disappointed that they were not to go alone, he did not show it.

"I will order the car to be brought round," he said. "Shall we have the hood down as it's a nice day? But you had better put something over your hair."

"I will get a scarf."

"And, by the way, I've not had an opportunity yet of saying how much I like it."

"Like what?" Ann asked, and then saw where he was looking. "Oh, my hair! There has been so much to think about, I really had forgotten all about it."

"It suits you," John said gravely. "Thank you for doing what I asked."

"You asked?" Ann echoed and then remembered. "Oh, yes, you did ask me to part it in the middle, didn't you? I didn't mean to do so, I liked myself as I was, but Charles made such a fuss about it that I thought I had better have it done before he returned with those wonderful clothes he has promised me."

As she walked towards the door the room seemed

suddenly very quiet. She looked back. John was watching her with a strange expression on his face.

"I will go and find the twins," Ann said quickly.

Twelve

"You look wonderful, quite wonderful," Charles said.

Moving forward with a swift grace which was somehow characteristic of him, he took Ann's hand and raised it to his lips.

"Didn't I tell you that I would make you a beauty?" he asked, "even though you are still—a sleeping princess."

Ann tried to laugh, but the touch of his lips on her hand was disconcerting and she felt the warm blood rising in her cheeks.

"Do I really look all right?" she asked at length, knowing the answer, yet childishly wanting to hear him tell her once again that she was beautiful.

"Haven't you looked in the glass?"

He raised his bent head, and now his eyes were teasing her.

"I've been staring at myself," Ann confessed, "but wondering where was the Ann I knew so well."

"She's gone, gone for ever," Charles told her. "Are you sorry?"

He was speaking lightly, but Ann answered him seriously:

"I think I am," she said. "I understood the old Ann. I knew what she felt and what she wanted out of life, but this woman is a stranger to me."

"She has a lot to learn," Charles told her; "of life—of delight—of love. And I pray that I am going to be the one to teach her—some of those things."

Beneath the look in his eyes Ann dropped her own.

"He is trying to flirt with me," she thought, and she knew that while she really ought to be shocked, she was in fact enjoying it.

"I must be careful," she cautioned herself; but at the same time it was difficult to be careful where Charles was concerned. He had done so much for her.

When she had looked at herself in the mirror, she had indeed realised that he had not boasted falsely when he said that he would make her a beauty.

At first she had been horrified at the clothes he had brought back from London. They were not in the least what she had expected. For one thing they were all in vivid, pronounced colours, which she had never imagined would suit her.

Soft blues she had always believed, were "her colour"; but the blue that Charles had brought her was deep and strong and somehow compelling.

"It won't suit me," Ann thought to herself until she slipped on the dress and went to the mirror to find how right Charles was in his judgment, how wrong she in hers.

She was wearing the blue dress now and she could not help feeling as she left her own room that for once Vivien would not have it all her own way and that she too could for the first time hold her own in the wealthy, luxurious atmosphere of Gulliver.

The dress was of chiffon, cut very simply, almost classical in line. It moulded her figure, revealing the soft curves of breast and hip, and great folds of the lovely material fell from the shoulder to the floor, giving the wearer an indescribable grace of movement.

The colour threw into relief the whiteness of Ann's skin, and the sculptured beauty of her arms.

It made her eyes seem vividly blue, while her hair, parted in the new way, seemed despite the allurement of the dress to give her sweet, serious face the unworldly, spiritual look of a young Madonna, such as one could find in the pictures of the early Italian masters.

"You are beautiful!" Charles told her again, and as they reached the drawing-room.

Ann wondered if John, too, would echo Charles's words.

John was handing his mother a glass of sherry as Ann entered. He looked up, walked quickly across the room to meet her and putting out his hand in greeting covered her fingers with his.

"I have been waiting for you," he said quietly in a voice meant for her ears alone, "because I want to be the first to tell you how charming you look."

Ann sensed that his words were sincere, and yet somehow they seemed dull and insignificant compared with the extravagant phrases she had already heard from Charles. John took her hand in friendliness, but Charles had raised it to his lips.

"A very pretty dress, Ann," Lady Melton said in her usual brusque manner. "I must admit that you have chosen well, Charles."

"Thank you for those few kind words," Charles replied.

But there was a sarcasm in his tone which caused Lady Melton to glance at him sharply.

"I'm glad you are looking your best tonight," John said. "Because we have been asked to drive over after dinner to Crockley Castle. The Marlows are very old friends of mine and I shall be very proud to show them my wife."

"Where are we going?" Vivien asked from the door.

Ann turned her head. She guessed that Vivien had deliberately waited until the rest of them were gathered for dinner before coming down. She had certainly dressed herself with a view of being competitive.

Her gown of gold tissue was far too elaborate for an informal evening at home, and yet worn with curious carved jewellery vaguely reminiscent of the Pharaohs, it gave Vivien an air of barbaric splendour with which it would have been difficult to compete had not the very simplicity of Ann's dress been the one perfect reply.

As if she took in the whole situation at a glance, Vivien advanced slowly.

"Well, Charles," she said, "I suppose I must congratulate you. What should we women do without him, I wonder?" she added, addressing herself to Ann. "You must be careful that you don't find him indispensable or even John might awake from his placidity and be annoyed."

John was annoyed. Ann sensed that by the sudden tightening of his fingers. It was then that she realised that his touch, warm and firm, was strangely comforting. Instinctively on Vivien's entrance she had clung to his hand.

Now, because she began to think about it, she felt embarrassed, and releasing herself moved from his side across to the fire-place where Sinclair was sitting, a quiet, silent spectator.

He smiled at her as she approached.

"It has been a full day, hasn't it?" he asked and she was grateful to him for not saying the obvious.

"The twins have gone off to bed," he replied. "They ought to be worn out. They have run their legs off inspecting everything and ended the evening by rowing on the lake."

"May I congratulate you on them instead of on your dress?" Sinclair asked.

Her heart warmed towards him, while her moment of vanity which had seemed so important slipped away into its proper perspective.

"Do you really like them," she asked, "or are you just saying that to please me?"

"When you know me better," Sinclair replied, "you

171

will learn that I have one horrible failing. I always tell the truth."

"Is that so horrible?"

"Many people are afraid of the truth."

"But I am all the more grateful for what you have just said," Ann answered. "I love the twins, but I am always nervous in case other people find them spoilt or precocious."

"I think they are both very delightful and very natural children," Sinclair reassured her.

Lady Melton caught the last word.

"Are you talking about Antony and Antoinette?" she asked. "I hope, Ann, that you will tell them to be more careful not to slam doors in this house. I saw Antony come dashing out of the library this afternoon and I quite expected the vibration of the door behind him to bring down one of the chandeliers."

"I will speak to them about it tomorrow, Lady Melton," Ann said quietly.

Her mother-in-law moved away and Ann's eyes met Sinclairs'. He smiled and she knew that he both understood and sympathised.

Dinner seemed to Ann a long-drawn-out, boring ceremony, at which conversation was made difficult by Lady Melton's dictatorial attitude on all subjects and Vivien's quite obvious desire to talk only with John.

The small elation which Ann had felt over the success of her dress died away and she felt depression creeping over her. Was this to be all that she had in life in the future, this background of ceremony, of convention and the underlying currents of jealousy and rivalry?

She thought of the noisy, animated meals they used to enjoy at home, of the arguments in which her father had joined with all the zest and vigour of a good opponent, of what fun it was and how at times they had all laughed helplessly, their sense of humour invariably aroused by the same things.

172

Could all the money in the world buy what had been theirs? Ann knew the answer.

She was aroused from her reverie by hearing Vivien say:

"You have not yet told me, John, what the plans are for this evening. I heard you say something about going to the Marlows as I came down to dinner."

"I am taking Ann over to meet them," John replied.

"Aren't we included in the invitation?" Vivien's voice was challenging.

"Of course, if you want to come. I had thought of taking Ann alone."

"How selfish of you," Vivien said accusingly, "and we can sit at home with our knitting or our patience cards, I suppose."

It was Charles who answered her.

"Ann and John are supposed to be on their honeymoon."

"I hope you will remember that, Charles," Vivien replied and glanced at Ann as she spoke.

To her own fury Ann felt herself flushing. Could Vivien have overheard the compliments that Charles had paid her she wondered; could she have seen him kiss her hand, or was she merely making a shot in the dark?

It was John who settled the matter.

"If anyone else wishes to come," he said, "there will certainly be room in the car."

"Then I think we will all go," Lady Melton said. "I want to see Mrs. Marlow about the Women's Institute at Crockley."

"Very well," John answered, his voice betraying no evidence of disappointment.

Ann felt a quick sense of relief. After what had occurred that afternoon she shrank from being alone with John.

"There is no need to hurry," Lady Melton said as they left the dinner-table. "We need not leave for another half-hour at least; the Marlows dine later than we do."

"I have ordered the car for nine-thirty," John said.

Ann slipped upstairs to say good night to the twins. Their lights were out, but they were certainly not asleep, and judging by the scuffling which occurred as she turned the handle of the door into Antony's room, they had been out of bed talking to each other through the communicating door which stood open between their two rooms.

"What are you up to?" she asked.

"Oh, Ann, it's you," Antony sat up in bed and switched on the bedside lamp, and a second later Antoinette came rushing in from next door.

"I say, isn't this fun?" Antony asked, speaking generally.

But Antoinette, being a girl, had noticed the difference in Ann.

"Is that your new dress? You do look gorgeous."

"Why aren't you both asleep?" Ann asked. "I thought you were tired."

"We're too excited to sleep," Antony replied. "Do you know what we have discovered? A whole room full of stuffed birds, animals and fish."

"Oh, yes, I know that room," Ann smiled. "John calls it the museum. His father shot a lot of the stags' heads and John killed some of the other things himself; you must get him to tell you about them."

"We found some bicycles and even a sledge in the stables," Antony said. "I wish it would snow, we could have some wonderful tobogganing in the park."

"You will have to wait a few months for that," Ann laughed. "What about doing some fishing tomorrow instead? There's lots of trout in the lake."

"Could we really?" Antony asked, while Antoinette put her arms round Ann's neck and squeezed her.

"We are so glad you married John," she said. "This is the wonderfullest place. We thought London was pretty exciting, but this is better."

"I'm glad you like it," Ann said, for the first time identifying herself with John's possessions.

"You like it, don't you?" Antoinette asked.

"Of course I do," Ann replied, hoping that her tone was convincing. But the twins were unusually perceptive.

"I expect it all seems a bit big at first," Antony said.

"And you miss Daddy, of course," Antoinette added. "I miss him too, I wish he could have come here with us.'"

Ann felt the tears come into her eyes. "You won't forget him, will you?" she asked.

"Of course we won't," Antoinette answered. "We talk about him lots, don't we, Antony?"

Antony nodded.

Ann found it difficult to speak, and then a sudden rush of affection made her draw Antoinette very close to her and put out her hand to Antony.

"All I want is for you both to be happy," she said at length.

"We are happy," they assured her almost in unison, and then Antony added: "You're not sick with us for not wanting to go on the films, are you, Ann? But Antoinette agrees with me. It's not the sort of things that a boy really wants to do."

"No, I understand," Ann replied. "I was only considering the money really and thinking how splendid it would be for you to have some of your own."

"But you've got lots now, haven't you?" Antoinette asked in surprise.

As she looked at the child's innocent face, Sinclair's words came back to Ann.

"He is right," she thought. "I'm making far too much fuss about mere pounds, shillings and pence."

First Myra, then the twins were taking it for granted that what was John's was hers and what was hers was theirs, and deep within her heart she knew the

175

reason for her revolt against their sensible and logical assumption.

Had she loved John, had they been really man and wife in the best and truest sense of the word, this question of money would not have arisen; and yet, however much she told herself she was being absurd, it was there now, a barrier which she could not surmount.

"You must go to sleep," she told the twins. "Get into bed, Antoinette, and I will come and tuck you up." She bent over Antony. "Good night, my darling; God bless you."

She kissed him; he reached up his arms to hug her, and then she turned out his light.

Antoinette was waiting for her, snuggled down against the soft pillows, the white linen sheet with its big embroidered monogram tucked under her little pointed chin.

"You will be good, won't you?" Ann pleaded. "I don't think Lady Melton is used to children. I don't want to upset her."

"We will try," Antoinette promised. "We like being here, Ann; we love being with you, so we will try to be good."

Ann pushed back the dark, silky hair so like her own from the smooth white forehead.

"There are a lot of lovely things we must do together," she said.

"You won't be too busy for us now that you are married, will you?" Antoinette asked.

The question with its wistful poignancy hurt Ann. She realised that the query might have been lurking at the back of Antoinette's mind for some time.

"Listen, darling," Ann answered, "whoever I am married to, whatever I do, I would never be too busy for you or Antony."

She saw the gladness in Antoinette's eyes, and then as she turned out the light and slipped from the room she thought to herself:

"And yet I might have had to leave them; they might have already gone to Aunt Ella's."

If that had happened, she would have been alone at this moment, yearning for them, longing for them, and not even knowing when next she would see them. For that alone she could never be sufficiently grateful to John.

"I must be nice to him, I must," Ann thought; yet she knew it would be hard while she was so afraid of him.

He was difficult and inexplicable. Why out of all the men in the world could she not have married someone easy and friendly—someone, for instance like Charles?

Ann went to her own room. The twins' unrestrained embraces had untidied her hair. She combed it out again, turning the ends as Lilith had instructed her.

There was a knock on her door, and expecting the maid, she called out, "come in," without turning her head.

Someone entered. There was the sound of the door closing and only then did Ann look to see who it was. To her surprise Vivien was standing there, a long fur cape draped over her golden shoulders.

"I came to see if you were ready," Vivien said, "and cousin Margaret suggested that I might bring this along for you to wear. She imagined that Charles had not started to buy you furs—as yet."

She threw a sable wrap down on the bed as she spoke.

"That is very kind of Lady Melton," Ann said, "I had not thought about it, but of course I have got nothing suitable to wear in the evening."

Vivien came across the room and stood near the dressing-table looking at Ann.

"Do you think you are going to be happy here?" she asked at length.

Ann had the impression that she had been premeditating her words for some time.

"I hope so."

Vivien stood watching her. Ann, glancing in the mirror because she was embarrassed, saw their reflections and thought how utterly in contrast they were one with the other.

"I wonder if you would mind if I asked you a question?" Vivien said at length.

"It depends what it is," Ann answered cautiously.

"It's quite a simple one really," Vivien replied. "I just want to know—how did you do it?"

"Do what?"

"Marry John."

For a moment Ann was too flabbergasted to speak. Then before she could be angry at Vivien's impertinence she realised that the girl's question was genuine. She was not being rude or provocative or any of the things she had been since they had first met; she was being for the first time completely frank and honest.

She wanted to know because it was vitally important to her. For the first time Ann thought of Vivien as another human being who could be hurt or miserable, and surprisingly she felt sorry for her. Instead of replying she asked a question.

"Do you love John very much?"

"I meant to marry him," Vivien said in a hard voice. "We might as well be frank with each other, you and I. I wanted to marry John and I was quite certain that sooner or later he would marry me."

"I'm sorry."

There seemed to Ann nothing else she could say. Vivien looked at her.

"What puzzles me is why he has married you instead of me. I thought I was everything that he wanted—the right kind of wife, interested in the same sort of things, friendly with his friends, intelligent about politics, *au fait* with his world; and yet you are . . ."

Vivien hesitated for a word.

178

"None of those things," Ann finished for her.

"Well, if you say so. . . . I was trying not to be rude."

"You're not rude. I am being as frank with you as you are with me. I don't know why I married John. I wish I did know the answer."

Vivien looked at her curiously, then she sighed.

"I suppose the answer is that he is in love with you."

Impulsively Ann would have blurted out denial, but something cautious and careful within her stopped her.

"This girl is your enemy," instinct told her. "Don't give her too much of your confidence; she will use it for her own ends. Be sensible."

Ann got to her feet.

"I don't really think we ought to discuss John behind his back, do you?" she said, but she spoke gently and the words were more of an appeal than a rebuff.

Vivien gave her a calculating glance.

"That means you don't intend to tell me any more. I don't blame you, but instead I will tell you something. I think you are the wrong wife for John. I don't think you are happy here, and I think sooner or later you will find that you have made a mistake."

She walked towards the door, her gold dress making a faint rustling sound as she moved. She reached the door, turned the handle and then looked back.

"If it's any satisfaction to you," she said softly, "my brother Charles thinks you are quite wonderful."

Ann said nothing. Long after Vivien had gone she stood staring at the closed door.

Then, as if it was an effort to force her feet to obey her will, she crossed the room, picked up the sable wrap which Vivien had left behind her, and went slowly, very slowly down the stairs to where John and his relations were waiting for her.

Thirteen

Ann read Myra's letter for the third time.

What she found there both puzzled and worried her. There was something wrong, what she did not know, but her instinct told her that there was something about the letter which rang false.

It was as loving as ever, and yet it seemed to Ann that beneath the demonstration of affection and behind the round almost schoolgirl writing something was being concealed.

She recalled the conversation she had had with Myra the day before. She had asked when she was coming to Gulliver. Myra had prevaricated and made excuses.

"I've got such a lot of engagements, darling . . . it is so exciting being here . . . people are asking me out . . . I went to a theatre last night."

"What sort of people?"

"Oh, friends of Dawson's." Myra had been vague.

Purposely vague Ann thought now, for she realised that the letter she held in her hand had been written after their telephone conversation and the whole purpose of the letter was to make as indefinite as possible both her plans and her arrangements for coming to Gulliver.

"What does it mean?" Ann asked, then blamed herself for not having insisted either on going to London to see Myra or on Myra's coming to her.

It was over a week now since she had seen her younger sister, a week which to herself seemed immeasurably long—so much had happened, so much experience had been packed into it that it might have been years.

Had it been the same for Myra? She felt it might well be, and her anxiety deepened. It had seemed obvious with the twins at Gulliver, that Myra should follow them; but when she had telephoned, there had come one excuse after another.

At first Ann had been content for Myra to stay away, she had even in a way been relieved.

She wanted to see Myra and wanted her younger sister with her, but at the same time she wished to establish herself at Gulliver, to find her feet.

Everything was new and difficult. It was hard enough, Ann thought, when one had to face it alone. With Myra, commenting and perhaps criticising, she felt it would be worse.

Then John had made it clear that two of Ann's most formidable difficulties—his mother and Vivien—would be eliminated in the course of a day or so. He had been very frank.

"I have been worried about you, Ann," he said quietly. "I have already admitted that I made a mistake in bringing you straight to my home for what was intended to be our honeymoon. I have been wondering whether it would be wise for us to go away together—alone."

If he noticed the startled glance that Ann gave him, he ignored it.

"But," he went on, "when I remembered the twins I thought perhaps you would not wish to leave them, and while I was wondering what to do for the best I learnt that my mother intends to go away next Monday. As a matter of fact she is going into a nursing home."

"Is she ill?" Ann asked.

"She has not been very well for some time," John replied. "The doctor warned her that she must take things more easily, but such a course is impossible as far as my mother is concerned. If she thinks some-

181

thing wants doing she can't rest until it is done, whatever the strain or exertion to herself.

"All through the war she didn't spare herself and I think, like many women of her age, she refuses to see that she is not so young and energetic as she was. Now at last she has been forced to admit her own frailty and is going into a nursing-home for an examination.

"I frankly know no more than that; and if she is any wiser she will, I am certain, refuse to share her knowledge with me. She is obstinately courageous about her health, but she has at last had to take her doctor's advice."

"I'm sorry," Ann said conventionally.

She felt that it would be hypocritical to say more when the thought of Lady Melton's being away gave her a sense of relief and escape.

"After Monday it seems," John continued, "there will be a general exodus. Vivien is going to the South of France, and Charles talks of accompanying her before paying some visits in Scotland. Sinclair will also be going to Scotland, to stay with some relations on the Spey. So, you see, we shall be alone together."

"With the twins," Ann said quickly.

"With the twins," John corrected, "and of course Myra when she chooses to visit us. I think we shall be happier here than if we tried holiday-making in some crowded hotel. What do you think?"

"I would rather stay here."

"That's what I wanted you to say. And now I want to talk to you about another house."

"Another?" Ann's eyes widened.

"I'm sorry," John exclaimed. "I should not have put it like that. I was referring to your old home at Little Cople."

"What about it?" Ann asked.

"Dr. Ashton was kind enough, as you know, to make himself responsible for seeing to your father's finances. He has written me very fully about them this morning.

"I need not bother you with all the details, but he has been able to sell the house for three thousand five hundred pounds.

"When your father's outstanding bills are cleared up, this will leave about three thousand pounds in hand for you, your brother and sisters."

"Three thousand pounds!" Ann exclaimed. "That's a lot of money."

"I hope you will always think so," John said with a smile. "I'm afraid it won't go very far in these days. I suggest that it's paid into your bank for the time being until we decide how it can be divided. I am also in the course of transferring some shares to your name.

"When this is completed I will get the bank to write to you formally so that you will know where you are."

"Thank you, John." Ann spoke with sincerity.

At least she had a little money of her own, something which was not John's, something to which she was really entitled. If things went wrong, really wrong. . . . She checked herself.

She must not think like that. Whatever happened, however difficult, she had got to make everything come right eventually.

On one thing, however, she was determined, that Myra must come to Gulliver before Monday. She would be glad when Lady Melton and Vivien left the house, but at the same time she shrank from the thought of being alone with John.

What would they do in the evenings when the twins went to bed? Sit together making conversation? Ann felt afraid, afraid not of being bored, but of something else, of John . . . of seeing that strange look in his eyes . . . and feeling his hands grip her shoulders. . . . Yes, she was afraid!

If Myra was with them, things would be better. Of that she was quite certain. Myra would enjoy every-

183

thing so much, would keep them laughing, steer them away from all that was serious—and frightening.

But Myra was being elusive, elusive in a way which told Ann far more clearly than any words that Myra was up to something. She turned the letter over in her hands and made a quick decision.

She went into the morning-room, closing the door behind her. Seated at the desk which, as Lady Melton had told her somewhat pointedly, was "kept for visitors" she picked up the receiver and gave the telephone number of John's house in London.

While she waited she looked out of the window across the grey stone terrace and on to the lake where it lay pale-gold in the early morning sunshine.

At the other side of it a Georgian owner of the house had planted an avenue of trees and flowering shrubs which led to a small Grecian temple, beautiful in its very simplicity. Suddenly the thought came to Ann what a perfect place this was for lovers and for those in love.

The gardens seemed to have been laid out with the idea of seclusion and privacy so that two people could escape, be together and find seclusion in the midst of great beauty.

Myra would love it, she thought, with her imaginative romancings and one day Myra might be in love and also be at Gulliver.

Ann was smiling at her own thoughts when a voice answered and she recognised the somewhat breathless tones of old Travers.

"Good morning, Travers; can I speak to Miss Myra?"

"Oh, is that you, m'lady? I am sorry to say Miss Myra's out."

"Out so early?"

"Yes, the gentleman called for her in the car. They were going to see something or other, I've forgotten what. Anyway she's out, but I am expecting her back to lunch, m'lady."

184

"Whom did you say she had gone with?"

"There now," Travers replied. "I had the name on the tip of my tongue. Major . . . I've forgotten it. He comes here often enough. Mr. Barclay would know. Shall I ask him, m'lady?"

"No, it doesn't matter, thank you. I will ring up at luncheon time."

"Very good, m'lady."

Ann put down the receiver.

Who was taking Myra out? she wondered. Who went to Berkeley Square often and yet of whom there was no mention in Myra's letters? There was something wrong here, Ann was certain of it.

It was unlike Myra to be reticent and to keep things to herself, and yet Ann realised now that her sister had been perfectly vague in all their telephone conversations.

"Friends of Dawson's"—"Dawson has arranged it"!! Ann picked up the receiver again.

The secretary's office in Berkeley Square had a different telephone number and Ann knew that she would speak to Dawson Barclay direct. It was only a few minutes before they were connected, and yet during that time she felt her anxiety about Myra growing until, when at last Dawson Barclay answered it was difficult for her to speak naturally and quietly.

"Hallo, is that you, Mr. Barclay?"

"Good morning, Lady Melton, I was just thinking how nice Gulliver must be looking and how hot it is going to be here as the day wears on."

"Mr. Barclay, I have rung you up because I'm worried."

"What can I do for you?"

"It's about Myra."

"Oh." There was to Ann something ominous in the monosyllable.

"I've just been speaking to Travers and he tells me that Myra's gone out already with a Major some-body. He couldn't remember his name."

185

"Major Rankin? Tommy Rankin."

"I understand that he's a friend of yours."

"Well . . . not exactly, Lady Melton."

"But I don't understand! Myra told me that she has been out with you and your friends all this week."

Again there was a pause. Ann could almost feel Dawson Barclay's embarrassment.

"I'm afraid that is not strictly true."

"Mr. Barclay, won't you tell me what's happening? Myra's only a child and I'm worried about her."

"To be honest, Lady Melton, I have been worried about her myself; in fact, I have been considering whether it wouldn't be wise to telephone you, but Myra told me that you knew exactly what she was doing and that you had given her your permission to stay on here, so I didn't like to interfere."

Ann made a quick decision.

"I'm coming up to London," she announced, "now, this moment. You will be there?"

"Of course I shall, and quite frankly I think it's the best thing you can do."

"I'm coming now," Ann said firmly.

She put down the receiver and ran from the room. In the hall she found Lady Melton interviewing the head gardener.

"Do you know where John is?" Ann asked, interrupting her mother-in-law without ceremony.

"I believe he has gone down to the farm," Lady Melton replied.

"Will he be long?"

"About an hour I should imagine, perhaps longer." She was about to turn to the gardener again when something in Ann's face stopped her.

"Is anything the matter?" she asked.

Ann's answer was instinctive.

"Nothing, thank you!"

She ran upstairs, picked up a coat and her handbag and came running down again. The hall was empty,

186

she left the house by a side door and hurried towards the stables.

In the yard the second chauffeur was cleaning John's car, polishing the big lamps until they shone like mirrors. He looked up as Ann approached and raised his finger to his forehead respectfully in a countryman's salute.

"Good morning, m'lady."

"I want a car to go to London in at once."

"Yes, m'lady, shall I fetch Mr. Barnet? I have got to take her ladyship to Crockley Cross in twenty minutes."

Barnet was the head chauffeur and Ann did not like him—for no good reason save that he always gave her the impression that anyone new at Gulliver must be suspect. Besides he was an oldish man and drove very slowly, while she was in a hurry.

"No, don't worry about Barnet," she said quickly. "I will drive myself."

"Very good, m'lady."

She got into the car, started it up and drove it, at first very slowly but with increasing confidence, down the long drive. She had never handled anything so powerful or so expensive as John's big open tourer, but she had driven her father often enough.

Anyone who could keep her father's small, cheap dilapidated car on the road, could, she felt, drive anything. Dr. Shefford had no car sense and he rattled over the country lanes until his cars fell literally to pieces from overwork and lack of attention.

"If I can drive one car I can drive another," Ann told herself and felt justified in her confidence as on gaining the main road the car seemed to leap forward beneath her hand, the engine humming smoothly with the purr of a contented cat.

The drive was uneventful except that her own urgency made her feel as if she was being carried along on wings. She drew up outside John's house in

Berkeley Square exactly an hour and twenty minutes after she left Gulliver.

Travers let her in and was astounded to see her. "It doesn't seem possible you could be here in person, m'lady," he said. "Why, it was only a few minutes ago as I was talking to you. All this speed ain't good for human beings! I've always said we shall all pay for it sooner or later."

Grumbling a little with the privilege of an old servant, he led her to the secretary's room situated down a long passage and opening on to the courtyard at the back of the house.

Dawson Barclay jumped up from the desk as she entered.

"You have been quick," he said holding out his hand. "Travers, will you bring her ladyship some coffee, or would you rather have a drink?"

"Coffee, please," Ann replied and sat herself down in one of the big leather arm-chairs with which the room was furnished.

"You must have come at a tremendous rate," Dawson Barclay said, offering her a cigarette from the big silver box embossed with John's crest. "How did you manage to galvanise Barnet? He always drives like a hearse when I'm with him."

"I drove myself," Ann said simply. "I was in such a hurry to get here that I couldn't even wait to be driven."

"It's not as bad as all that," Dawson Barclay said simply, and then he too sat down.

He was a tall, thin young man, with dark hair brushed back from a pronounced forehead and horn-rimmed spectacles which gave him a permanent expression of wisdom.

Only when he removed these did Ann realise that he was much younger than she thought and that he had when he smiled a boyish look which was disarming and attractive.

188

"Please tell me everything about Myra," Ann pleaded.

"Well, quite frankly," Dawson Barclay began, "it has been difficult for me. You see you and John left your family in my care, but I was not quite certain how far my authority extended. Where the twins were concerned it was easy. But Myra is different—she considers herself a grown-up young woman."

"She is nothing of the sort," Ann exclaimed. "She's very young and very inexperienced. Don't let's beat about the bush. Who is this man?"

Dawson Barclay smoothed his hair with a helpless air.

"His name is Rankin as I told you—Major Rankin, and to be honest I'm afraid he is rather a bounder. The unfortunate thing is that Myra met him in my sister's house. He was brought to her dance by some people whom we had invited, but he was not a man to whom knowingly either my sister or I would ever offer hospitality.

"He knows a lot of people, but whether they are friends or merely acquaintances it is hard to judge. He is well known on race-courses and usually can be found in the latest and most up-to-date night club.

"He lives, I imagine, if you would call it living, on his wits. I can't say that I know anything really bad about him, but he's just the type that I'm sorry to see attached to any nice young girl."

"And Myra thinks she is in love with him, I suppose?"

"I'm afraid so!"

"And he . . .?"

Dawson Barclay hesitated.

"Well, he is certainly paying your sister a great deal of attention. How much of that is due to Myra's own charms, and how much to the fact that she is John's sister-in-law, I can't tell you."

"John's sister-in-law!"

Ann obviously had not thought of this aspect before.

189

"I don't believe that Tommy Rankin has much money. That may be the explanation, but at the same time I wouldn't like to say that he is not genuinely attracted."

"And how long has this been going on?"

"Ever since the dance at my sister's. I do want to say how awful I feel about this, Lady Melton; I had no idea that Myra was not telling you of everything that she was doing. She certainly gave me the impression that you knew and approved."

"It isn't your fault, it's mine really. I might have guessed, knowing Myra, that something like this would happen. Myra always imagines herself to be in love. To be honest, I thought it was you who attracted her."

Dawson Barclay smiled.

"I wish under the circumstances it had been."

"What's this Major Rankin like, apart from what you have told me? Could I appeal to his better nature?"

Dawson Barclay shook his head.

"I doubt if he has one." The door opened and Travers came in with the coffee.

"Sorry to keep you waiting, m'lady," he said, "but I sent out for some cream. The cook thought you might prefer it to milk."

"Thank you," Ann said. "How kind. Will you thank cook?"

She got up and poured herself a cup.

"Are you not having some?" she asked Dawson Barclay.

He shook his head.

"I am usually working too hard to think of elevenses."

"I suppose John keeps you very busy?"

"Things are a bit easier at this time of the year when Parliament is not in session and most people are away for their holidays."

Ann sipped her coffee.

"Myra will be in at lunch-time," she said. "Travers told me that he was expecting her."

"Yes," Dawson Barclay replied. "I made inquiries after you had telephoned and found that Major Rankin had taken Myra down to Greenwich. They've got some special demonstration there this morning. I don't quite know what it is. Something to do with the naval cadets I believe."

"It sounds harmless enough," Ann remarked.

"I should imagine it was Myra's idea. I don't believe that the Major is much of an early riser as a rule, but Myra has been determined to sight-see and he has constituted himself her escort."

"I will wait and see her," Ann said, "and I shall soon find out what's wrong. In the meantime I mustn't interrupt you if you have got work to do."

"My answer to that, Lady Melton, is—that it's a pleasure."

Ann looked at him with a little frown.

"Must you call me 'Lady Melton'?" she asked. "You call John by his christian name."

"We were at school together," Dawson Barclay answered. "I was his fag his last term. But thank you, I should love to call you Ann. I have heard so much about you that I feel I know you very well indeed."

"The twins have been chattering, I suppose?"

"And Myra. I don't think any real harm will come to her while she loves you as much as she does."

Ann smiled a little tremulously.

"I feel I ought never to have left her here all by herself."

"You couldn't help that. You had to think of yourself and John."

"Yes, of course."

Ann put down her empty coffee cup and walked towards the window. The traffic was moving slowly through the Square.

There was an air of tired dusty depression about the trees and the worn grass, all that remained of what had once been a private garden for the aristocratic inhabitants of the great houses, most of which had long since been converted into flats and offices.

She turned back and looked into the room. Dawson Barclay was standing by his desk and there was an expression on his face which she could not fathom.

He looked worried, and for a moment Ann wondered if he had withheld some information from her which she ought to have. Then he saw that she was looking at him and he smiled quickly, rather too quickly, as if it was an effort.

"How's John?" he asked.

"Very well."

Ann hoped that her voice did not sound stiff, but somehow she found it almost impossible to speak naturally of her husband.

"He's an amazing person," Dawson said reflectively, "but of course there's no need for me to tell you that."

"Why amazing?"

"His grasp of detail for one thing," Dawson said. "The way he tries always to see the other man's point of view. I've got a memorandum of his here which he wants me to have ready for him when the House reassembles.

"An extraordinary piece of work; he has taken an endless amount of trouble in compiling it, and all through I can see how earnestly he is striving to be absolutely just both to the man in authority and to the man who has to take his orders.

"Shall I be honest and tell you that I don't believe that John will ever be a famous politician because of that quality in him; but he will be, and for that matter is, a great humanitarian."

"I wish I knew more about his politics," Ann said impulsively.

"He has never spoken to you about them?"

She shook her head.

"That is like John, an extraordinary reserve. It is always difficult to know what he is thinking, owing

192

a great deal, I suppose, to his upbringing. But I can promise you one thing, Ann, he is a wonderful friend."

"I'm glad of that." Ann tried to speak naturally. "And I think he is very lucky to have you to work for him."

Dawson looked at her and then quickly, as if he had not got time to choose his words, he said:

"I wish you had not said that."

There was so much feeling in his voice that Ann stared at him in surprise; then, because from her earliest childhood she had grown used to coming into contact with people who were worried, in trouble, or ill, she knew that something was wrong . . . very wrong with Dawson.

All that was understanding and maternal in her came to the forefront; her own troubles were forgotten.

"Won't you tell me what's worrying you?" she asked.

"How do you know that I am worried?" Dawson asked and added before she could reply, "But of course you would know. Can I do a very indiscreet thing and ask your advice?"

"But of course," Ann said. "Why don't we sit down comfortably?"

She moved across the room and Dawson followed her.

"I ought not to talk to you like this," he said. "I oughtn't to burden you with my problems; but somehow, as I told you just now, I feel I know you so well. Your name came naturally to the twins whatever they saw or felt or heard.

" 'Ann would say this, Ann would tell us that' until finally I got to know you.

"It was almost a shock this morning when you came in and I realised how ridiculously young you are. I have been thinking of you as the little mother of all the world, at least of all the people with whom you come into contact."

"Have years got anything to do with it?" Ann questioned.

"I don't think they have," Dawson replied, "and so, will you believe me when I tell you that at the moment I feel younger and more lost than Antony, and that I want your advice and help just as much as he does?"

"Tell me what's the matter," Ann suggested.

"It's this," Dawson began. "I've been offered the chance of becoming a candidate for a South London borough. I know the people there well. I have run a boys' club in the roughest part of the constituency for over six years. I have worked amongst the poorest of the poor and I understand their difficulties.

"Now they want me to put my name forward for the by-election which is going to take place in two months' time. The present member is retiring owing to ill health."

"And of course you will accept?" Ann said.

"Should I?" Dawson asked. "That is the point. You see, first of all I shall have to tell John that I am leaving him, secondly that my politics are in opposition to his.

"That may seem crazy to you," he said as he saw the surprise in Ann's face, "but although I admire John, although I am as fond of him as I might be of an elder brother, I don't see things from his angle.

"I've always been the under-dog and I suppose I have the under-dog's point of view. I've never told John that I am not entirely in sympathy with his political faith and his ideas and ideals. I have done my best to help him and I have, I hope, served him loyally.

"Now I shrink from telling him the truth. I don't believe he would mind, but at the same time none of us care for those we have helped to strike out independently especially when their opinions are in opposition to our own."

"I don't suppose John would mind that a bit," Ann

exclaimed, and then instinctively she asked: "Isn't there anything else?"

"Yes, there is something else," he replied, "and this I hardly know how to put into words. I've made my desire to leave John and be independent sound very altruistic, but I am also ambitious! Yes, terribly ambitious! I want to succeed and I want to succeed quickly because . . . well, because I'm in love.

"I've got to be successful. The seat I have been offered is by no means safe—in fact the present member belongs to John's party and not to mine. If I fail in the election I am finished. I shall have used a part, if not all of my savings.

"John would not be able to take me back into his employment even if he wanted to. I should have to start again—having lost everything."

"Including the girl you love? But surely she . . ." Dawson sighed.

"She doesn't love me. At least she loves me but not enough to stand by me either now or in the future if I am a failure. There is only a chance—but a chance I like to believe in—that she will come to me if I am successful.

"If I once get my foot on the rung, I believe I can make good. I can make enough money. I have enough conceit to be certain that ultimately I shall win through, but is this the right moment to take the risk? To put all my eggs in one basket, to lose my position, my reputation, and . . . and her if I fail? That is what is worrying me, Ann; and if you can give me the right answer to that problem, well, then, I will bless you all my life."

Ann hesitated a moment, then she asked softly:

"You feel it is the right thing to do, that if you do represent these people you have worked with you can help them, that you can do good?"

"I know I can," Dawson spoke forcefully, "that is the one thing of which I am sure. It is, too, an opportunity of a lifetime—but at the same time I have got to ask myself—can I afford it, dare I afford it?"

Ann smiled at him.

"I know the answer to that," she said. "I remember years ago my father being asked very much the same question, and he answered:

'Never let money stand in the way of opportunity'."

"He was right!" Dawson said. "Of course he was right, and yet I will be honest with you, I know what is the right thing to do, but—I am afraid."

"Aren't we all afraid of something?" Ann asked, "and isn't it because we have so little faith in ourselves?"

Even as she spoke the words, she felt they came from another source other than her own brain. Dawson looked at her, she saw him absorbing the idea.

" 'Oh, ye of little faith . . .'," he said slowly; "how true that is of so many of us! Thank you, Ann, you have made up my mind for me."

"You will do it?"

"I shall do it."

"Then I am certain you will succeed," Ann said. "If one cares enough one will always get what one wants."

"You believe that?"

"When I am talking about your problems I do," Ann answered honestly; "when it comes to my own I, too, am afraid."

He held out his hand simply and she put hers into it.

"Thank you," he said. "The twins gave me to believe that you were a wonderful person; now I know they are right."

"And this girl you love?" Ann asked.

"Perhaps faith will help me there," he said. "I know deep down in myself that whatever she says, whatever she does, we really belong to each other.

"Every day for the last two years I've been expecting to hear that I have lost her, and yet she is still

196

free, and as long as she is free I shall go on hoping. Perhaps we have both been blinded by the same things, both been fearful because we believed that money was so important.

"I have condemned her for it often enough, and yet I have fallen into the same trap myself. You have shown me the way out."

"I should give her the opportunity to fight with you," Ann said. "Perhaps that is what she is waiting for, for you to be decisive."

Dawson sighed.

"If you knew her as well as I do . . ." He stopped, looked away, and then looked back at Ann. "I've told you so much, Ann, perhaps you had better learn the rest. It can't do any harm. You know the girl I love."

"I know her?"

"Yes, it is Vivien."

"Vivien! But she has . ." Ann spoke without thinking. Dawson interrupted her.

"Yes, she has been trying to marry John, I know that. She wanted to marry him because he is rich, because he could give her all the things that I can't and yet I am convinced that I am the only person she has ever loved and the only person she ever will love."

Ann had nothing to say. It was all so unexpected that she could only stare at Dawson.

"Will you do one more thing for me, Ann?" he went on. "You have been so kind already that I am going to trespass still further on your good nature. Will you tell Vivien that I am leaving John and why?

"I want her to hear it from you and not from anyone else. John's mother and perhaps even John himself may call me all sorts of a fool, but you will understand and you will tell Vivien for me why it matters so much."

Still dazed, still bewildered, Ann did not reply and Dawson asked her again:

"Will you do this for me, please?"

"Yes, Dawson, I will," Ann said quietly.

As she spoke, the door was flung open and Myra came rushing into the room.

"Oh, Dawson, I have come back to say I shall not be in to . . ." she stopped suddenly, saw Ann, and just for a moment it seemed to her elder sister as though the expression on her face held not only surprise but something else—something secretive, defiant!

Then with a cry of joy Myra ran across the room.

"Ann, darling, how wonderful to see you! Why didn't you let me know you were coming up?"

Fourteen

Myra's arms were round Ann's neck.

"What have you done to yourself, darling? You look different!"

It was with difficulty that Ann prevented herself from saying the same thing, but certainly not in the generous tone of admiration which Myra had used to her. For a moment she could not think of what to say as she gazed at her younger sister.

She remembered then that she had always had to curb Myra's taste in the past, and she realised how crazy it had been to leave the girl alone to make her own choice with the money John had given her.

Myra was wearing a flowered silk dress, with a flamboyant pattern, which somehow contrived to look both vulgar and cheap.

Over it she wore a box coat of scarlet cloth trimmed with gold buttons; in the button-hole was a nosegay of feather flowers. Not content with so much gaiety, she had added a hat which Ann felt must have been sold to her as "a perfect summer creation"!

A medley of flowers, ribbon and tulle, it was perched over Myra's right eye, giving her what she imagined was a sophisticated appearance, but which in reality verged on the comical side, for she looked what she was, a very young girl atrociously over-dressed.

Ann had time in one swift glance to notice, too, the elaborate open-toed shoes, the fish-net gloves, and the huge black patent-leather handbag.

Poor Myra! She would have been sorry for her had she not been so vitally concerned with far more important matters than mere clothes. Before she had time to speak, Myra was chattering on.

"Oh, I wish I had known you were coming, darling; I meant to ring you up last night, but I went out early to a film. As it is I have really got an engagement for luncheon and the afternoon. That's why I rushed in here to tell Dawson I wouldn't be in for lunch."

Myra spoke breathlessly in her usual quick, vivacious way; but Ann, familiar with every mood, knew all too well that there was an undercurrent of embarrassment and perhaps a suspicion of guilt.

Quickly, and with that instinct which had always served her where the children were concerned, she made up her mind exactly what to do.

"Oh, I am sorry you are busy," she said. "What a pity! You see, I came up from Gulliver especially to fetch you."

"What for?"—Myra's tone was suspicious.

"A party," Ann replied. "John has got some people coming to dinner tonight who are particularly exciting! We thought we might dance afterwards and if it's warm enough to go on the lake in boats. All very romantic!" she smiled.

She paused for a moment to let her words sink in and then added:

"But of course, if you can't come, darling, I quite understand. It is a pity though, because very shortly everyone will be going off for their holidays."

Myra wavered.

"It does sound lovely and of course I'm dying to see Gulliver, but it's just that I had promised Tommy . . . Tommy Rankin—he's a friend of mine—to motor down to Henley with him this afternoon and stay for dinner."

"Oh, well, of course if you prefer to do that . . . John will be disappointed and so shall I, and there are two or three fascinating young men whom I wanted you to meet. But never mind, I dare say we can arrange something of the sort in the autumn."

Ann spoke regretfully but with quite an impersonal note in her voice. It succeeded, as she had believed it would. Myra hesitated and was lost.

"It does sound too fascinating to miss," she said. "I will explain to Tommy; I'm sure he will understand. I suppose," she paused a moment and then obviously plucked up courage for her request. . . . "I suppose it wouldn't be possible for him to come too?"

"I don't think it would be this time," Ann replied apologetically. "I'm sorry, darling, but I'm certain we shall have a lot of men over as it is."

"Oh, well, he will understand, at least I hope he will. He has been awfully kind to me."

"Has he? How nice."

"Would you have a word with him and explain?" Myra asked.

"Of course I will," Ann answered. "Is he here now?"

"Yes, he's in the drawing-room waiting for me."

"Well, I could easily talk to him while you are packing."

"Would you? That would be marvellous."

200

"You had better go ahead and prepare him."

Myra ran out of the room, her absurd and ridiculous little hat nodding on her head. Ann turned to meet Dawson Barclay's smile.

"I think you are wonderful" he said.

"Keep your fingers crossed," she answered, "we're not out of the wood yet."

Then after glancing through the door, which Myra had left wide open behind her, to make certain that they were not overheard, she added: "Ring up John for me. Tell him I am here, and tell him that he must arrange some sort of party for this evening. There are lots of people round about, he must ask them in. Tell him I will explain why when I get back."

"Leave it to me," Dawson said and added somewhat anxiously: "Do you think you can deal with Tommy Rankin?"

"I'll have a try," Ann replied.

She went along the passage to the drawing-room hoping she looked braver than she felt.

Major Rankin was standing in front of the fireplace, his hands in his pockets, his feet apart, in what Ann felt was a characteristic attitude. He was listening to Myra who was perched on the arm of a chair.

He was a man of at least thirty-five, and Ann knew at a glance that he was just the type of rather suave, polished man-about-town who would appeal to Myra at this particular phase in her development.

He had a way of smiling which showed too much of his teeth. He had dark expressive eyes which Ann was quite certain that Myra would find fascinating; and he had, too, rather over-impressive manners which made him spring forward almost dramatically as she entered the room.

"Lady Melton, this is indeed a pleasure!"

"How do you do, Major Rankin. My sister has just been telling me about you and how kind you have been to her."

"I'm sure the boot is very much on the other foot.

201

Your sister has been very kind to me. I can't remember when I have enjoyed myself as much as I have these last few days."

"How nice," Ann said with a smile; "and has she told you that she is going to desert you for tonight at any rate?"

"She has just been breaking the sad news," Major Rankin replied. "Of course I'm devastated and bitterly disappointed, but at the same time I understand. If you and Sir John have got a party . . ."

"It is only a small one," Ann said quickly, "but we would like Myra to be there."

"Of course you would," Tommy Rankin exclaimed, "and Myra tells me she has not yet seen Gulliver. It must be looking perfect at this time of the year."

Ann guessed that he intended to angle for an invitation. Without answering she turned to Myra.

"Run upstairs and pack, darling; we must be down in time for luncheon; there is so much to do this afternoon."

"It won't take me long," Myra answered; then she looked at Tommy Rankin with something wistful in her eyes. "You won't go till I come down, will you?"

"Of course I won't," he replied heartily, and sprang across the room to open the door for her.

As she passed him, Myra raised her eyes to his, while he inclined his head towards her with his flashing, rather theatrical smile. As he closed the door behind Myra and turned to walk back across the room.

Ann found herself gripping her fingers together and murmuring a little prayer in her heart that she would do the right thing, and that she could save Myra from . . . this.

"May I tell you how fascinating I find Myra?" Tommy Rankin asked with an easy familiarity which made Ann still more apprehensive than she was already.

"I'm glad you think so," she replied. "She is, of course, very young and very inexperienced as yet."

"That is what makes her so . . . well, shall we say unique?" Tommy Rankin replied.

Ann drew a deep breath.

"I want to tell you how grateful I am to you," she began, "for looking after Myra and giving her such a good time this week. She will be coming back to London very shortly, and I hope, if it is not asking you too much, you will continue to be kind to a little country cousin!"

"You don't have to thank me, Lady Melton," Tommy Rankin said. "It's early days to talk about it yet, but I think you will already have guessed that I am very attracted by your sister."

"As you say," Ann answered smoothly, "it's early days to talk about it, but I'm sure Myra will be very glad of a friend. I'm afraid it's going to be very dull for her living in London alone, and hostel life is never, I believe, particularly entertaining."

"Hostel life?" Tommy Rankin questioned, raising his eyebrows.

"Yes, hasn't Myra told you?" Ann continued. "She is going to do a commercial course, shorthand and typewriting and all that sort of thing; John thinks it will be best for her to be on her own. After all, if she has got to earn her own living, she might as well face the fact from the very beginning."

Major Rankin looked nonplussed.

"I thought," he said slowly, "I thought as Sir John's sister-in-law . . ."

"That he would provide for her?" Ann inquired. "Oh, no, I'm afraid you don't understand my family. We are very proud. We all of us intend to stand on our own feet. Myra is going to be entirely self-supporting.

"We decided that even before I married John, and the twins as soon as they are old enough will also earn their own living. I think and all three agree with me that it is absolutely degrading to live on somebody else's charity, even if it is a relation by marriage."

There was no pretense about the surprise in Major Rankin's face, and Ann guessed that he was calculating in his own mind just how near the truth this might be.

"Myra will be completely independent of John," Ann stated firmly. "I expect she has told you that he has most kindly advanced her a little money so that she could buy some new clothes; but even that is not a gift, that is part of the hundred or so we are each to receive from the sale of my father's house.

"Our one bit of capital, Major Rankin," she added with a smile. "But what does money matter when one has one's health and strength?"

Major Rankin coughed. Ann knew that he had no words at that moment to express either his astonishment or his own feelings.

"But of course," she went on, "it will be wonderful for Myra having someone like you to take her about. I shall be terribly worried about her in case she doesn't get enough to eat.

"But I expect really she will be quite capable of looking after herself. She seems to have been clever already in finding someone as kind as you."

Major Rankin got to his feet and helped himself absentmindedly to a cigarette without asking permission. Ann could see all too clearly what was going on in his mind.

To take out Sir John Melton's sister-in-law, to give her a good time with the prospect of being invited to Gulliver, perhaps even of marrying a girl with such a safe background, was a very different proposition from befriending a young woman who had chosen independence in a hostel in Kensington and had only a commercial career in front of her.

He made an effort.

"If you will forgive me saying so, Lady Melton, I think you will find that the life you suggest is rather hard for a young girl. Are you quite certain that your sister would not be better off living with you? After all, you can't pretend there isn't room either here or at Gulliver."

Ann gave an affected little laugh, which she hoped sounded sophisticated.

"My dear Major Rankin, however big the house in which one lives, there is seldom room for another woman when one is first married. Besides, quite frankly I think I have mothered my young sister long enough. It is time she learned to look after herself."

She thought how awful she sounded and she prayed that it might be convincing. What did it matter if this unpleasant man thought her jealous, self-seeking or anything else, so long as he went away and left Myra alone?

With a sense of relief she saw him stub out the cigarette from which he had taken only a few puffs. He looked at the clock over the mantelpiece and then at his wrist watch. . . .

"I wonder if you would think me awfully rude, Lady Melton, if I asked you to say good-bye to Myra for me? I had promised to meet a friend soon after twelve. . . ."

"Oh! Myra will be disappointed!"

"Tell her I shall be seeing her," Tommy Rankin said lightly and vaguely.

"I will give her your message," Ann said, "and thank you once again. I can rely on you as soon as Myra goes to her hostel?"

"Yes, yes, of course. Just let me know. Myra knows my address."

He took her hand, holding it automatically a little longer than was necessary.

"You know, Lady Melton, I should have liked the opportunity of congratulating Sir John both on his bride and on his sister-in-law."

"You and Myra must come to dinner one night when we get back to London," Ann said graciously.

Major Rankin was defeated and he knew it.

"Good-bye, Lady Melton."

Standing in the hall Ann heard him start his car and listened to the sound of it driving away. Then, and then only, did she feel the tension of her nerves relax and she knew how desperately hard she had fought for Myra. She thought of her father. She could hear his laughter, see the twinkle in his eyes!

"Have I done well, Daddy?" She almost said the words out loud.

There was a "coo-ee" from the top of the stairs.

"Is that you, Ann? I'm ready. Tell Travers to send someone up for the luggage, will you?"

Ann walked back into the drawing-room and rang the bell. By the time Travers had climbed slowly from the basement to the hall Myra had run downstairs.

"The housemaid helped me, that's why I've been so quick." She looked around. "Where's Tommy?"

"He remembered he had an appointment just before twelve," Ann replied; "he was sorry to rush away, but said that he would be getting in touch with you."

"Did he really say that?"

Ann nodded.

"That's all right then. I expect he knows the telephone number at Gulliver."

"If he doesn't, he has only to look it up in the telephone book."

"Yes, of course! He didn't sound annoyed or anything? What did you talk about?"

"I merely thanked him for being so kind to you," Ann answered truthfully, "and said I hoped that you would see a lot of him when you came back to London."

Myra slipped her arm through her elder sister's.

"He's rather exciting, isn't he?"

"Is he?"

"Don't you think so?" Myra asked. "He's frightfully experienced, there's nothing he has not done."

"Yes, I should imagine that," Ann replied, hoping that she had kept a note of irony from her tones.

"I will tell you something," Myra said, lowering her tones in case anyone passing through the hall should hear. "He thinks me awfully pretty. Do you think I have improved in looks?"

There was something so childish and ingenuous in the question that Ann could not bear to tell the truth and damp Myra's enthusiasm.

"I think you have taken a lot of trouble with yourself," she prevaricated.

"That's true," Myra answered. "And I want to show you all my clothes. My evening dress is wonderful—black lace over rose-pink satin, and it's cut frightfully low. You'll be stunned by it."

Ann was certain of that, but she was wise enough to say nothing.

"What about saying good-bye to Dawson?" she asked.

"Yes, of course we must," Myra replied, and ran along the passage shouting his name noisily.

"She is still only a schoolgirl," Ann thought.

All the way back to Gulliver Myra chatted happily while Ann drove, saying very little, but listening intently. Was this serious, she asked herself, or was Myra just in love with love, in love with being young and having a good time?

How easy on top of the excitement of new clothes, dancing and meeting new people to add the sensations aroused by Major Rankin's fulsome compliments and flashing smile and to believe it to be love—real love!

Would Gulliver make Myra forget or was her heart really touched by the first swashbuckling buccaneer to come swaggering into her life?

If she did forget, Ann thought, never for one moment must she guess that she had been saved from herself.

If Myra was suspicious of being tricked, unduly influenced, her confidence might be destroyed and some of that honest, open-hearted frankness which had always been one of her most engaging qualities would vanish.

"Do you know, Ann, I was half afraid you wouldn't like Tommy," Myra was saying. "Wasn't it silly of me? I really think he put the idea into my head. He seemed to think that you and John would think him too old for me. I could see that he was quite surprised when you were so nice to him."

"Why shouldn't I be nice to him when he has been kind to you?"

"Oh, Ann, you are sweet. I will always tell you everything, I will really." There was a moment's pause, and she added in a small, rather quiet voice: "He kissed me, you know!"

"Did he?" Ann asked easily, "and did you like it?"

She heard Myra draw a sharp breath, as if for a moment she had been afraid of her confession.

"It was disappointing somehow. I thought kisses were more thrilling!"

"Perhaps some kisses are."

"I expect it was because I felt shy and uncomfortable," Myra said in a common sense sort of voice. "Besides, I couldn't quite get the idea out of my mind that it was wrong for Tommy to kiss me. Maybe that was because I hadn't told you about him."

"Maybe that's what it was," said Ann, her eyes on the road ahead of them.

"I will tell you everything in future," Myra repeated, "everything!"

As they drew up at the front door only a quarter of an hour late for luncheon, Ann felt suddenly tired and a little exhausted.

It had been a long morning with a great deal of strain about it, but at the same time she knew it had been a good morning's work, and she was prepared to brave Lady Melton's frown at their lateness, content in her own mind to know how unimportant it was.

To her relief no one was in when they arrived except

208

John who welcomed them with a smile and Ann saw by the look that he gave her over Myra's head that he understood the whole circumstances.

Dawson must have made his explanation cleverly, for John's first words after he had greeted Myra were:

"I'm so glad you were able to come down to our party tonight."

"It sounds thrilling!" Myra said, "and oh, John, this house is wonderful. It is even better than I imagined it would be."

"Aren't we ever going to have any luncheon?" Charles asked from the doorway.

"It's my fault," Ann said. "Myra, I want you to meet Charles Lynton, John's cousin. Charles, this is my sister Myra."

It was with faint amusement that Ann realised what Charles would think of Myra's get-up. Luckily she had taken her hat off in the car and despite the vulgarity of her coat and dress she was with her hair blown about her face extraordinarily pretty.

"Let's go and eat at once," John said. "Bring your cocktail with you, Ann."

"Where is Lady Melton?" Ann asked.

"She's gone out to luncheon," John replied, "and Vivien has gone with her; they are opening a flower-show or some such gaiety this afternoon."

"And the twins?"

"They are down at the farm helping with the harvest. The farmer's wife promised them a meal to reward their labours, and they took four bottles of ginger beer with them—to be on the safe side."

"At least they won't be thirsty—which I am," Charles cried plaintively.

As they moved towards the dining-room Sinclair joined them in the hall.

Myra was already chattering away to John, perfectly at her ease, exclaiming at everything she saw, and was in fact so unaffectedly happy that she raised everyone else's spirits, too.

Luncheon was indeed the most enjoyable meal that Ann had had at Gulliver. When it was over and John suggested that he should take Myra on a tour of the house, she drew Charles to one side.

"I want to speak to you," she whispered.

He nodded, and as the others moved off they slipped into the morning-room.

"Charles, you've got to help me," Ann said without any preliminaries.

"But of course, you know I am always ready to do that."

"I rushed up to London this morning to rescue Myra from a perfectly horrible man."

"I guessed there must be something like that about it. She's a pretty child; but ye gods, what clothes!"

"I know, almost as bad as mine."

"No, worse, much worse! Yours were dull, but these . . ." Charles made a gesture of despair.

Ann laughed.

"It's another job for you."

"So I'm to dress Myra?"

Ann nodded.

"Anything else?"

"Yes, I want you to help me make Myra forget this man who has been running after her. I told John to invite a party here tonight, it was the only way I could get her to leave London. See that she has a good time, Charles. You know the people and I don't."

"And what's she going to wear?"

"Black lace over rose-pink satin," Ann told him and laughed again as he made a grimace of horror.

"Don't tell me any more; I can imagine it."

"Well then, you must save her from herself."

"Leave it to me," Charles said. "I will transform her."

"You will get very good at this Cinderella business by the time you have finished," Ann teased.

"I thought I told you what you were."

"All right, I remember, don't say it all again," Ann replied.

"And what about my payment for all this work you are giving me?" Charles asked.

For a moment Ann took him seriously.

"John said . . ." she began, and then she realised that he was not speaking of money. "What payment do you require?"

"That is what I am wondering," Charles said slowly. "At least I know what I want, but I am wondering if I dare ask for it."

His eyes held hers for a moment, and though the blood rose in her cheeks Ann contrived to speak lightly.

"You are not trying to flirt with me, Charles?"

"Are you suggesting that I should attempt anything so commonplace?" he asked in scorn.

"Then what are you trying to do?"

He hesitated for a moment.

"Mightn't I be trying to teach you a little about that elusive but very wonderful thing called . . . love?"

"No, you mustn't do that."

"Why not?"

"You know the answer as well as I do."

Charles sighed. "I suppose so; at the same time it is stupid always to do what is right and proper."

"It would be equally stupid to do what is wrong and improper—even once."

"Would it? And am I to work for nothing?"

"For nothing, Charles," Ann said firmly.

"I wonder." He looked at her contemplatively for a moment, and then he smiled. "Somehow I still believe there's some justice somewhere."

He moved swiftly taking both her hands in his. He turned them over.

"Such sensible, capable little hands," he said, and before she could stop him he pressed a kiss into the palm of each one.

"That's just a little on account," he said, and then, before she could say anything, he held open the door for her with a flourish.

"Go and find John and your little sister!" he said. "I have got some telephoning to do if your commands are to be obeyed."

Ann went without saying a word, and it was only when she found herself in the hall and the door had closed behind her that she stood very still. It was very quiet.

She half fancied that she could hear her own heart beating . . . but she was not sure.

Fifteen

"Darling, it's been wonderful, simply wonderful!"

Myra put her arm round Ann's waist and gave her an affectionate squeeze.

"Do you know, that nice Captain Marlow said that I looked like Persephone. I couldn't remember at first who she was until Charles whispered in my ear 'Spring'; so it was a compliment, wasn't it? It's all been absolutely gorgeous!"

Myra gave a sigh of utter contentment, and Ann, holding her close for a moment, said softly:

"I'm glad you were happy, darling; I was awfully proud of you."

"You were really?"

"Really!"

"If someone had told us two months ago that we should be at Gulliver and I should be dancing with all sorts of important people in the most beautiful dress in the world, well, we should have laughed at them, shouldn't we?"

"We might even have thought it was one of your romanticisms!" Ann teased.

"But they have come true, haven't they?" Myra asked. "You used to laugh at me; but you see, time has proved me right. Oh, Ann, I'm so glad you married John."

"Are you?"

There was a change in Ann's tone and she released herself from Myra's affectionate arms.

"We must go to bed," she said, "it's after one o'clock."

"Who cares?" Myra retorted, but all the same she stifled a yawn. It had been a long day.

"Aren't you two girls ready for bed?"—Charles spoke from the doorway.

"Myra is pretending she isn't tired," Ann replied.

"Well, I know I am," Charles answered; "John is speeding the last parting guest."

"And Vivien is helping him, I suppose?" Ann said.

She could not help the slight sting in her tone, although she meant the remark to be merely humorous.

"Vivien, as you say, is helping him," Charles said slowly.

It seemed to Ann there was some meaning in his voice which for a moment she did not understand; but Myra, preoccupied only with herself, whirled across the polished floor.

"Oh, Charles," she cried, "I've had such a lovely evening, and I know it's due to you. I see now that the dress I bought would have been all wrong. I was hurt when you told me so this afternoon, but that was before I had seen this."

She picked up her filmy skirt of white lace.

"It is lovely, isn't it?" she asked, speaking in awed admiration as though the dress was not particularly hers but just something of beauty that she must admire.

She was right, it was a lovely frock, and Ann on

213

seeing Myra in it had reiterated that Charles was a genius where women's clothes were concerned.

The dress he had chosen which had arrived by special messenger from London only half an hour before dinner-time, might have been specially created for Myra's romantic nature.

A great bouffant skirt of white lace was caught at the waist with the palest and most delicate spring blossoms. There was a necklace of the same flowers, and tiny bracelets for each of her wrists.

When Myra was dressed she looked the personification of all that was young, lovely and unspoiled; and Ann was not really surprised when she overheard several of John's guests exclaiming at Myra's looks and saying that she would undoubtedly be one of the most beautiful débutantes of the winter season.

One person had added:

"I believe these two Shefford girls will be acclaimed as famous beauties; what is more, I hear there's a third hidden away somewhere."

"Famous beauties!" Ann echoed the words to herself, and then almost laughed out aloud.

It seemed ridiculous somehow that Ann and Myra, the daughters of an obscure country doctor, should be spoken of in such terms, and she knew that much of the appreciation they were receiving was due to Charles.

He had indeed produced them. He had, to quote the simile he had himself used, put the picture in a decent frame.

She wondered what the people now busy paying Myra compliments would have said if they had seen her earlier in the day in her common little red coat and fly-away hat, or if only a fortnight ago they had seen the new Lady Melton of Gulliver scrubbing the floor of the kitchen in an old overall.

Would they have thought them beauties under such circumstances? Ann doubted it.

What was more important than anything was that

Myra had enjoyed her evening. If she had thought of Tommy Rankin, she certainly showed no signs of missing him or of being lonely without him.

Charles had been true to his promise and had done everything in his power to ensure Myra's success.

It was not only the dress itself, it was not only the charming things which he had said to her which made her eyes sparkle and gave her confidence, it was the way he had taken her under his wing and been in attendance the whole evening.

He had rescued her from the dull old men who were all too willing to monopolise a pretty girl if they got the chance. He had seen that she had the opportunity to dance with the nicest and most popular of the young men and that never for a moment did she find herself alone or neglected.

Ann had watched him and had been grateful, so grateful that she had not realised that she herself had been a little neglected in consequence. Now as she watched him smile at Myra in his irresistibly attractive manner, she found herself feeling a tiny pang of loneliness.

Without Charles how difficult, how big and frightening Gulliver would seem!

"Well, have you enjoyed yourself?"

It was John speaking from the doorway, as Ann turned at the sound of his voice she was surprised to find that he asked the question of her rather than of Myra.

"Very much, thank you; it was a delightful party."

"Personally I was disappointed." Vivien's cool, clear tone seemed to Ann to shatter the quiet, pleasant, contented atmosphere.

She came slowly into the room, her dress of silver lamé glittering mirror-like beneath the lighted chandeliers.

"I'm sorry about that," John said gravely, but there was a note of irony in his voice.

"I expect I'm getting old," Vivien yawned. "I find the exuberance of the very young somewhat tiring."

"You should have gone to bed early and got your beauty sleep," Myra said.

Ann was amused to note that Myra had very quickly taken Vivien's measure. She was not in the slightest upset or disconcerted by Vivien's rudeness.

Instead she was apparently perfectly prepared to take up any challenge that the older girl wished to throw down.

If Vivien and Myra were to remain under the same roof it was obvious that there were likely to be some exchanges of wit in which it was by no means certain that Vivien would be the winner.

Now, because it was late and she wanted the evening to end on an harmonious note, Ann spoke soothingly.

"We must go to bed," she said, "and by the way, your mother retired very early, John."

"I'm afraid she was feeling ill," John replied, "although her excuse for leaving us was that she felt you were quite a sufficient chaperone of such a young party."

"I'm sorry if she felt ill," Ann said, "as long as she was not still angry."

John laughed.

"The twins really excelled themselves tonight!"

"I was furious with them," Ann confessed, "but at the same time I could not help laughing. I should have wanted to do the same thing when I was their age."

The evening had started badly. Ann felt that Lady Melton was not particularly pleased when she and Vivien returned from the flower-show to find that quite considerable festivities had been arranged in their absence.

Not only were twenty people coming to dinner, but treble that number had been asked in to dance afterwards, and John had arranged for a dozen or so to stay the night. It was not that there were any difficulties from the domestic point of view; the servants at Gulliver were used to large numbers and short notice, and once the orders had been given, everything proceeded with the smoothness of clockwork.

But Lady Melton liked to hold the reins very tightly in her own hands. If things were to be arranged she liked to arrange them herself; and Ann knew that, though she said very little, she was in reality both annoyed and affronted.

She tried to explain the circumstances as best she could without either being disloyal to Myra or putting her young sister in an unfavourable light; and by the time a number of people had arrived and they went upstairs to dress for dinner Ann believed that she had been, in part at any rate, successful in appeasing her mother-in-law.

In her own room Ann undressed quickly and wrapping her dressing-gown round her passed through the door which led to her bathroom. Everything was laid out as usual.

The big pink towel open on the chair, the bath half filled, the water exuding the fragrance of bath salts scented with stephanotis.

Then, as she went to slip off her dressing-gown, she stood spell-bound, not certain whether to scream or run. It took her a moment to understand what it was she saw, for out of the water of her bath rose the ugly snout of a monster pike.

Then as she stared she remembered she had last seen that very same pike in a glass case hanging on the walls of the museum. She stepped forward and picked it out of the bath.

Was she the only person on whom the twins had played such a trick? She hoped so!

It was only when all the guests gathered for dinner that Ann learned only too forcefully that she was not alone in being victimised.

Lady Melton had found a small alligator concealed in the bottom of her bath, and had not known it was

there until she put her foot on it. Vivien—and Ann
admitted to herself that the twins had shown a precocious sense of character here—found an adder coiled
up in the silk underclothes she was about to put on.

A giant-sized cobra in Mrs. Marlow's room, a guest
who had come over for the evening, had frightened
the lady so much that she had practically had a heart
attack before she had realised that it was not alive.

Sinclair had gone to dress to find cuddled side by
side on the pillows of his bed the heads of a roaring
tiger and a small wide-eyed gazelle.

With the exception of Charles, who had been let
off with nothing worse than scorpions in both his shoes,
Sinclair was the only person to see the humour of the
whole thing.

The other guests, some of them staying at Gulliver
for the first time, had all found something in their
bedrooms or bathrooms.

One, a middle-aged woman who had a name for
being a thruster in the hunting field, had rushed
screaming into the passage because the twins had left
a stuffed monkey peeping over her wardrobe.

"It will do everybody good. This house needs waking
up," Charles had said soothingly after Ann had apologised over and over again and everyone had spent
the beginning of the evening describing their sensations.

More than one of the older members of the party
had made it their duty to tell her innumerable stories,
usually long and rather boring ones, of practical jokes
which had gone wrong, in consequence either causing
the death of those who perpetrated them or being
responsible for sending the unfortunate victim straight
into a lunatic asylum.

Ann had gone up to have a final word with the
twins after dinner, but it was no use; they were quite
unrepentant.

"It was funny, Ann, you must see it was funny!"
Antony laughed. "We listened outside some of the

bedrooms. I only wish we could have seen as well as heard."

"The women shrieked like anything," Antoinette giggled.

"You are very naughty, both of you," Ann remarked. "You have given a number of kind, nice people a terrible shock; besides I am certain you have damaged some of the animals, especially the ones you put in the baths."

"John won't mind," Antoinette retorted lightly. "He said the other day that everything in the museum ought to be burnt."

"Well, I don't care what he said, I'm furious with both of you."

"Not really you aren't," Antoinette pleaded winningly; "besides we heard you laughing when you were talking to Charles about it."

"You shouldn't listen at doors," Ann said, trying to be severe and failing utterly.

She had gone downstairs again feeling that after all it was only a childish escapade and that perhaps Charles was right—Gulliver did need waking up!

When she reached the ballroom to find Myra with a look of ecstatic enjoyment on her face, she thought that nothing mattered as long as her own little family were safe and well.

Yet she was too sensitive not to mind if people were genuinely upset.

"Don't you worry," Charles told her later. "It gave some of the stuffed shirts a bit of a shock, but they will be able to dine out on the story for months. It will be the talk of the county by tomorrow morning, and I promise you it will lose nothing in the telling."

"It is Lady Melton that worries me most," Ann said.

"Lady Melton is not going to be pleased with you whatever you do."

"Why not?" Ann questioned.

"You are John's wife," Charles said shortly.

"That's no answer."

219

"It's the complete answer really."

"But why? She can't be jealous. I have never seen anyone show so little affection towards their only son."

"It's not what people say that matters," Charles answered, "it's what they feel. Haven't you learned that by now?"

"Isn't it the same thing?" Ann asked innocently.

He laughed.

"One day you will wake up, and when you do that—you may even grow up."

"What nonsense he talks," Ann thought.

She would have told him so if they had not been interrupted at that moment by the announcement that supper was served.

"I have eaten too much and danced too much and had too much of everything," Myra said now, "but I can't bear to think that the evening's ended."

"There will be other evenings," Charles said soothingly.

"You promise me that? I'm so frightened that this is a dream."

"Shall I pinch you, and if it hurts you will know it's the truth."

"You will find as you get older that these things are all very much the same," Vivien said in a blasé voice. "In fact one dance at Gulliver is very like another."

"We must all go to bed," Ann said again, "or you will soon be persuading us that we have not enjoyed ourselves at all. Good night, Charles, and thank you."

She moved from the room with Myra beside her. They went upstairs slowly, Myra chattering and calling back over her shoulder to the others who were following.

"I am going to swim in the morning," she told Ann, "and Charles has promised to show me how to row."

"That will be lovely," Ann said, noting with relief that no mention was being made of Myra returning to London.

220

She stopped at the top of the stairs and kissed her sister affectionately.

"Good night, darling, you looked lovely."

"Not half as lovely as you did," Myra whispered, and there was something so sincere in her voice that Ann felt the tears come to her eyes.

Dawson had said that Myra loved her. She knew it was true; the child made no attempt to hide her feelings, and the kiss she pressed against her cheek came from an overflowing heart.

"God bless you." Ann said the words softly, and turned towards her own room.

It was only as she closed the door behind her that she remembered that she had not yet kept her promise to Dawson.

There had been no opportunity, for although she had wished to seek Vivien out, they had not had a word together the whole evening. Ann hesitated for a moment, then decided that it would be impossible to sleep with the thought of that message hanging over her.

She was more nervous about it than she cared to confess even to herself. Myra might stand up to Vivien, but Ann knew that she herself was frightened of her. She did not seem human; she somehow seemed something fashioned not from flesh and blood, but from all the arts and graces and pretences of that social world of which she—Ann—knew so little. Yet it had to be done!

Quickly Ann opened her door, crossed the landing and moved down the wide, beautifully proportioned corridor which led to Vivien's room.

It took courage to bring herself to knock; and as she waited for the sound of Vivien's voice bidding her come in, Ann wished that she had never listened to Dawson or given him her promise.

"Come in!"

Now it was too late. Ann turned the handle of the door.

Vivien was seated before her mirror, removing from her neck the carved jade necklace which had flattered her skin, making it in contrast seem very white and transparent.

"Oh, it's you!"—there was surprise in Vivien's voice as she turned her head.

"Can I speak to you a moment?"

"Of course, come in."

Ann shut the door and walked across the room.

A lovely room, she thought, and a perfect setting for Vivien. It was decorated in pale green, the hangings of the big four-poster bed were of green also, while most of the furniture in the room was carved and gilded.

The dressing-table itself was a great slab of pink marble supported at either end by gold dolphins and mermaids. It was an exotic room, but it had both character and originality.

Ann wondered whether John had paid to have it specially designed for Vivien or whether she had chosen it from the many beautiful rooms at Gulliver.

"Sit down," Vivien suggested, and indicated a chair covered in green velvet.

Ann did as she was requested and wondered how she was to find words to begin.

"You wanted to see me?" Vivien asked.

Ann nodded.

Vivien looked at her and narrowed her eyes.

"I wonder if I can guess why you have come?"

"I doubt it," Ann said quietly.

"It's about John?" Vivien suggested.

Ann shook her head.

"No, you are quite wrong, it's about somebody very different, somebody who has asked me to give you a message."

Vivien looked surprised, and then without prevaricating further Ann said:

"I went to London today to fetch Myra. While I was there I had a long talk with Dawson."

222

"Oh, Dawson." Vivien looked away quickly.

There was something in her tone when she spoke Dawson's name which told Ann that whatever else she might be, Vivien was not indifferent.

"Dawson," Ann went on, "has come to a very important decision. He wanted you to know about it; and because he honoured me with his confidence, he asked me to tell you what he has decided to do before you heard it from anyone else."

"Why should you know?" Vivien inquired.

"I happened to be there this morning at a moment when Dawson was trying to make up his mind. When he had decided his first thought was of you."

Vivien said nothing. She turned her head away from Ann and sat staring at her own reflection in the mirror.

"He has been asked if he will stand for a South London borough. He has decided to leave John and to take a chance of winning the seat, and . . . of winning you."

Ann's voice dropped on the last word. She was half afraid of what she had said, and yet she knew she had done what Dawson wanted of her.

Why he loved Vivien she could not understand, for what good, she thought, would this hard, brittle creature be to him in the life he had chosen? He cared for the people amongst whom he had worked—the poor people, the people who needed a champion.

He was prepared to work for them, to fight for them. It had been there in the light of his eyes, when he spoke of them, in the ring in his voice. But Vivien . . . what would those people mean to her?

And then Ann saw that her fingers with their long crimson nails were lacing themselves together nervously.

There was a silence, a silence in which Ann watched Vivien, and Vivien stared at her own reflection. Then at last, abruptly, with a movement that was somehow jerky and unlike her usual exquisite grace, Vivien got to her feet.

"He's crazy," she said sharply, "crazy to leave John! What will he live on?"

"His salary when he is a Member of Parliament," Ann replied, "and I have a feeling that he won't be a backbencher for very long."

"You have a feeling," Vivien said sneeringly. "What do you know about Dawson?"

"Very little," Ann answered quietly, "but I know sincerity when I meet it. He means to succeed, he wants to succeed, and what's more he is bound to succeed if you stand by him while he is fighting the hardest battle of his life."

"I stand by him?" Vivien who had moved across the room turned round suddenly. "What could I do about it?"

"He loves you."

"Yes, I know that." Vivien spoke almost impatiently.

"And you love him?"

For a moment Ann thought that Vivien was going to deny it, was going to scream at her in sudden rage. She stood still and tense, a look of anger on her face that was almost frightening; and then quite suddenly her anger passed and instead a look of help-lessness, almost of despair, came to her face.

"Yes, I love him," she said, and her voice broke, "but what can I do about it?"

"Can't you marry him?" Ann asked the question softly.

She had forgotten in that moment all her fear of Vivien. She only knew that here was someone suf-fering, someone in trouble.

"How can I?" Vivien asked the question throwing wide her arms in a gesture of despair. "How can I marry a man with no money, with nothing . . . nothing to offer me?"

"Except love."

"Will love feed and clothe us?" Vivien asked, and there was ironical cynicism in her tones now. "Will love give us cars and jewels and holidays in the

South of France? Will we be able to entertain our friends, to live in a civilised manner? Can love provide servants and a comfortable home? You know it can't."

Ann said nothing. Vivien started to walk about the room, her hands clasped tightly together, her head thrown back a little, her eyes wide as though she would defy them to shed the tears which were so very near the surface.

"I love Dawson," she said more quietly as if she spoke to herself; "yes, I love him. I've tried hard not to. I have tried to forget him, to escape even from the memory of him. Yet for some reason that I can't fathom I still go on being in love with him.

"Why, tell me why, do people fall in love? He's not particularly handsome, he's not amusing, he's not gay. He's serious, he's idealistic, he's interested not in the people and things I like, but in those he believes are needy and suffering. I know it all—everything that is crude and harsh and unpleasant.

"I want to shut my eyes to it; and yet I love Dawson. How absurd it is, how ridiculous, but I still love him!"

Vivien stood still and looked at Ann.

"I'm a fool to tell you all this," she said. "How you must be laughing at me! I meant to marry John—I still mean to marry him if I can get him away from you. John can give me money and power and position and security."

"And happiness?"

"I should be happy with all those things," Vivien's answer was a challenge.

Ann's reply came quickly:

"While you are still in love with Dawson? Don't deceive yourself—you would be miserable. You belong to Dawson and he belongs to you. Do you suppose that for one moment things can make up for people?"

"I won't be poor, I won't." Vivien almost shouted the words.

"Why are you so afraid of poverty? If you are happy it doesn't matter."

"You can't convince me of that."

"I shouldn't attempt to try," Ann replied; "but I can tell you the truth that I have been wonderfully happy all my life. We have also been frightfully poor."

"But you are different." Vivien's voice was scornful.

"Am I? Are any of us different in one way? We are all human, we all want to love . . . and to be loved."

Even as she said the words she realised the message they held for her as well as for Vivien.

"We are all human."

Yes, even Vivien was human, Vivien of whom she had been so afraid, who had seemed so hostile, so utterly alien from anything she had ever known.

But Vivien, hard, glamorous and exotic, who had frightened her since she first came to Gulliver, had now changed into a woman distraught by suffering, a woman who cried out suddenly in a voice piteous in its intensity:

"Yes, I too want to be loved—Oh, God, what am I to do?"

Sixteen

Abruptly Vivien sat down on the stool in front of her dressing-table, but this time she sat with her back to the mirror facing Ann.

For a moment she did not speak; then, as if it was an effort to recapture her self-control, she said:

"You may think that I am being hysterical, but you have no idea what I have suffered all my life from fear . . .yes, fear of insecurity. You have been poor but at least your poverty had the virtue of being continuous. Our lives, Charles's and mine, were very different."

She paused a moment putting her crimson-tipped fingers across her eyes as if the memory of the past still had the power to frighten and disturb her.

"Even when I was a child," she went on, "I was always afraid of finding myself hungry and naked. I suppose all children are imaginative; but while for most of them that means living in a world of fantasy and fairy tales, for me it meant the horror of imagining myself dying of cold, starving for want of food, being ragged because I had no clothes. That sounds exaggerated, but I assure you it was true.

"My father, who was one of the most attractive men I have ever seen in my life, had one hopeless and incurable vice—he was a gambler.

"He would bet on anything and everything, not only horses and cards but on anything else which came to his attention. I believe once he staked some hundreds of pounds that the fly he chose on the windowpane would reach the sill before the one chosen by another man.

"He was quite insane where gambling was concerned. I was brought up on the story that once he had even wagered me when I was a baby on the turn of a card against another man's retriever.

"Unfortunately—and I choose the word deliberately—on that occasion he won! But he was not always so lucky!

"My mother died when we were quite young, and my childhood was spent in a bewildered chaos of fluctuating circumstances which at first I did not

227

understand, and which was, therefore, all the more terrifying.

"For many years my father retained by some miracle the family house, and that constituted for us our home, but the four walls and the roof were about the only things which did not change with my father's fortune.

"One month there would be magnificent furniture, pictures, silver, glass, and a bevy of servants to wait on us. Overnight, or so it seemed to me, they would all vanish and we would be left with just the bare necessities on which to sleep and with which to eat. And the servants would go, all of them with the exception of our old housekeeper who had been with my mother when she first married.

"Charles and I never liked her, but nevertheless she was for us the only static thing in a changing, incoherent world.

"My nannies, and I loved some of them dearly, were snatched from me to leave behind bitter-sweet memories because in those days I was an affectionate, even demonstrative person.

"I grew older, and while I suppose in some ways I grew a tougher and harder outer skin, I still remained inside vulnerable and afraid.

"I learned to get money out of my father when he was in funds and to hoard it by me so that I could afford to buy clothes and even food when he was down and out. I had, of course, little education; governesses came and went even as my nannies had.

"Once I was sent to a fashionable school, but I was forced to leave at the end of the second term because my father could not find the fees for the third.

"Charles was more fortunate as he was sent to Eton by an uncle who paid the school fees direct, not trusting my father with the money.

"That was the life I lived until I was twenty-one when my father died suddenly and Charles and I found ourselves faced not only with a mountain of debts, but also with the possibility of a most unsavoury and unpleasant Court case.

"I am not mincing words when I tell you that at the end of his life my father was a crook. He gambled not only with his own money but with other people's."

Ann gave an exclamation of pity. Vivien looked at her.

"You have no idea what it was like," she said in a hard voice. "I wondered what to do, wondered where I could turn for help, and then John came to the rescue.

"I suppose I ought not to tell you this, but I have said so much that I may as well continue to be frank.

"Long before I even saw John and he was only a name, almost a legend to us as a distant cousin—so rich, distinguished and powerful—I made up my mind to marry him. John and Gulliver meant security, security from all that I had loathed and detested all through my life."

Vivien stopped speaking, then she covered her face with her hands. There was silence, a long silence, until at length Ann said in a voice warm and deep with sympathy:

"It must have been ghastly; I am so sorry for you."

Vivien took her hands from her face.

"You have every reason to be," she said, and a bitter little smile curved the corners of her red mouth. "I should have married John if you hadn't come along. He didn't love me, but he was growing used to having me here. His mother wanted the marriage and sooner or later he would have come round to our way of thinking."

"And now, what are you going to do?"

As if the question brought her swiftly from the past back to the future, Vivien stiffened, and then made a gesture of utter hopelessness.

"What can I do?" she asked, and added cynically: "Rich men don't grow on gooseberry bushes."

"And Dawson?"

Vivien's face softened.

"Poor Dawson; yet what help would I be to him? I should make him a bad wife, you know that."

"Not if you loved him."

"I do love him. That's exactly why I shouldn't saddle him with anyone so incompetent, so selfish and so completely unsuitable as I am myself."

"But need you be all those things?"

"I've got to be them as far as Dawson is concerned. Never again could I face that ghastly insecurity, that horror of dreading what tomorrow may bring, of having so much one moment and losing it the next. Heavens above! Why, of all the men in the world, did I have to fall in love with Dawson?"

Vivien looked across the room at the great bed with its green hangings, she moved her hand and the gesture was echoed in the mirror behind her and two long gold-framed mirrors on the other side of the room.

"This is what I want," she said softly as though she was speaking to herself. "This."

"Alone?" Ann's question sounded almost sharp.

Vivien turned her head but did not answer.

"Won't you be lonely?" Ann asked. "You say you love Dawson, and yet you are afraid of poverty with him. I have been poor too; and though perhaps my poverty has been less eventful than yours, I found in it tremendous and unceasing happiness."

Vivien smiled scornfully.

"What sort of happiness?"

"The happiness of being with the people one loved," Ann answered. "The happiness of having the same jokes, laughing together, sharing things, of having fun, real fun, and that feeling of unity which is unbreakable . . . except by death."

230

"Fun," Vivien repeated. "Can you imagine me enjoying that sort of fun?"

"Why not?" Ann asked. "What fun do you have here? Look at this room. It's beautiful, lovely; but surely if you are to come to it alone night after night, you will forget the beauty and know only the loneliness of it?

"Gulliver is big and magnificent, but how often do you all laugh? You talk to each other, you discuss things, but you never appear to me to be really enjoying yourselves.

"You are putting on an act, talking for the sake of talking, not because the chatter is bubbling spontaneously out of you and because you can't bear not to share that particular knowledge or joke with people who love and understand you.

"If it comes to that, how much love have you found at Gulliver?"

Ann spoke challengingly, there was a ring in her voice and a light in her eyes, that Vivien had never seen before.

"I've been happy here, I tell you," Vivien said half defiantly.

"Have you?" Ann asked. "Have you been really happy with that deep, springing joy which makes everything in the world seem wonderful because the people for whom you really care are with you, near you, touching you and loving you?"

"Must we have that to have happiness?"

"Yes, if it's to be real happiness," Ann answered. "You tell me you are in love with Dawson, and I know he is in love with you. Have you ever found anything here in this great empty house to equal the emotion you feel for him when you are together?"

Vivien got to her feet and moved restlessly about the room.

"What's the use of talking about it?" she asked almost savagely. "I'm trying to forget Dawson. I have not seen him for months. Sometimes John mentions

231

his name, but otherwise I have tried to forget his very existence."

"You can't run away like that," Ann said. "Can't you see that is what you have been doing all your life?"

"Running away?"

"Yes, running away. You have been afraid of poverty. Instead of facing it you have tried to escape it. When you do that, sooner or later fate always catches up with you. Perhaps poverty is a lesson that you have got to learn, perhaps an experience that you have got to pass through some time in this existence.

"Whatever it may be, running away is not going to help you; fate to prove its point has sent you Dawson. Now you are running away from him and trying to escape your own destiny."

"Damn you, leave me alone." Vivien stamped her foot in a sudden rage.

Then almost before she had spoken, her anger was shattered by a sudden tempest of tears.

"Why do you torture me?" she cried. "Oh, Dawson . . . Dawson . . . I can't bear this!'

She threw herself down in an arm-chair, her head bowed between her hands, her shoulders shaking. Impulsively Ann sprang up and went across the room to her. She knelt beside her, putting an arm round her shoulders, talking to her soothingly as one might to a child.

"Don't, Vivien, don't," she pleaded.

"I'm such a fool," Vivien sobbed, "such a damn fool and yet I can't help it. I want him so. I love him. I ache for him. I've tried to stop myself, tried and tried, but it's no use. I want him more than anything else in the whole world."

She raised her face; it was streaked with tears, and yet it seemed to Ann that she looked more beautiful than she had ever looked before.

"I love him," she repeated brokenly.

232

"I know you do," Ann said, "and you are going to marry him, aren't you?"

"I suppose so," Vivien said dully.

"You're right, I'm sure you are right."

"I'm afraid—really desperately afraid."

"You needn't be," Ann said. "Dawson will look after you, I'm sure of that. He will never let you down. If you help him he will succeed. Somehow I know—I am utterly convinced that he cannot fail."

Vivien gave a little sob, then she drew a deep breath.

"If only I had faith like you," she said, "things might have been different a long time ago." Then, as if a thought struck her, she asked: "And yet, though you know so much, you yourself are not happy."

"Perhaps that's because I have left my poverty behind me," Ann said with a faint smile.

Vivien got to her feet and walked to the dressing-table in search of a handkerchief.

"It's so ridiculous if you think of it," she said. "If our roles were reversed we should both have had what we wanted. You would make a wonderful wife for Dawson, while I should be eminently suitable for John."

Quite suddenly she laughed.

"Oh, Ann, who would have imagined two hours ago that we should be talking to each other like this?"

"I was afraid of you," Ann said, rising to her feet.

"And I hated you because you had taken everything that I wanted."

They both laughed together, and Vivien, looking at herself in the mirror, said:

"I've made a freak of myself; but for once in my life I don't care."

"I thought when you were crying," Ann said in all sincerity, "that I had never seen you look more beautiful."

233

"You're crazy," Vivien exclaimed, but Ann could see that she was pleased. "I've tried never to let myself cry."

"And so you have bottled it all up inside . . ." Ann suggested.

"Until tonight when the cork came out of the bottle. What a fool I've been, and I'm not certain that in saying I will marry Dawson I am not being even more foolish. If I am, it's your fault. You have made poverty sound attractive, though how I don't know."

"Only poverty with Dawson," Ann suggested.

Vivien smiled. "Yes . . . with Dawson."

"When are you going to tell him?"

"Now, at once, tonight, before I change my mind. Before I lie awake in that big comfortable bed and think what a damned fool I am to exchange it for a straw mattress in a garret."

She spoke lightly, but Ann knew that in some extraordinary way her fear had already diminished, that now she was only playing at fear while before it had been desperate, real and agonising.

"If you are going to telephone Dawson," Ann said, "I will leave you alone. Good night, Vivien. God bless you, dear."

She spoke the last words almost automatically as she might have to Antony and Antoinette if they had passed through a crisis and come at last to the haven of forgiveness and quiet contentment. But Vivien seemed startled.

"You mean that?" she asked in a very low voice.

"Of course I do," Ann said, "and I think He will. If one does the right thing, His help is never far away."

Vivien stood very still.

"I shall need that help, shan't I?" she said softly. "I hardly know how to say it, but I have forgotten how to pray."

"You will remember," Ann said, "because you

want so much for Dawson as well as for yourself. It's easier to pray for someone one loves."

Vivien nodded, and suddenly she moved forward and kissed Ann.

"Thank you," she said, "and you will help me, too, won't you?"

"Of course I will," Ann said.

She moved towards the door. As she reached it, she looked back and saw that Vivien was already sitting at the side of the bed and had taken up the telephone receiver. There was a radiance on her face, and her mouth was soft and tremulous. It was the face of a woman who had passed through deep waters and suddenly found peace.

It was the face of a woman who loved.

Ann closed the door behind her and went softly along the now darkened passage towards her own room. There was only a dim light showing in the hall to guide her, but she went slowly, holding her hands in front of her for fear she would bump into a piece of furniture.

In her own room the lights were burning brightly. As she opened the door, she had a momentary impression that another door, the door in John's room, had closed softly.

Then she imagined she must have been mistaken.

He had never come to her room since her first day at Gulliver. Occasionally he would call through the door or knock to tell her that he was going downstairs; but otherwise they met only in other parts of the house, and Ann was grateful that he respected the privacy of her bedroom.

She undressed slowly; somehow her thoughts went back not so much to the extraordinary and amazing interview she had just had with Vivien as to Vivien's face as she had left her. It was hard to believe that it was the same girl she had hated and feared.

She wondered how long they would talk together—there would be so much to say, so much to plan.

Vivien would have awakened Dawson from his sleep, if he had been asleep.

He might have been lying awake thinking over the big decision he had made this morning, the decision on which his whole future rested. And now his courage had won not only the opportunity of a great career, but also the woman he loved.

Suddenly Ann felt very lonely. She had spoken to Vivien of love and of happiness, but she had been speaking of the past.

She had Myra and the twins, it was true, but she knew that she also wanted the companionship that she and her father had enjoyed together. How close it had been, how satisfying in every way!

Yet would it always have proved enough? Ann asked herself the question.

Would she not as she had grown older have wanted more? Might not she have also fallen in love, have found a man to whom she could give her heart and soul?

She thought of how when she was very young, she had imagined, as all girls do, the face of the man she would marry.

He would be tall and handsome, she had been sure of that, and he would love her and want her, and she would be able to do things for him, look after him, help him, guide him and encourage him by her faith and trust.

She had imagined all that, and yet none of it had happened. She had never met a man who had made her heart beat fast, she had never fallen in love, and there had been little time for men to fall in love with her.

One or two had undoubtedly been attracted, but she had not considered them seriously, she had been too busy with her little family, with her father and the cares of the household.

Then John had invaded their home. That was the

right word ... he had invaded them, though it had been no choice of his.

Was perhaps fate working on her behalf, even as it had worked for Vivien? Ann asked herself the question but did not know the answer.

She only knew that something within her ached and longed to experience that ecstasy that she had seen for a moment on Vivien's face.

She, too, wanted to be transformed, to know the quivering wonder of awaking love, to know that moment of surrender when one gave oneself into a man's keeping.

She slipped on her nightgown and got into bed. The linen sheets were cool and smooth and she felt for a moment as though she must shiver; then as her limbs relaxed she knew she was very tired. She reached out her hand to turn out the bedside lamp.

She had asked Vivien if she would not feel lonely when she was alone in her great room. She dare not ask herself the same question.

Resolutely Ann closed her eyes. It had been a long and tiring day, so much had happened, and yet in some ways it had all been very wonderful. Myra was back with her, and she herself had made two new friends. She wanted friends, and she knew that Vivien and Dawson would prove themselves such in the future.

She closed her eyes; the waves of sleep were creeping slowly over her when suddenly there was a click as of a door opening.

She was so tired that it was an effort to force herself back to consciousness, and then she realised that light was invading her room, a long shaft of golden light. It came from the open door which led to John's dressing room.

Instinctively Ann lay still.

She was awake now, and her heart was beating quickly with fear and apprehension of the unknown. Someone was coming into the room.

She knew who it was and she forced herself to keep her eyes closed. The steps, so soft that she could hardly hear them, grew nearer to the bed.

She was aware of him standing there looking down at her.

The light from the open door fell softly on her face. She lay so still that she hardly dared to breathe, and only as the moments passed was she aware that she had clenched her hands beneath the bedclothes so tightly that the nails were biting into the skin.

John did not move.

Ann waited, waited with every nerve in her body tense in case he should touch her, in case he should speak her name. Then softly, very softly, he sighed, and the footsteps retreated—back, back to the door.

There was a gentle click followed by utter silence.

For some moments Ann did not dare open her eyes. At last she raised her lids very slowly. The room was in darkness, and she was alone. Then only was she conscious of the throbbing of her pulses.

She sat up in bed, looking into the soft darkness wondering why he had come and what it meant. Was this the first time, or had he been there before?

She did not understand it, and she wondered now why she had pretended to be asleep. Why had she not frankly and openly told him she was awake and asked him what he wanted?

Again Ann could find no answers to her own questions. She lay down again, turned restlessly from side to side. Her own questions seemed to haunt her. They were like ghosts at her bedside questioning her, questioning her.

"I shall never sleep," she told herself, and fell into a dreamless slumber even as she thought it. . . .

In the morning the memories of what had happened during the night came flooding back to her after she was called. Ann lay for a long time while her early morning tea grew cold thinking of that strange visitation.

Resolutely she tried to treat it as something quite ordinary and commonplace; she who had prided herself on her own common sense could surely find an explanation for this?

Might not John have come to her room earlier in the evening and then, wondering what had happened to her, had come once again to make sure she had returned?

Perhaps he had wanted an aspirin or some other remedy for a headache or sleeplessness.

There were many explanations she told herself, but she knew that not one of them rang true or was in the slightest convincing.

"What does it matter?" she asked finally, metaphorically shrugging her shoulders and trying to force her thoughts to centre on Vivien, on Myra and the twins.

There were so many things to think of, and it was indeed the thought of Myra which finally made her spring up, dress quickly and go downstairs a good quarter of an hour before the breakfast gong was sounded.

Lady Melton breakfasted in her own bedroom and so did Vivien, but Ann had said firmly that she preferred breakfast downstairs as had been her habit, all her life. Besides, she liked to superintend the twins, seeing that they ate and drank the proper things.

This morning she had another reason for being down early.

The post at Gulliver arrived about ten minutes to nine, ten minutes before the hour scheduled for the breakfast gong. The letters were sorted by the butler, and those for the members of the household who came downstairs were laid aside beside their places at the breakfast table. Would Tommy Rankin have written to Myra? This was the question Ann asked herself, and she hurried down determined to see for herself. She was so early that the post had not yet arrived.

Instead, the letters written the previous day, which the postman used to collect when he called, were stacked ready in a neat pile on the big table by the front door.

Ann looked at the pile wondering if she would ever have such a voluminous correspondence as was Lady Melton's.

Suddenly a thought struck her. Looking quickly round to see there was no one watching, she went through the letters. Halfway down the pile she found what she sought. A letter in Myra's big, schoolgirlish writing addressed to "Major Tommy Rankin"!

Half ashamed of herself and yet convinced in her own heart that what she was doing was for the best, Ann extracted the letter and going into the morning-room shut the door behind her.

She looked at the envelope.

What has Myra said? she wondered.

It seemed hardly possible that the girl had found time yesterday to write to anyone. Had she done it last night before she went to bed or had she got up very early this morning?

Ann found herself afraid, as she had been afraid yesterday, for Myra, for her sweet untouched youth. She remembered the expression on Tommy Rankin's face when she had made it clear that Myra was to be independent. She guessed that it might be easy if Myra's heart was not too deeply involved, to shake him off and get rid of him now; but if Myra was tenacious, hanging on to him, wanting him, what then?

Ann made a decision.

Quickly she tore the letter still in its unopened envelope into small pieces.

Then she laid it at the side of the hearth and taking a box of matches, burnt it slowly, piece by piece. Myra's writing curled and quivered at her as the flames rose, but she forced herself to concentrate only on the burning of the paper and not to read a single word. In that at least she would be honourable to her sister.

"One day she will thank me," Ann said shakily as

she looked down at the little pile of charred ashes. Then she put the matches back in their place and went from the room into the hall.

The post had arrived and Barker was sorting the letters.

"Good morning, m'lady."

"Anything for me, Barker?"

"No, m'lady."

"Anything for Miss Myra? I don't know whether she will be down to breakfast after such a late night. I was just going up to her room."

"No, nothing, m'lady."

Ann drew a sigh of relief, then quickly she ran upstairs.

She opened the door of Myra's room softly. Myra was still asleep, the curtains had been drawn back, and her early morning tea stood untouched beside her. Her hands were raised behind her head, and with her eyes closed and her face in repose she looked very young and defenceless.

Ann stood looking at her.

"Oh, darling," she murmured in her heart, "I hope I have done the right thing for you. It's dangerous to interfere with other people's lives, and yet what I have done I have done because I love you."

Myra stirred suddenly. Her eyes opened; instantly there was a smile on her face.

"Hallo, Ann, am I frightfully late?"

"It doesn't matter a bit," Ann said. "Would you like to have breakfast in bed?"

"Good heavens, no. I'll be down in a jiffy. Is Charles waiting for me?"

"There's no sign of anyone yet," Ann said, "but why Charles?"

"We are going bathing; I told you, don't you remember?"

"Oh, but not till much later in the morning. Nobody here gets up very early. You forget you are living amongst the idle rich!"

Myra laughed as she jumped out of bed.

"Goodness, money is enjoyable, isn't it? When I think what fun last night was I could shout for joy, and I am going to have lots more fun today, too."

"With Charles?"

"With Charles," Myra nodded. "I think he's a very attractive young man!"

She skipped across the room in her nightgown and into the bathroom.

"I'll be down in ten minutes."

At that moment the deep notes of the gong vibrated through the house.

"I won't wait for you," Ann said.

"Well, keep some breakfast for me," Myra shouted, "I'm hungry."

Certainly no one ever sounded more heart-whole or less lovelorn for the man she had left behind her.

"Perhaps I've been unduly fussy," Ann thought to herself.

Nevertheless she was glad that she had burnt the letter to Tommy Rankin. Let Myra concentrate on Charles!

"She will come to little harm there," Ann thought to herself; and she smiled secretly at the thought of him.

As she reached the top of the stairs, she saw John standing in the hall below her. He raised his eyes and saw her.

Suddenly and inexplicably she felt the blood rising in her cheeks in a burning crimson wave.

Why . . . why . . . had he come to her room last night?

Seventeen

Ann looking out of the neatly curtained window saw the rain falling in a gentle summer drizzle over the garden with its geranium-filled flower-beds and tidily clipped box hedges.

The grey skies made the room in which she waited seem shadowed and chill and unconsciously she shivered and turned from the window to look around her.

The room gave the impression of being furnished with souvenirs.

There was a beaten brass tray from Benares, a rhinoceros horn from Africa, a model of the fat-stomached, laughing god of good luck and various small pieces of crested china, some inscribed with "A Present from Blackpool" or "A Memory of Southend".

Were these, Ann wondered, sincere expressions of gratitude? If so, what were the people like who chose them?

The room, however, made up in personality what it lacked in taste. There were innumerable photographs on the writing-desk; there were two or three amateurish but charming water-colours on the walls and there were flowers everywhere.

The flowers were arranged without much sense of decoration, but they gave the impression that they had been chosen because the person who picked them loved to be surrounded by their colour and fragrance.

And yet despite the scent of the flowers in the room there was another smell which slowly and insidiously impressed itself so that it was impossible to escape from the realisation of what it was . . . anaesthetic.

Ann looked at her watch. She had been told to be at the nursing home at eleven-thirty; it was now twelve o'clock, and she had not yet been allowed to see her mother-in-law.

"How I should hate to be here myself!" she thought; yet looking round the matron's room she could well believe that whoever entered these walls would have not only the attention, but the affection of those who ministered to them.

She had seen the matron and liked her warm, smiling Irish face. She had liked too, the way she spoke of each of her patients as though he or she were a clever and beloved child.

"Lady Melton's been wonderful," she told Ann. "I have seldom had a more courageous patient in my care."

"She knows the whole truth then?" Ann asked.

Matron nodded.

"She insisted on being told almost at once. With some people it's better to be frank. Your mother-in-law is one of them."

Ann thought how she was dreading the interview which lay ahead and wondered exactly what she would say, how she would express her sorrow.

She was used to sick people, used, too, to those who knew they were to die; but they had been her father's patients—village people—Lady Melton was different!

It was hard to think of that efficient, busy woman facing the fact that the months ahead of her were numbered. It was all so bewildering and had happened so quickly and even now Ann could hardly believe that there was not some mistake.

It was rather horrifying to remember that all the time she had been at Gulliver Lady Melton must have been in pain, suffering when those around her had thought her merely sharp and disagreeable.

That irritability was understandable now when one
244

became aware that it was but the natural reaction to hidden torments.

Ann sighed and moved restlessly about the room. Would they never come downstairs to fetch her? She wanted to get it over.

"Mother wants to see you," John had told her yesterday, "and to see you alone."

"Alone?" Ann echoed the word.

"Yes, she particularly said that she would like to see you alone," John replied.

Ann longed to ask him why, or if there was any particular reason for this request, but somehow she felt that the least she could do was to acquiesce agreeably in whatever was suggested. John himself was so reserved that it was difficult to know if he was desperately upset about his mother or not.

When he told Ann the doctor's verdict, he had spoken gravely and seriously as was somehow characteristic of him, and it had been impossible to detect how emotionally he was disturbed by the prospect of his mother's death.

It had come as a bombshell to Ann, for she had had so much to think about that she had hardly noticed her mother-in-law's departure nor indeed given more than a passing thought to the fact that she was going into a nursing home.

At the time Antoinette had a touch of the sun, nothing very serious, but enough to give her a temperature and to make her very sick and sorry for herself. Ann had kept her in bed, but she had come up one evening to find Antoinette, who should have been asleep, romping about the bedroom scantily dressed in only her nightgown. Of course she had caught a cold and had run another and more feverish temperature which had worried Ann considerably, and which the doctor diagnosed as "summer 'flu".

This time Ann decided to take no chances on Antoinette making herself worse, and she moved upstairs, sleeping with the child and tending her both

245

day and night. John had protested that he would send for a trained nurse, but Ann had refused.

"I have always looked after the twins when they were ill," she told him, "and they would hate to have a stranger fussing over them. If you will keep Antony out of mischief, I shall be more than grateful. Don't worry, I will soon have Antoinette on her feet again."

"I was worrying about you more than Antoinette," John replied.

Ann smiled at him.

"That is very nice of you, but I would rather do things my own way. After all the twins are my responsibility."

"Very well, if that is what you wish," John answered.

Ann had moved upstairs, hardly leaving Antoinette's room even for a breath of air until the fever had subsided and Antoinette was her old self again.

"We might as well isolate ourselves while we are about it," Ann said. She remembered how particular her father had been about isolation when any of the children had an infectious complaint, however slight.

Being therefore out of touch with things she was surprised when she came downstairs a week later to find that Sinclair and Charles were still at Gulliver and had not left for their holiday visits as she had anticipated.

"I didn't expect to find you here," she said to Charles.

"John was very firm that you did not wish to see us," Charles said, "otherwise I should have braved the bubonic plague on your behalf."

"But why haven't you gone away?"

Charles looked grave.

"I think John ought to tell you that himself; you will find him in the library."

Curious, but putting duty first, Ann went in search not of John but of Antoinette, who wrapped up in a warm coat was ready to take her first walk in the sunshine. Myra and Antony were with her and they were talking eagerly.

"Hallo, darling, it's lovely to see you," Myra exclaimed.

"I'm glad to see you, too," Ann replied. "Antoinette and I feel as though we have been marooned on a desert island. What have you been doing? What has been happening?"

"I've been having a wonderful time," Myra said quickly. "I've got such lots of things to tell you. Charles and I motored to the sea yesterday and had a bathe; it was perfectly scrumptious, and he's promised to go again and take Antoinette as soon as she's well enough. Would you like that, poppet?"

"It would be heavenly," Antoinette cried.

"I thought Charles was going away?" Ann questioned.

"None of them have gone,'" Myra said. "Haven't you heard?"

"Heard what?"

"About Lady Melton."

"I've heard nothing," Ann replied.

"She's ill, frightfully ill."

"Why, what's the matter with her?"

"Fancy you not knowing," Myra exclaimed. "I thought John would have written to you even if you did make all that fuss about seeing none of us."

"He didn't," said Ann shortly, "so suppose you tell me."

"Well, you know she went into a nursing home to have an examination. Apparently, although she didn't say so, it entailed a sort of operation even to examine her.

"The doctors rang up afterwards and that was the first time that John or anyone realised how serious it was.

"They said that Lady Melton's condition was very grave indeed and they wanted to see him at once.

John went off immediately and when he came back he told us that his mother had . . . cancer."

"Cancer!" Ann exclaimed, "How terrible!"

"It's awful isn't it?" Myra agreed, "and they have given her only a few months to live. They can't do much for her, she's past the stage where a proper operation would do any good."

"But Myra, this is ghastly!" Ann exclaimed. "I must go and find John at once. Why didn't somebody tell me?"

"What could you have done anyway?" Myra asked with practical common sense. "What can you do now for that matter?"

"I don't know," Ann said, "but I feel I ought to have been told."

She realised that Myra and the twins were taking this tragedy to John's mother in a philosophical, practical manner, which was, of course, the inevitable result of their upbringing.

They were so used to hearing of people being ill and dying that it meant precisely nothing to them unless the person concerned was a very close friend. But Ann's reaction lay particularly in the knowledge that she had never liked her mother-in-law.

There was something sinister in knowing that someone one had disliked—almost indeed hated—was to die quickly and unexpectedly. In some ridiculous manner Ann almost felt responsible.

This, she knew, was only the fantasy of overwrought nerves, but she went white-faced in search of John.

John, as Charles had told her, was in the library. He welcomed her appearance and then confirmed what Myra had already related, speaking of his mother calmly and with what seemed to Ann a singular lack of feeling.

"Supposing it had been Daddy," she thought and knew it would have been hard to restrain her agony at the thought of him waiting patiently yet irretrievably for death.

Better that he had died the way he did than this. There was something horrible about the idea of waiting, waiting for the inevitable.

The door behind Ann opened. She turned quickly as Matron came in.

"I'm sorry to have been so long," Matron smiled; "the doctor came unexpectedly. I was not expecting him until this afternoon, but now at last your mother-in-law is ready for you."

Bustling ahead she led the way across the hall and up the thickly carpeted stairs to the first floor.

It was a nursing home which had a name for being the last word in comfort and for individual attention, yet it seemed to Ann that it had, as had every other home she had ever known, that atmosphere of impermanence which made one feel that one was not a person, but just an occupant of a room—coming with the fear of not going out. . . .

Matron opened the door of a bedroom.

"Here is your daughter-in-law, Lady Melton," she said in bright clear tones which the professional nurse so often assumes when speaking to a patient.

Ann followed Matron into the room.

There were clean, shining walls, a bay-window overlooking the garden and there were flowers everywhere—flowers which Ann recognised as having come from Gulliver.

They were very different from the simple, jumbled bunches in Matron's sitting-room. Here there were orchids, carnations, lilies and every possible hot-house flower.

There were great bowls of fruit, too, arranged on the table at the side of the bed. Lady Melton was propped up against the pillows which matched the bedspread of oyster-satin and antique lace.

For a moment Ann thought it was ridiculous even

249

to have imagined that she could be ill, for she looked so very much as usual.

Her grey hair was dressed neatly on top of her head, and she wore a deep purple velvet dressing-jacket trimmed with narrow bands of sable which was infinitely becoming.

Lady Melton was watching as Ann walked across the room towards the bed, and as usual she felt small and insignificant with her mother-in-law's eyes upon her. Matron brought her a chair and she sat down.

"Now I will leave you two for a nice gossip," Matron said. "Don't talk if you feel tired, Lady Melton, and ring for a nurse if you want her; the bell is beside you."

"Thank you." Lady Melton's voice was quiet.

The door closed behind Matron, and the two women were left alone.

Ann made an effort.

"I don't know how to tell you how sorry I am," she said nervously. "I wanted to write to you, but John said you would much rather not have letters."

"I have had quite enough of them," Lady Melton replied, indicating a large pile which lay on the bed at her side.

"I'm sorry, so terribly sorry," Ann repeated rather lamely.

"That is good of you," Lady Melton replied.

It seemed to Ann there was a curious inflection in her voice.

There was a pause which Ann found infinitely embarrassing, and then her mother-in-law spoke.

"I asked you to come over this morning, and I told John that I wanted to see you alone."

"Yes, he told me."

"I have a reason for that request."

"Yes?"

"John will have told you that I have not very long to live, Ann; it may be three months, it may be six," Lady Melton went on. "It depends how quickly the growth develops, but I have insisted on knowing the truth. For the last month or so at least I shall be under morphia most of the time and know very little of what is going on."

She spoke without any emotion in her voice whatsoever. She might have been speaking of some third person in whom neither of them was particularly interested.

"I'm sorry," Ann murmured again.

It was all she could think of to say.

"What I wanted to ask you," Lady Melton continued, "was if you minded my coming back to Gulliver. I would, if it is possible, like to die there. I want you to be perfectly frank. If you think it will upset you, if it will overshadow your future, I will stay here."

"But of course you must come." Ann stammered, surprised almost beyond words at the request.

"No, don't answer me like that," Lady Melton said. "I want you to consider what you are saying."

She smiled, and it seemed to Ann that the smile was softer and more gentle than anything she had seen on her mother-in-law's face before.

"I am well aware, Ann, that I have not been very kind to you. There's no reason why you should consider me now."

"But you mustn't say that," Ann said quickly.

"Why not, when it's true?" Lady Melton asked. "My dear child, I have been many things in my life; but I have never been a hypocrite and I have never pretended to myself. I know where my own discrepancies lie, and since I have been here, digesting all the doctors have told me, I have seen many things more clearly and perhaps I might say more humanely."

She looked away from Ann across the room where the great vases of flowers banked the ugly mantelpiece and made it almost a bower of beauty.

"I suppose it's a shock for everyone when they are told they are going to die," Lady Melton said softly.

251

"We all want to live, and we all believe that death is so far ahead that we needn't worry about it. And yet one faces up to it, one's whole perspective changes. Things fall into their right proportion—many of them which seemed so vitally important become very small and trivial."

Lady Melton paused. Ann said nothing; she could only sit still and tense, her eyes on her mother-in-law's face.

"And yet, when one is faced with death," Lady Melton went on, "one has the relief of knowing one need not pretend any more, one need not even strive, one can just lie back and be honest both with one-self and with other people. It is quite a relief, I find."

She looked at Ann and smiled again. She seemed to be waiting and nervously Ann broke the silence.

"But of course you must come to Gulliver; John would want that."

"Will he? I don't really know," Lady Melton said. "I have not made it a particularly happy place for John, that is why now I want you to make it a home for him in the future."

"Me?"

Somehow the monosyllable escaped Ann's lips before she thought.

"Yes, you, my dear. Who else?"

Ann dropped her eyes.

This whole conversation was bewildering; she was not quite sure where it was carrying her.

"Listen, Ann," Lady Melton was speaking again, "I want to tell you something. Vivien came to see me yesterday. She told me that she is going to marry Dawson and that it is due to you.

"She told me how much they both owe to you for the happiness they are certain is going to be theirs in the future. I began to think after that, to think very seriously of John's future, and yours.

"I've been cruel to him. It seems funny for me to

252

say that to you, doesn't it? but as I have said, one stops pretending at moments like this.

"Yes, I've been cruel all through my life to John—my only child."

Ann raised her eyes once again. Lady Melton was looking at the flowers.

There was no particular emotion in her voice while she spoke; it was clear and precise; yet Ann had the feeling that the older woman was at this very moment passing through some deep crisis.

"It seems funny," Lady Melton continued, "to want to explain myself to anyone, but I do want to explain myself to you. I don't suppose anyone has told you much about me. They haven't told you, for instance, that I came from an obscure country vicarage in Yorkshire, from a poverty-stricken home, and that I was one of a family of six girls."

Ann looked surprised.

"I had no idea."

"I made, of course, what was called a brilliant marriage. You can perhaps understand the excitement there was when John's father, Sir Frank Melton, rode over from his grandmother's house where he was staying and formally asked my hand in marriage.

"I was in the seventh heaven of happiness. One moment I had been a household drudge, the eldest, on whom many of the household cares and responsibilities rested, the next I was the envy of my family and friends, the girl who had captured the richest and most distinguished young man who ever came to our neighbourhood.

"What was more, I was in love. I had adored, almost worshipped Frank ever since we had played together as children.

"We got married, and it was only after I married that I learned the reason for my good fortune.

"Perhaps for a modern young woman who is more capable of looking after herself it would have not been such a shock, but when I learned that my husband had married me out of pique and because the woman he really cared for, being married to someone else, would not risk a scandal for his sake, I wanted only to die.

"Even after all these years I can still remember my utter despairing misery . . . the bitterness of my tears . . . the anguish I suffered. . . .

"Then pride came to my rescue. Our family is an old one, I had a tradition behind me. I was, too, the daughter of a clergyman who believed utterly in the sanctity of marriage. I was determined that whatever other people knew, no I would never give them the satisfaction of even guessing that I was unhappy. I was 'Lady Melton of Gulliver'. That, I told myself, should be sufficient for me.

"My husband neglected me; I expect in reality he found me gauche and a bore after the very polished perfection of the woman he really loved.

"At any rate, he left me very much alone. I was resolute that no one should be sorry for me. I was only twenty-two, but I decided there and then to make myself powerful and formidable.

"People should never pity me—better that they should be frightened of me than that.

"Now, looking back, I'm sorry for that young bride. Gulliver seemed very big, and she was very much alone!

"Even as I steeled myself not to show my wounds, not to acknowledge even to my closest and most intimate friends the hurt I suffered day after day by my husband's indifference, so I taught myself never to ask affection or to give it.

"When John was born, it was a week before my husband left London to come down to visit me and see his son. In that week my bitterness caused me almost to hate my child as much as I told myself I hated my husband. In reality I loved them both . . . desperately . . . hungrily.

"It was, I suppose, during those first years of my married life that I grew to be afraid of affection; it

254

night have broken my determination, destroyed the armour in which I faced the world.

"I brought up John never to be demonstrative. I would not let myself kiss him when he was a baby, and he was rebuked if he kissed me. His nurses were given strict instructions not to encourage any sort of sentiment in the child.

"Now—now I have begun to wonder what I have done! Are you wise and strong enough to break down the barriers of reserve which I have created in him?

"Strange though it may seem to you, I love my son. I have always loved him, but now that I have got so short a time ahead of me to right the things that I have done wrong,

"I am beginning to be afraid in case I have destroyed his happiness."

"Do you think he is unhappy?"

"Do you think he is happy?" Lady Melton asked the question softly, and Ann had no answer to give her.

"And you," Lady Melton went on, "I know you are not happy. That I can understand. I, too, have been overpowered by Gulliver, I, too have suffered there."

Ann did not answer. There was sympathy in the older woman's voice which made her feel perilously near tears. Lady Melton sighed.

"I wonder if it's too late for me to put anything right?" she asked, and there was something wistful and almost pathetic in the question.

"Perhaps it will all come right in time," Ann said.

She could not pretend, could not in the face of her mother-in-law's utter frankness answer her with lies—pretend to her that she and John were happy, or that she had been mistaken in her shrewd assumption of the position.

"You think so?" Lady Melton's expression lightened for the moment, and then she sighed.

"Don't be proud," she advised. "I was too proud; but now when I need friends, when I need love, when

I need the affection of those who belong to me, realise that instead they can give me only admiration An admiration for what?—for efficiency, for my powe for the position I have created for myself. 'The form dable Lady Melton', yes, I have heard them say of me, and I know now just how much it means."

"But you mustn't be sad," Ann said quickly. "Peopl do admire you. I have been afraid of you. It was stupi of me, but . . ."

"Not stupid," Lady Melton interrupted. "It wa what I wanted you to be, what I liked most peopl to be, because it kept them at arm's length.

"Can't you understand that even as Vivien has ru away from poverty all her life, so I have run awa from love. I have wanted love, so much that I hav been afraid of it, afraid of my own desire for it."

Lady Melton put out her hand.

"I want you to forgive me, Ann," she said, "an I want you to help me in these last few months tha I am allowed to live to try to put some things right You advised Vivien. In the short time that you hav known her you have managed to alter her life an given her happiness. I have known her much longer I was fond of her in my own way and yet I coul not do that.

"I could only encourage her to want what I knev in my heart of hearts were not the right things but which I was too proud to admit were the wrong.'

Ann slipped her hand into her mother-in-law's It was strange to feel the other woman's fingers thin and chill, press her own.

"Try to make John happy," Lady Melton whispered "I love him even though I have been foolish enougl to hide it all these years. Now, when it's too late, want to give him the affection he has always missed.'

"I will try," Ann promised, but even as she saic it she felt almost ashamed of her promise.

How could she make John happy, how could she feeling as she did about him?

As if Lady Melton sensed her thoughts she said: "John loves you."

Ann answered her quickly. "He has never said so."

"Perhaps that's my fault, perhaps he, too, is afraid to express his own feelings."

Ann took her hand from her mother-in-law's and pressed her fingers together in her lap. Somehow she could not bear to continue this conversation about herself and John.

Why she did not know, but she shrank from it, feeling that it laid bare the secrets of her own heart which were better hid.

Lady Melton sighed again and then asked her original question.

"So I may come to Gulliver?"

"Of course."

"And when I do we will be friends, you and I, Ann, until—the end?"

It was a question, but Ann answered it simply. "Thank you."

There was a knock on the door. A nurse came in.

"Matron says she will get into trouble with the doctors if your visitor stays much longer, Lady Melton."

Ann looked at her watch. It was a quarter to one. "I must go home," she said and got to her feet.

"I am rather tired," Lady Melton confessed. "But I hope in a day or two the doctors will let me come home."

"Is there anything you want?" Ann asked.

"I have got everything, thank you," Lady Melton replied. "Good-bye."

Ann hesitated, and then impulsively she bent over and kissed her mother-in-law's cheek. For a moment she thought the older woman was going to repulse her, and then a very faint flush stained the pallor of her skin.

"Thank you, dear," she said. As Ann turned away she knew Lady Melton had been pleased at her gesture.

Driving back to Gulliver, she found herself going over the conversation, even more astonished now when she had time to consider it than she had been at the time.

It made so many things seem clear; it explained so much that had been merely frightening. Suddenly it seemed to her that she heard her father chuckle and heard his voice ask humorously:

"Didn't I tell you that everyone is human once you get under their skin?"

Eighteen

Ann came downstairs after having tucked the twins up for the night.

It was a warm summer's evening, and the hall door stood open. Outside there was twilight, the lake reflecting the deepening sky in which the first evening stars twinkled.

She could hear voices in the drawing-room, but the utter silence and peace outside drew her. She walked across the hall to stand at the door, conscious that the night breeze on her cheeks was cool and fresh after the heat of the day.

The breeze stirred the soft chiffon of the dress she wore, making her feel as if it caressed her and drew her away from the world into the mystic unknown. She felt something stirring within her, she had the idea that something was about to happen, what she did not know.

Was it merely a prelude to a thunderstorm or something more personal, something which might occur in her own life?

"I am growing fanciful," Ann thought.

Yet she did not move away, but leaned closer against the grey stone of the house.

She thought of all the tumultuous events of the last few weeks; she thought of her mother-in-law and how an enemy had become a friend. She thought also of Vivien to whom she had spoken earlier that evening on the telephone.

Vivien was in London, "garret hunting", she had told Ann laughingly, but there was something proud and tremulous in her voice, too, and Ann knew that however poor the house or flat that Vivien and Dawson were to live in, Vivien would make it a home because at last she loved and was loved.

"How happy they are!" Unconsciously Ann sighed.

Upstairs in her drawer were two letters, one from Dawson and one from Vivien.

They had written to thank her, telling her how much they felt they owed her, and how they would never forget their gratitude in the years to come. It made her happy to read their letters and she knew that they were written with both sincerity and affection.

How much had happened lately! But Ann could not help thinking that her own life remained the same.

She and John were still strangers, still acquaintances who met and were polite to each other, but who got to know each other no better.

She had tried to see him in a new light since Lady Melton's revelations, but it was hard.

It was one thing to imagine the loneliness of a little boy whose mother kept him at arm's length, who had no affection and no love offered to him, only the grandeur of an historic home and the cold consolation of an honoured name.

Ann knew maternally that she could yearn for that little boy, long to pick him up in her arms and cuddle him, to watch his face light up, to feel his kisses warm upon her cheek.

It was a very different thing to remember that

same small boy was the grave, serious John of whom she was so inexplicably afraid.

It was no use arguing with herself—she was afraid of him, she knew it in that tingling consciousness that was hers when he came into the room; she knew it by the tenseness of her muscles when he came near her, by the beating of her pulses when she remembered that strange mysterious visit to her bedroom when he had thought she was asleep.

She wondered if he had ever come again, and often at night she would lie wide-eyed in the darkness, listening for the click of the door; but if he did come she did not know it, and morning came without her being disturbed.

"What do I want?" Ann asked herself now and shrank from the question.

Inevitably the answer showed her Vivien's face, ecstatic and quivering, with that look of radiance which only love can bring.

It was growing dark now, the trees in the park were deep shadowed, the lake was the colour of molten silver, steel beneath a sable sky. Ann turned to go into the house, and as she did so the drawing-room door opened and Charles came out.

"Ann," he exclaimed. "I wondered where you were; I was just coming to look for you."

"Do you want me?" Ann asked.

"I always want you," Charles answered; "but particularly so at this moment."

Ann smiled. "Well, I am here."

"So I see."

He looked at her appraisingly, his eyes travelling from the top of her beautifully groomed head down to the crimson toes of her satin shoes peeping beneath the folds of her dress.

"I suppose it would be banal of me to say that you look lovely?"

"You can't say it often enough," Ann retorted.

"Strange though it seems, I like hearing nice things about myself."

"I suppose by that you are inferring that you don't hear enough?" Charles asked. "My dear, don't get conceited; one of your most charming qualities is your lack of selfconsciousness."

He spoke so seriously that Ann had to laugh at his tone.

"I don't think you need worry," she said. "You and Antony are the only men in the house who pay me compliments. They are rare, and because they are rare I appreciate them."

"You will have all the compliments you want when John takes you to London," Charles said; "and when you are the great success of the social world, you will look back and laugh to think that you even so much as listened to my feeble efforts."

"Why this sudden modesty?" Ann teased.

"I am feeling humble," Charles told her. "That is what I want to talk to you about. Let us go into the orangery; we shall not be disturbed there."

Curious as to what he wanted, Ann led the way. The orangery at Gulliver was built out from the south wall and had been originally designed in the reign of Charles the Second.

It had been added to since; but perfectly proportioned and exquisite in every detail, it was one of the most famous and beautiful features of the house. The flowers, too, were breath-taking, and Lady Melton had gone to immense pains to see that their arrangement by the gardeners enhanced rather than detracted from the architecture.

The windows looked directly on to the lake, so that sometimes one had the illusion that one was at sea, floating in a ship of flowers over silver water.

Ann led the way to a comfortable sofa situated in an alcove where they often sat after meals.

There were big orange-coloured cushions, and she

put one behind her head as she settled herself comfortably.

"What are you going to tell me?" she asked. "Is it good news or bad?"

"That is for you to say," Charles replied enigmatically.

Ann raised her eyebrows.

"Am I concerned in this?"

"Very much so," Charles answered.

Ann was suddenly aware that in some way he was different. She looked at him and realised what it was. For perhaps the first time since she had met him, Charles was looking serious, almost grave.

She was so used to his smile, to the twinkle in his eye and the slightly mocking quality in his voice that Ann realised that this was a new Charles, one she had never known.

"I want to tell you about myself," Charles said—"and Myra."

"Myra!" Ann echoed the word.

Charles took a deep breath.

"I want your permission to marry your sister."

Ann was too startled for the moment to say anything. She could only stare at him, and then at last she ejaculated:

"But she's much too young!"

"I felt you would say that," Charles replied, "but will you listen to me for a moment, Ann? I am twenty-seven, nine years older than Myra. I have lived, as you very likely know, a lazy, useless life ever since I grew up. It is very easy to make excuses for oneself, I know that, but I took the line of least resistance.

"People always told me that I was no use at anything, and so I believed them, or at least I made no effort either to contradict or disillusion them.

"I might have done something decent in the war if I hadn't been wounded fairly early on and found it quite impossible to get a medical board to let me fly again; and so I loafed around enjoying myself to a certain extent, but at the same time being just as lazy and improvident as people seemed to expect me to be.

"You are your father's son all over again," people would say, shaking their heads at me. "He never did an honest day's work in his life!"

"As long as John was prepared to keep me, I didn't see why I should trouble myself unduly. I liked being here, I liked being able to spend the little money I made one way and another on myself and where it suited me.

"I designed dresses because it amused me. I could, I suppose, have struck out on my own and made a name for myself; instead I was prepared to let my friend take the credit.

"In fact, Ann dear, I saw no reason to exert myself in any way until I met Myra.

"I admired you; I thought you were one of the loveliest people I had ever seen. I liked you, I wanted to make love to you, but I was never really in love with you. I don't think I ever have been in love in the way I am—now."

"And Myra?" Ann asked the question quickly.

"Myra loves me," Charles replied. "I know what you will say to that, that she has been in love with other people; but not in the same way, and I promise you one thing, that Myra's love for me will be a real and lasting thing because I love her so tremendously."

There was a deep emotion in Charles's voice, but Ann looked at him with troubled eyes.

"But, Charles, are you certain this is wise? Myra is so young, she has seen so little of the world."

"Myra wants looking after," Charles answered. "You know that better than anyone else; and Ann, don't you understand? that is what is so wonderful. For the first time in my life I have found somebody who wants to rely on me.

"Up to now I have always been looked after; now

263

for the first time I am the responsible person. I am the man, and I know that whatever I undertake I shall not fail, because Myra will be dependent on me!"

Ann smiled; it was impossible not to be impressed by his sincerity.

"I suppose," she said, "that in reality you and Myra have fixed everything up and there is nothing left for me to say."

"Oh, Ann, you're magnificent," Charles explained. "No one but you could have carried the conversation so far and not asked what we are going to live on.

"You are concerned with what we feel about each other, and that I promise you is really the only thing that matters, but only one person in a million would have refrained from inquiring how I propose to keep a wife.

"As you have not asked me that, I will tell you. Two or three days ago, when I knew that Myra loved me as much as I love her, I went to London. I looked up various people and followed up contracts that I had made some years ago, with the result that I have been offered—I have the letter in my pocket at this moment—the chance of heading a trade mission to South America.

"The dress designers and textile manufacturers of this country want someone to go out and see that their goods are put in a favourable light. They have offered me the job of arranging the whole thing. I chose my own staff, I do everything.

"If I make a success of this, and I shall, there will be undoubtedly a very wide field open for me on my return."

"And Myra?" Ann inquired.

"Myra will go with me, of course. Can't you see that she will be one of my biggest assets."

Charles smiled, but Ann looked at him in something nearing astonishment. This was indeed a man she had never known before. There was determination and drive in all he said. Already it seemed to her there was a note of authority in his voice.

She knew without his telling her any more that Charles had at last found his right métier. He may have been lazy in the past, but now he seemed galvanised with energy.

"Oh, Charles, I'm glad for your sake," she cried. "It all sounds very exciting."

"We shall have to be married very shortly."

"It wouldn't be better to wait until your return?"

"And leave Myra here alone to fall in love with someone else? Not on your life," Charles replied. "I want her, she wants me; but I'm not such a fool as to think that anyone so attractive or so young as Myra would not be liable to forgetfulness if one was out of sight.

"No, Ann. I am marrying Myra now and taking her with me. One does not leave lovely valuable things lying around unattended."

"It is all arrranged then? And yet you have asked me my permission. Thank you, Charles, for the formality."

"We want your good wishes and your help now and always."

"You know you will have both," Ann said softly, "and oh, Charles, I am glad, really and truly, I am glad."

"I promise you one thing, Myra shall not regret marrying me, I will make her happy or die in the attempt."

His words were in the nature of a vow. Instinctively Ann held out both her hands to him; he took them and raised them to his lips.

"Thank you, Ann; and now, there is only one thing we want to ask you."

"What is that?"

"We don't want you to tell anyone else as yet."

"Why not?"

"I want to have the whole position clear and the contract in my pocket before I spring an engagement on an astonished world," Charles smiled. "You know what business men are like, they may feel that if I am getting married I shall not be able to give so much attention to their concerns.

"Actually, as you know, it's entirely on Myra's account that I shall work, but they are not to know that, and it is a wise precaution from a business point of view first to catch your hare."

"I understand," Ann said. She could not help faintly smiling to herself at Charles's thinking all this out, considering every detail. It was so unlike his usual casual acceptance of anything the day might bring.

Indeed, "Take no thought for tomorrow" might have been Charles's motto in the past. Now he was leaving nothing to chance.

"Myra wanted you to know at once," Charles said, "but we want your promise that you will tell no one, not even John."

"But of course you have my promise," Ann replied. "I agree with you. You must make every effort to ensure success."

"And it will be a success," Charles assured her.

He stood up and held out his hand to her. "Let us go and find Myra. I want to tell her that you have not raised any objection to our engagement. Tomorrow when I go to London I am going to choose her a ring, but she mustn't wear it on her finger until we can let the cat out of the bag."

Ann stood up. "It still seems ridiculous, in some ways, to think of Myra being married."

"She is so sweet. What I love about her is that she is so utterly unspoiled—so childlike in many ways and so sensible in others."

"You will look after her always, won't you?" Ann asked. "If Myra's heart was ever broken I don't think I could bear it."

"I have promised you, Ann," Charles replied. "I love her with all my heart and soul and I will never let her down."

"Bless you." Ann felt the tears prick her eyes, and then impulsively she bent forward and kissed Charles on the cheek. "It will be wonderful to have you for a brother."

He put his arm round her shoulders and kissed her cheek in return, and she knew that he was moved beyond words, a man dedicated to a new life. They drew apart, and then Ann raised her eyes.

Coming through the doorway at the end of the orangery were John and Sinclair. For a moment she wondered if they could have seen, and then as they advanced talking quite naturally, she dismissed the thought from her mind.

"How lovely it is here," Sinclair remarked, and they talked of the effect of light on the water and of the flowers while Ann noticed that Charles slipped away quickly, obviously in search of Myra.

Soon it was time for bed, and Ann went first to Myra's room to kiss her and tell her how thrilled she was at the news.

"Oh, it's all so wonderful," Myra cried. "I'm so happy. I hardly know what to do with myself. You aren't angry, are you?"

"Angry?" Ann echoed; "of course I'm not."

"I think Charles was afraid that you would say I was much too young; but, Ann, I don't think age one way or another has much to do with it when one meets the man one really loves, do you?"

"As long as you are sure."

"I am sure; Charles is going to look after me, and I, though he doesn't know it, am going to look after him. We shall be happy together, you can be certain of that."

Ann put her arms round Myra.

"Love him and go on loving him! That is all that matters." Myra nodded.

"You have taught me that," she said, "and though I seemed awfully feather-brained in lots of ways, Ann, I have watched you. I have seen how you look after people, how you guide and influence them without seeming to do it, and I am going to try to be just like you."

Ann kissed Myra with a heart too full for words. When she was in her own bedroom she thought of what her sister had said and she knew that no compliment could be greater.

She undressed and put on her nightgown, and over it a négligé of white satin and chiffon which Charles had chosen for her quite recently.

"Your lingerie should always be white," he told her. "Pink and blues and colours are suitable for other women, but not for you. White expresses you, and white is what you must wear."

Ann had been thrilled with the beautiful things he had sent down from London.

Chiffon and lace, combined together by skillful fingers, satin, velvet and soft frills of net, but all in white and soft ivory, which Myra told her laughingly made her look like a nun.

Now she moved about her room, turning off the lights on the dressing-table and leaving only those burning beside the great four-poster bed. She drew back the curtains from the window.

Outside darkness had fallen, somewhere an owl hooted, otherwise it was very quiet and still. Then there was a click as of a door opening, and startled she turned round.

John had come into the room. He stood there in the doorway, the light behind him, and she saw he was still in his dinner-jacket.

He said nothing for a moment and she came from the window across the room towards him.

"Do you want me?" She asked the question formally, surprised by his presence.

He turned and shut the door behind him.

268

"Yes, I want you."

There was something ominous in his tones which disquieted her.

She waited, pulling with a quick nervous movement her dressing-gown closer across her breasts. John moved to her side and stood looking down at her.

"I think the time has come," he said, "for us to talk frankly to one another."

"Don't we always?" Ann asked, raising her eyes to his.

"Are you frank with me?" he asked the question sharply.

"Well, I think so."

"You lie!"

The word was like a pistol report.

Ann quivered.

"I don't understand," she stammered.

"I think you do," John said grimly. "I saw you tonight as I came into the orangery—saw you with Charles."

"Oh, that!" Ann spoke lightly,

Then swiftly the memory came to her of the promise she had given Charles.

"Yes, that."

There was a bitterness in John's tone.

"Listen, John," Ann began, "I can't explain, but. . ."

"I want no explanation. What I saw is quite sufficient."

Suddenly his arms reached out and once again he held her by the shoulders, gripping her with all his strength. Ann felt a sudden fear shoot through her, the fear she had known before and which she had dreaded experiencing again.

"I've been a fool," John was saying, "a fool! I married you because I loved you. Yes, I loved you from the very first moment I saw you. I thought you were different from all the women I have known.

"I saw you giving yourself to your family, I saw you mothering them and comforting them, and I knew that that was what I had missed all my life—affection love and tenderness.

"I knew then that the one thing I wanted in the whole world was you. I was prepared to wait, to woo you slowly until you came to love me even as you loved your father and the children; but circumstances were against me, events happened too quickly. I was afraid of losing you and so in my bungling fashion I tried to find a solution. You agreed to marry me and once again I believed that if I gave you time you would learn to love me. Instead, because I have been slow and stupid, another man has been able to take what should have belonged to me."

"But listen, John, you must listen. . . ." Ann interrupted.

"I won't listen," he said roughly. "I see now so many things that I didn't see before. I see now what has been going on behind my back.

"I was afraid of your purity and your innocence, yes, afraid. I was afraid to approach you in case my love and my passion frightened you, and all the time you whom I imagined so perfect were carrying on an intrigue behind my back, a flirtation with my own cousin."

The scorn and bitterness in his voice seemed to whip her.

"It is not true," Ann said desperately, "you must hear what I have got to say. . . ."

She struggled, trying to free her shoulders from his grip, but as if her efforts inflamed him, John's fingers tightened.

"Am I not to believe my own eyes?" he asked furiously; "but if another man can make love to you, so can I—I who am your husband."

He swept her into his arms, with one hand he tilted back her chin so that her head lay against his shoulder, her eyes agonised and pleading looked up at his.

"Please, John . . . please. . . ." she begged, but it was as though she had never spoken.

For a moment he looked down at her, helpless, a prisoner in his arms, and then his lips came down on hers, and she felt herself quiver beneath the fierce possessiveness of their passion.

She attempted to struggle, but it was no use. She felt as if deep waters were closing over her head. She was drowning, lost, conscious only that John seemed to draw her very soul between her lips and make it his. . . .

He kissed her mouth while time seemed to stand still.

She felt as if she lost her identity. He drew her life from her and left her empty . . . then at last his lips left hers and she felt him kiss her neck.

She felt the soft satin of her dressing-gown rip as he tore it from her shoulder.

He lifted her in his arms, and then, only then, as he carried her across the room towards the shadows of the great bed, did she cry out again.

"No, John. . . . No. . . ."

He paused for a moment, and it seemed as though her piteous cry had been heard.

He looked down at her, her head thrown back, her eyes staring up at his, her hands fluttering across her breasts. His eyes held hers; she saw the passion in them, a fierce, burning furnace which seemed to scorch her.

As suddenly as he had lifted her, he put her down. He took his arms from her, and she put out her hands to steady herself against the pillar of the bed. She clung there for a moment as he looked down at her, a strange expression on his face that she was too bewildered to fathom. . . .

Then he turned, the door closed behind him, and she was alone.

Nineteen

How long Ann stood staring across the room at the closed door she had no idea.

She only knew that she was throbbing all over, that every nerve in her body was quivering.

At last, as if she awoke from a kind of stupor, she pulled her torn dressing-gown across her shoulders and then suddenly slipped down to the floor, hiding her face against the softness of the silk bed-cover.

She crouched there for a long time, until, chilled with cold, she rose to creep into her bed in search of warmth; but there was no chance of sleep and she lay wide-eyed in the darkness hearing the clock in the hall strike each succeeding hour.

At last the dawn light began to show between the curtains and she slipped from between the sheets moving softly and swiftly across the thick carpet.

She dressed; and when at length she was ready, she stood for a moment looking out of the window. The sun, golden-fingered, was already rising over the horizon, the faint mists over the lake were dispersing.

It was very quiet and it seemed to Ann as if a hush lay over everything, making the beauty of green lawns, still water and the verdant foliage of spreading branches even more poignant.

With a sigh Ann turned from the window, took a few things from the drawers, pulling them open softly as if she was afraid that her movements would be overheard. She filled a small bag, and then tiptoed from the room, closing the door noiselessly behind her.

The great staircase and the hall were still wrapped in dusky twilight. The curtains had not been pulled.

Ann hesitated for a moment, then went along the passage. At the far end of the south wing were Sinclair's rooms.

When she reached them, she paused again as if to screw up her courage and then knocked on the bedroom door.

She heard Sinclair's voice say "Come in," and she entered to find him, as she had half expected to do, sitting up in bed reading.

Sinclair only slept a few hours a night, and the one solace for his suffering body was that he could lose himself in the books which he so often said were not only his best friends, but also the finest antidote to pain.

"May I come in?"

"But of course, Ann."

Sinclair's smile was in itself a welcome.

Ann crossed the room and stood by his bedside. He waited for her calmly, expressing surprise neither at her sudden appearance, nor at the fact that she wore a hat and coat and carried a bag.

"Sinclair," Ann began nervously, "I am going away."

"For long?" he asked the question gently.

"I don't know. Perhaps I shall come back this evening, perhaps not. I can't tell you. I have got to think . . . that is all I know for certain. I have got to think, and I can't think here."

"And what do you want me to do?"

"I want you to tell Myra and the twins that I am all right, that they are not to worry about me, and perhaps . . ."

Ann dropped her eyes before Sinclair's and then with an effort continued, "perhaps . . . you had better tell John as well."

"I will do that. You will be taking the car?"

"Yes, I don't suppose John will mind."

"I will tell him that you have taken it, and that you will take care of it and—of yourself."

273

Sinclair spoke with intent, and Ann looked at him understanding the message he was conveying to her.

"You can tell him that," she said.

"Thank you, my dear, and God bless you. We shall miss you until you come back to us."

"You seem certain that I will come back."

"I know you will. You are perhaps right to go away; it is hard to listen to one's own heart when there are so many other things to hear."

Ann looked at him in some surprise.

"You think that is what I am going to do?"

"I am sure of it." Sinclair smiled again, and then as Ann still hesitated he added: "I think all your life you have listened to your heart where other people are concerned, now it is your own turn. Good-bye, my dear."

Feeling somehow as though she had been dismissed, Ann turned towards the door. As she reached it, she looked back.

"Thank you, Sinclair," she said softly.

He smiled at her and raised his hand, a gesture of farewell, and yet she felt as though he blessed her. It even seemed to her, as she went through the darkened house, that already some of the turbulent tempest within her breast had subsided.

Nevertheless, it was with a sense of urgency that she wakened up the sleepy chauffeur and obtained the key of the garage. The big car started at a touch and she was away, speeding down the drive, Gulliver left behind her, the sunshine growing brighter ahead.

How long she drove she had little idea. She had no set plan, only the desire to put as many miles as possible between herself and John.

She kept away from the high roads, turning aimlessly down lanes and roads which bore no signposts. About two o'clock she stopped to fill up with petrol and saw a small wayside café upon the opposite side of the road.

For the first time she remembered that she had

274

ad no food since the night before; so she left the car, and entering the café ordered some tea and bread and butter and was persuaded by the young proprietress to have a new-laid egg.

"We keep our own hens," she said proudly, "that's why most of our customers come here. They know what they will get will be fresh and appetising."

Automatically Ann agreed with her suggestion because it was less trouble than making an effort to refuse.

When the egg came, brown and lightly boiled, she ate it, hardly aware of its flavour or of the crisp home-made bread that accompanied it.

When she had finished she paid her bill, got back into the car and started off again.

It grew hotter as the afternoon wore on, but still Ann drove on and on, passing through open country, along narrow shady lanes, beside wide rivers and twisting, willow-fringed streams.

She had no idea where she was, but still she journeyed onwards.

Whenever she came to a highway she turned aside, avoiding the big towns, knowing that something within her was crying for isolation, for a place where there were no people, no sign of human habitation.

It was late in the afternoon when, as at last she became aware of aching eyes and a cramped body, she glanced at a sign-post and saw one name standing out clearly, almost like a direction shouted in her ear—Melchester.

She knew then where she was, knew, too, where all her journeying had led her—instinctively without conscious thought she had come home.

Half an hour's drive and she was on the outskirts of Little Cople. Home! The word seemed to cry itself aloud within her heart.

This was what she had intended without knowing it, this indeed had been why the urge within her had been so forceful. She had escaped to find comfort and solace in all that was familiar and dear.

Then she remembered that the house had been sold. John had given her no further information; he had only handed over the money.

How could money, she asked herself, have bought anything so dear, so beloved?

Slowly Ann turned up the village street; she looked at the cottages nestling close together, the thatched roofs cheek by jowl with more modern ones, diamond-paned windows in close proximity to broad, ugly sashes, and yet beneath those roofs and behind those windows, picturesque or grotesque, dwelt friends.

Something warm rose phoenix-like within Ann's heart. How she loved them, those people whom she had known since childhood!

The old ladies who had revered and respected her father, the young married women he had attended at their first confinements, the children he had brought into the world and for whom he had prescribed in every childish complaint.

Ann found herself repeating their names as she drove past—Eric Geary . . . Molly Robinson . . . Vera Hull . . . Doris Draper. . . .

There was the little grey stone church . . . there the village shop with its tempting bottles of sweets which had presented such a variety of choice when one had pocket-money to spend . . . there was the schoolmaster's house, the ugly red-brick school enclosed by spiked railings, and there . . . at last, surrounded by trees, was . . . her home.

The drive gate was open; she turned in and drew up at the door.

Whoever owned the house now, she thought, would surely not refuse her the privilege of walking through the garden, of sitting under the cedar tree, of looking at the rooms where the happiest years of her life had been spent.

She got out of the car and was conscious of a terrible weariness. She walked up the steps and rang the front-door bell, hearing the shrill clanging of it far away in the depths of the house. She waited, but no one came. She rang again, and finally decided there was no one at home. This was better than she had hoped. She went round to the side of the house, and there she saw that the curtains of the sitting-room windows were drawn, also those on the bed-room floor above.

The house was obviously empty. Ann felt her heart leap. She went round to the back. How well she knew the defective catch of the pantry window!

It was a way in which they all had used on more than one occasion when they had shut themselves out or had come back after a holiday to find that Mrs. Briggs was ill and no preparations had been made for them.

It was only a matter of seconds for Ann to get the window open and to climb inside. She moved from the pantry into the kitchen.

It appeared to her as if nothing had been touched. Everything was as she had left it.

Eagerly she moved along the passage, looked round the hall and went into the sitting-room.

She pulled back the curtains and opened some of the windows, the light flooded in, and now at last she could look round and see the rooms which held so high a place in her affections.

How shabby the covers were, she thought, and dirty too! She ought to have sent them to be cleaned.

Had there always been so many holes in the hearth-rug, and how often had she reminded herself to have the hinge on the bookcase repaired?

She walked round the room, moving the chairs a little, patting the cushions, dusting the face of the clock, and then almost mechanically winding it up. The wallpaper was stained and peeling in one corner where a pipe had burst.

Surely it should have been repaired? In fact the whole room needed a coat of paint.

She stopped suddenly! Could she be really criticising, finding fault with her own home?

Was it the perfection of Gulliver, which revealed the shabbiness and poverty of the home she had adored?

Quickly, as if ashamed of insulting a beloved friend, she decided to go upstairs. But she walked slowly; it seemed to her that the house was speaking to her, there were voices in the silence, memories of the past that she must recapture in the faint, fusty atmosphere.

On the landing she turned towards her own room. Here, too, the curtains were drawn. She pulled them back and saw the small, narrow bed in which she had slept for so many years, the muslin-flounced dressing-table, the wardrobe which had held her clothes.

When she pulled it open the dresses she had left behind when she married John were still there.

At the sight of these personal, familiar garments something seemed to grip her throat. They had been so intimately a part of her.

She turned from them, leaving the room to cross the landing to where her father had slept.

In the room there was the scent of tobacco, of Scottish tweeds and of hair-oil, mingling together, making that unmistakable smell which recalled her father so vividly that Ann could only stand on the threshold and cover her face with her hands.

She felt as if her father must be there, have been waiting for her until just this moment when she would come home.

"Oh, Daddy, Daddy . . . !"

Involuntarily she spoke the words aloud and the sound of her own voice startled her.

She turned blindly and went from the room back to her own.

There she felt herself shaken by tears which had

been too long suppressed and flung herself face downwards on the bed and cried, sobbing as though her heart would break, her whole body being shaken by her utter abandonment. . . .

It was a long time later that she became aware that her tears had dried and that she had been lying for some time utterly exhausted, her face hidden in the pillow.

Aware that she was cold she moved and as she raised her head saw that darkness had fallen.

The room was in gentle twilight; outside in the garden she heard the high whistle of the bats as they swooped round and round in their nightly flight.

Cramped and stiff, Ann moved to the window; her eyes were weary from weeping and yet strangely enough she felt curiously at rest.

Her misery had gone, and something else had gone too, that chaotic tumult which had seethed within her all day and all the night before.

She was at peace; it was as if her tears had washed away everything save a calm gentleness—infinitely tender, infinitely comforting.

Now at last she felt she could think, could face without panic the thought of what had occurred the night before.

Now she could remember without horror John's coming into her room, his accusations and his fierce possessiveness. Had her terror indeed gone? She asked herself the question, and then swiftly came another question: had it been terror?

Step by step, with her head against the lintel of her window, she reconstructed what had occurred.

She remembered John's face as she advanced across the floor towards him; the hard, almost brutal grip of his fingers; the questions he had asked her, and then, yes, then, she remembered his mouth upon hers, his lips holding her prisoner even as she lay captive in his arms.

She felt her heart give a startled throb, her pulses

quickened and she knew what she felt was not fear, but something else. . . .

She thought of the tones of John's voice, the raw emotion which had rung out when he told her that he loved her.

At that moment his reserve had vanished, the iron control he had exercised all his life had broken. It was not surprising that she had been afraid—but had she been? Again she asked herself the question, and truthfully knew the answer!

Clearly, like the pieces of a jig-saw puzzle falling into place, Ann saw herself, saw her whole life winding like a silver stream up to that moment.

Why had she run away from John for so long, why had she been afraid of him? Now in the darkness of her own bedroom she understood.

She saw herself looking after her family, loving her father, being loved in return; and yet always she had been the giver, she had been the one to pour out the bounty of her love.

It was to her they turned in trouble, on her they relied. Hers had been the power, and she the benevolent giver of gifts.

She remembered John coming to the house; he had seemed to the others to offer so much, but she had shrunk from his generosity and tried to force his departure. Why, why?

Ann knew the truth, and dropping her head hid her face in the curve of her arm. She had been afraid, not of John's strength, not of his money or of his position, but of herself.

She had been afraid of being conquered, of having to give up her throne, because her heart might come to him in sweet surrender.

Yes, that was the truth, she had been afraid of her own feelings, afraid of the emotions within herself that were aroused by his very presence; always she had fought him, always she had defied that inner onviction that whispered here was a man from whom he must "take".

Humbly Ann admitted how desperately she had failed her own ideals, and now she knew there had been no horror within her last night, when John had held her close to him, when his kiss had claimed her.

She loved him, loved him not with the calm affection she had given to her father and her brother and sisters, but with that strong passionate love which burns fiercely within the heart, consuming with a leaping flame all that is cheap and unworthy of its sanctity.

"I love him"—Ann caught her breath and looked over the garden.

Yes, she loved him, and he was her master. She knew now that she had no pride, that had only been an excuse to escape from what her instincts had always recognised must be the final surrender.

She wanted him, she knew that they would become a part of one another, one flesh.

This was love, this tingling ecstasy, this mystic rising spirit reaching out for the perfect consummation of souls.

She knew then that she would go back, soon . . . very soon . . . back to John, back to her real home which lay with him . . . within his heart.

For a long time she sat by the window. It grew darker and darker, and yet it seemed to her that light was pouring upon her, a light shining brilliant and beautiful beyond words.

She was no longer pulling against the stream, but flowing with it in harmony and inutterable joy. . . .

At last the needs of the human body were too strong to be ignored. Sleep lay insistent upon her eyes, and almost too weary to walk.

Ann crept from the window to her bed. She slipped off her clothes, rummaged in the drawer and found a nightgown, and slipping into bed closed her eyes and was asleep even as her head touched the pillow.

She slept the sleep of utter exhaustion.

Only once in the night did she think that she hear a sound far away in the depths of the house.

"It must be a door slamming in the wind," sh thought dreamily, and fell asleep again, a smile o her lips because of the happiness within her.

When she awoke, it was to find the sunshine pour ing through the uncurtained window warm upon he face. She stretched and was instantly awake, tremu lous with excitement.

Today she would go back to Gulliver, back t John, back to the man whom she loved. Bricks an mortar could not make a home, this home she ha loved so much was only a shell, where John wa there for her would be home.

Ann jumped out of bed, ran across the passage t the bathroom, and drew herself a bath. The wate was cold, and yet as she rubbed herself dry she fe the chill of it give way to a tingling sense of healt and well-being.

She was hungry, very hungry she told herself, an going back to her bedroom she dressed, slipping o not the clothes she had worn yesterday, but the blu linen overall she had always worn in the morning when preparing breakfast for the family.

She found a comb in the drawer and ran it throug her hair and then smiled at the flushed cheeks an shining eyes which looked back at her from the mir ror.

Humming, she went downstairs to the kitchen. Sh was not hopeful of finding anything to eat, but sh knew that unless Mrs. Briggs had taken it, there woul be an unopened tin of coffee at the back of what ha been her store-cupboard.

Nothing had been touched, the coffee was there There was even a spoonful of sugar in the bowl.

Ann was opening the tin on the table when sud denly she heard footsteps coming down the passage

282

he stopped what she was doing and raised her head
lightly.

Several questions shot through her mind. Was this
the new owner of the house?

Then, as the footsteps came nearer, she stood, her
eyes fixed on the door, apprehensive, and even a little afraid. The door was pushed open. . . .

"I, at least, have been wise enough to bring my
own breakfast with me," John said.

Ann could only stare at him as he stood there
holding in his hands a bottle of milk and a basket
which she could see contained eggs and various other
packages.

"Where have you come from?" Her voice sounded
high and astonished.

John put the milk down on the table and faced his
wife across it.

"I arrived last night," he said. "Far too late to disturb you, but I came through the sitting-room window
and made myself quite comfortable. In fact I think
I must have slept nearly as well as you have. We
are both disgracefully late."

"You slept here—last night?"

"Yes, don't look so scandalised. It's a perfectly
respectable action as we happen to be married."

John was laughing at her. There was a twinkle in
his eyes and a smile on his lips.

Quite suddenly Ann found herself flushing, the
blood rising in her cheeks like a crimson tide. Her
eyes fell beneath his, she was conscious only of the
humiliation of a flush which could not be hidden.

"You must be hungry," John said quietly. "Shall
we have breakfast first and talk afterwards?"

She glanced up at him with a question in her eyes.
He sensed what she asked and answered her.

"Sinclair gave me your message. Charles and Myra
have let me into their secret; but never mind that
now, I'm hungry and you must be too."

283

"But how did you know where I would be—I didn't even know myself."

"I guessed you would come—home."

"But it isn't my home now . . . it is sold."

"Yet it is still yours!"

"You mean . . ."

Ann questioned in bewildered tones.

"That I bought it for you. I thought we might need it one day for a holiday . . . or a honeymoon."

Again Ann's eyes fell before his—she felt herself tremble.

"What about breakfast?"

There was a lilting happiness in John's voice she had never heard before.

She took the eggs from the basket, finding there was also a great pat of yellow butter, a pot of marmalade and a loaf of bread.

"How will you have your eggs done?" she asked him.

She made an effort to escape from her own embarrassment, from the shyness which was creeping over her like a tidal wave, a shyness which was somehow exciting and rather thrilling.

"I leave the choice to you," John replied. "Shall I lay the table?"

Briefly she told him where to find a table-cloth and where the knives and forks were kept. As she cooked she watched him surreptitiously.

He was concentrating on his job as she had seen him concentrate on other things; and yet, she told herself, there was something different about him this morning.

He seemed younger, more elastic, less staid and stiff, certainly not the awe-inspiring autocrat with whom she had frightened herself so long. The coffee was boiling over . . . quickly she turned to it, and then they were sitting at the table eating and drinking together like an old married couple.

They spoke little, but Ann was very conscious of

ohn's gaze upon her, and more than once she looked
p to meet his gaze, then looked away again. At
ast they were finished. Ann got to her feet.

"We ought to put some water on for washing up,"
he said, and John laughed.

"We are not going to do any washing up; we will
end for someone else to do that later. Come with
ie, I want to talk to you."

He took her hand, and without argument Ann let
im lead her down the passage through the hall into
ie sitting-room.

She expected him to stop there, but instead he
rew her across the lawn, and she knew then that he
as leading her to her own favourite place, the seat
nder the cedar tree, where, so long ago it seemed
ow, he had asked her to marry him.

They reached the tree; John looked at her, and
or a moment held her eyes. Ann drew an unsteady
reath.

"Sit down," John said gently, and his voice was
eep with some inner emotion.

She did as she was told. John sat down beside her,
nd reaching out took her hand in his. His fingers
vere very warm and strong, and she felt as though
he was content to leave her hand there for ever,
ecure in the strength of his protection.

Then he spoke.

"I am going to say now, Ann," he said, "what I
ught to have said when we were here last and I
sked you to be my wife. I was slow and stupid, and
iy only excuse is that I was afraid of frightening
ou, afraid of letting you see how deeply my own
eelings were involved."

His fingers tightened on her hand.

"I love you," he said. "I love you with all my
eart."

Ann felt her breath come quickly, but as she did
ot speak, John reaching out with his other hand
ook her chin gently and raised her face to his.

285

"I love you, Ann," he repeated, "and now I wan you to tell me that you love me."

It had been easy last night in the darkness to con fess her love, but now that the moment was upon he Ann felt herself quiver, felt the last resistance of he pride rush to stem the words which rose to her lips. He eyes dropped before his.

"You see, darling," John went on, "even befor Charles gave me an explanation of what had occurre in the orangery, I knew that you loved me. I knew when I felt your lips respond to mine, when I hel you in my arms.

"I knew then how much I had missed, what a foo I had been to hesitate. I could have taken you ther and then and made you love me, but I was afraid o my own passion, afraid of the violence of my ow feelings.

"I wanted you to come to me of your own free wil to tell me that you were mine, even as I am your. But the knowledge of your love broke the chain which have held me all my life.

"I became a man in that moment, Ann—a man wh needs you and is not ashamed to claim you for hi own . . . his woman.

"Look at me, Ann, look at me and tell me tha you love me."

There was a pause in which Ann could feel hi will compelling hers. She knew him then for her mas ter, knew that she had no choice in the matter.

Her heart was beating, she was weak and helpless utterly at his mercy; she was trembling, but not wit fear.

Very slowly she raised her eyes. She looked int his and saw there an utter tenderness joined with th strength of passion and of perfect love. Her lip moved, and for a second no sound came.

"Tell me what I want to hear . . . say it, m darling."

His was a command which must be obeyed.

286

At last she spoke in a voice tremulous and broken and so gentle that John must bend his head to hear.

"I . . . love you . . . John."

The last barrier was down.

For a moment timeless and eternal they looked at each other, and then with a cry of triumph and of wonder John took her into his arms.

She felt a glory beyond all words encompass them both and with a sob of unutterable happiness she turned her lips to his.

of the paper-thin bread-and-butter from the plate beside him.

The Shefford sisters were unlike anyone he had met in his life before. He was used to seeing beautiful women and they made little or no impression on him. He was used, too, to the chatter of girls socially ambitious, to the machinations and schemes of their mothers who looked on him as a very attractive matrimonial catch.

But Sir John seldom met complete and absolute frankness or unsophistication such as Myra's, which proclaimed real innocence as well as naïvety, or anyone like Ann. . . . He thought about her.

Upstairs in the twins' bedroom Myra was sitting on the edge of the bed telling them the news.

". . . he has a polo ground, a covered tennis court and a swimming bath which holds more water than any other private bath in England, while the house has hundreds of bedrooms, literally hundreds! And he is rich, frightfully rich! Oh, I wonder where that magazine is which showed pictures of Gulliver; we must find it!"

There was a step outside the door, then Ann's voice saying, "Aren't you coming down to tea?"

Myra jumped up and ran to the door.

"Oh, Ann, isn't it exciting about Sir John? I was just telling the twins."

"I don't see much to get excited about," Ann said quietly. "He came here by chance and he will be going very shortly."

"He is in no hurry; he told me so," Myra said defiantly.

"Even if he isn't, what is there to get so worked up about?" Ann inquired. "I don't suppose it will bring Daddy any more patients if we do put a sign over the door—'Physician-Extraordinary to Sir John Melton.'"

She was teasing, and Myra, who hated being teased, turned petulantly towards the door.

"All right," she said. "Have it your own way. Rich

patients mean nothing to us, of course! They are always popping in unannounced; and we aren't interested in the most famous house in England or in the man who owns it! I think you are very unimaginative and commonplace!"

She slammed the door behind her, leaving Ann and the twins looking at each other with something like dismay on their faces.

"Oh, dear," Ann said, "I didn't really mean to upset her."

"She will get over it," Antony answered. "I say, Ann, what did old Mother Burrows say about us?"

"She has forgiven you," Ann answered. "But you are both to write a letter of apology, a proper one. And oh, twins, don't do anything like that again—at least, not to the tradespeople to whom we owe money. We simply can't pay Mr. Burrows at the moment."

"We never thought of that when we did it, did we?" Antony asked.

"No, and we're sorry, Ann, we really are."

Antoinette ran forward and put her arms round Ann's neck.

"It is all right, darlings. When I looked at that awful Eric snivelling and shuffling in his mother's best arm-chair, I really didn't blame you. But you know what things are at the moment so far as money is concerned."

"Yes, we know," Antoinette said. "But . . ."

"If that man downstairs is as rich as Myra says he is," Antony interrupted, "I hope Daddy charges him properly for his board and lodging."

"He will have to stay here for ever if we are to pay off all our bills," Ann replied, "and I don't think he is likely to do that. Oh, dear, what a nuisance money is! And Antony, you do need a new suit."

Antony looked down at his grey flannels.

"The boys started shouting 'Patched pants' at me again yesterday," he said; "but I gave one of them